Look for t

MW01538832

Published by Carina Press

Sound's Familiar

TERRA NOCTEM BOOK 1

BY
DANA MARIE BELL

DM
B

Dana Marie Bell Books
www.danamariebell.com

Sound's Familiar
Copyright © 2019 by Dana Marie Bell
ISBN: 9781694983916
Edited by Tera Kleinfelter
Cover by Leah, OA Book Covers

First Edition electronic publication by Dana Marie Bell: September 27, 2019

Dedication

To Mom, who finally learned how to text on her phone. Gods help us all.

To Dad, who doesn't bother reading his texts. For him, it's call or nothing.

To Youngest Son, who'd rather text than do ANY other form of communication. Geez, you've got a mouth for more than feeding yourself, ya know. And dear lord and lady, the *memes*…

To Eldest Son, who doesn't care, he's gonna tell you all about what he's interested in RIGHT. THE. FUCK. NOW. Seriously, kid, I don't play Warhammer! But I'll admit that If the Emperor Had a Text To Speech Device *is* pretty hilarious.

And to Dusty, who thinks the whole thing is damn funny. Keep bringing me my coffee in the morning and I'll forgive you (almost) anything.

Glossary

Angel: A creature of the plane Angelus, they have wings and are beings of order. They prefer maintaining and preserving the status quo, and often find themselves in conflict with beings from the plane Infernus because of this. See *Demons* below.

Anima/Animus: Like yin and yang, anima and animus are the two forms of magic that fill every living thing. Sorcerers use anima/animus to cast spells, while familiars use it to transform into their animal counterparts. Most sorcerers need a familiar to help balance out their magic, or they run the risk of slipping into blood sorcery. The two are interchangeable, neither male nor female, just two halves of a whole.

Blood Sorcerer: Blood sorcerers are those who eschew forming a bond with a familiar. Instead, they pull anima/animus from the living, using blood rituals and human sacrifice to absorb the power. This sort of activity has a cost, however. Blood sorcerers run the risk of becoming withers, creatures of Terra Noctem that thrive on absorbing the magic of others. See *Sorcerer* and *Withers* below.

Demon: A creature of the plane Infernus, they are creatures of fire and chaos. They often have horns and red or bronze skin in their demon form. They prefer change and invention to maintaining the status quo, which often leads to conflict with denizens of the Angelic plane. See *Angel* above.

Dimen: Often confused for demons, dimen (pronounced dye-men) are simply interdimensional beings from the different planes who have chosen to make Terra Mundus their home. See *Planes* below. Dimens are angels, demons, elementals, elves, fairies, and merfolk. Some lump shapeshifters among the dimens, while others argue that they are originally from Terra Mundus, and therefore not dimens.

Elemental: A being of one of the four elemental planes, they often bear characteristics from their home dimension.

Air elemental: Often has flyaway hair, blue or gray eyes, and when using their powers, wings. Often called sylphs.

Earth elemental: Brown- or black-haired, brown- or green-eyed, they are often strong and big-boned. When using their powers, their skin will sometimes turn earth-colored as well. Their nickname is gnome.

Fire elemental: Reddish hair and brown eyes often mark these creatures. When using their powers, their skin turns ruddy. They are known as djinn.

Water elemental: Pale-haired, with blue eyes, these creatures are often called merfolk. Scales appear on their skin when they use their powers.

Elf/Fairy: Elves and fairies are creatures of Terra Dryadalis, aka the fairy realm. Elves often have the power of healing as well as the power to force other dimens from the plane the elf resides in. Some believe that familiars were used in the elven war against the Infernal plane, and that their magical changes to the familiars created shapeshifters. This is the source of the rumor that shapeshifters are actually dimens.

Fairies have the ability to hex others, causing mayhem among both humans and dimens. It is said that fairies are the outgrowth of elves who bore demon children, either voluntarily or involuntarily, both during the war and at other times.

Familiar: Familiars are people capable of changing into animals but who also bond with sorcerers to balance out their magic. Sorcerers and familiars are said to be cousins, familiars being born out of necessity. They cannot cast spells, but they can amplify their sorcerer's spells and make them more stable. A familiar does not, however, need to bond with a sorcerer in the same way that a sorcerer needs a familiar, as all of their magic is directed inward rather than outward.

Familiar House: Familiar House is both the advocate for and home to familiars. A familiar looking for a sorcerer will form a temporary bond with the house, allowing them to set up the meet and greets where sorcerers come to look for potential partners. Familiar Houses set the rules that both sorcerers and familiars use to regulate the bond.

Gate: Extremely difficult to open, gates are how sorcerers can move between planes. This is only recommended if proper preparations are made to survive the plane that the sorcerer wishes to travel to.

Gods: The gods are said to have created the planes of existence. They have their own plane, removed from almost all of the others. Only one pathway exists to the realm of the gods, and only certain creatures, such as demons, angels, and planewalkers, can travel there. It is impossible for a sorcerer to form a gate to the plane of the gods.

Human: Natural-born residents of Terra Mundus, humans are both numerous and capable of channeling the magic of the other planes. Sorcerers are always born of humans. Because of their ability to channel, they need familiars to help ground them and balance out their magic.

Ley Line(s): The primal force of a world, ley lines flow much like air currents and can be tracked by those who can tap into them. Unlike humans, elves use ley lines to cast their spells, as do gnomes, merfolk and other dimens.

Mana: The generic term for the magical power used by humans.

Necromancer: A sorcerer whose focus is the dead, necromancers can communicate with the spirits of those residing in Terra Noctem, the night realm. They do *not* raise the dead, but their association with the realm of the dead causes others around them to feel uncomfortable in their presence.

Pathways: Pathways are the connections between the planes. Each plane has its own set of pathways to and from the various other planes. (Diagram coming!)

Plane: There are ten planes (aka "Terras") of existence, including the plane of the gods:

Mundus: The "human" realm, a place where creatures from the other planes can also exist in relative comfort. Only the gods have no presence on Terra Mundus.

Dryadalis: The fae realm, home of the elves and fairies.

Infernum: Home of demons and realm of chaos.

Angelus: The angelic realm of order.

Ignis: Plane of fire, home to djinn.

Aether: Plane of air, home to sylphs.

Tellus: Plane of earth, home of the gnomes.

Aqua: Plane of water, home of the merfolk.

Noctem: The night realm, realm of the dead, home to withers and ghosts. Often believed to be the source of the belief in purgatory.

Caelestes: Realm of the gods.

Planewalker: The only being who can walk between the planes without having to perform gate spells or prepare for survival. Planewalkers are believed to be descended from the gods and are very rare.

Shapeshifter: A human who can shift into an animal but is *not* a familiar. Most are predators. Shapeshifters can sometimes lose control over their beasts, called "going feral." Predator familiars have acquired a bad reputation due to the shapeshifters that go feral, despite the fact that they cannot due to their magic.

Sorcerer: A human who can channel the magic of the planes, sorcerers are imbued with powerful anima/animus. Most sorcerers bond with familiars, stabilizing their magic, while others view familiars as chains around them. These sorcerers become blood sorcerers. See above.

Vampire: A creature of both Terra Mundus and Terra Noctem, vampires are the only true undead. They reside exclusively in Terra Mundus and require infusions of anima/animus to survive. This magic is absorbed through the blood of the donor. Laws are in place regulating how and where a vampire may feed. One must either register with the authorities to be turned or be able to prove that there was no other way to sustain their life. Some people have undead wills, allowing them to be turned in cases where the human may not be able to give conscious consent.

Chapter 1

Carol Voss yawned widely, startling the gecko that had been sitting on the arm of the sofa and sunning itself in the light from the nearby window. Stacey hiss-screamed, the noise geckos made when they were threatened.

Carol snorted at the tiny lizard. It was just instinct on her friend's part. Stacey understood she was safe around Carol, even when they were both shifted, as they were now. Carol didn't eat sentient beings.

Carol huffed an apology and nuzzled Stacey. Stacey promptly climbed onto Carol's snout, making Carol cross-eyed as she tried to keep her gaze on the gecko. Stacey wouldn't fall off, but Carol didn't want to accidentally hurt her friend.

Carol glanced slowly around the room, making Stacey stumble a bit before the lizard lay down, sprawled over Carol's nose, her little limbs dangling on either side and her head over the tip of Carol's nose. She'd have to be careful to warn Stacey before she sneezed. The last time that happened, Stacey wound up with a broken arm when she hit the wall.

She hadn't spoken to Carol for a week. Carol wound up making chocolate-covered strawberries to appease her. She'd thought about making chocolate covered crickets but…

Ewewewewew. She shuddered, almost dislodging Stacey. Just the thought of touching bugs made her want to hurl. She loved Stacey like a sister, but dear God it would take something more than not talking to get Carol to ruin perfectly good chocolate that way.

Chasing off thoughts of chirping chocolate, Carol glanced around again. The room was filled with a mix of human and animals, all of them familiars. The San Fernando Valley Familiar House was about to hold its monthly Saturday meet and greet, and she was eager to catch a glimpse of those who showed up. Sometimes they got some pretty famous people roaming through, looking for a partner their magic could work with.

Carol had never matched with a sorcerer before. They all passed her by with a cursory glance at best. She was twenty-three and still hadn't broken her magical cherry.

Some of the other familiars teased her about that, but Carol did her best to let it slide. Matching with a sorcerer could be difficult as a large predator. Most wanted something small and portable, like Stacey, whom they could carry in their pocket or on their shoulder. Ravens, owls, cats, and even rats were far more popular than wolves and the larger familiars. She had a theory about that, having to do with the shifter community. Sometimes larger shifters turned feral, running amok and causing a lot of damage to people and property. But Carol wasn't a shifter.

She was a familiar, and that made all the difference in the world to anyone who understood exactly what that meant. No matter what happened, going feral wasn't possible when you were as closely bonded with your animal as familiars were.

One of her friends, Brent, was a freakin' polar bear. He'd only matched once, to a sorcerer on an arctic expedition. After the year and a day contract was up, the sorcerer had returned with Brent in tow, saying he didn't need the polar bear any longer as he was done with his expedition.

Carol had wanted to claw the man's eyes out. Brent had been heartbroken, but while the familiar picked the sorcerer, the sorcerer didn't have to keep the familiar, no matter how well their magic might mesh. Both had to be on the same page before a long-term bond could form.

"Okay, everyone, listen up!"

Carol turned her head toward the doorway, her thoughts interrupted by the overly happy female voice. She needed to pay attention to the woman who was in charge of today's meet and greet. Carol couldn't remember her name. She was new, and so chipper she made Carol wince.

The woman smiled and practically bounced in place. It was way too early in the morning for that level of perkiness. "We have some pretty important people lined up to visit today, so be on your best behavior." The woman frowned at Carol— who'd chosen to spend the day in her wolf form—the tiger, and Brent, who'd also shifted into his bear. "No peeing on or eating the sorcerers."

Carol rolled her eyes. She'd only done that once, and that was because the guy was bullying Stacey, trying to force her into his pocket. But no, pee on someone's shoes *once*, and you never got to live it down.

Only for Stacey and her other friends would she be willing to put herself out there like that. She needed to be careful though. She'd finally graduated from the police academy and was preparing to work for the LAPD. She prayed she'd eventually go to the MCU—the Magical Crimes Unit, a special police unit that dealt with magical crimes of all types—maybe even as the partner of one of their officers.

It would be a dream come true, but right now she needed to listen, or Perky Patty was going to rap her nose with those rolled-up papers she was holding.

"Some of the attending sorcerers you may recognize from the newspapers so, please, don't fawn all over them. You'll know if they're meant to be your sorcerer, so don't be shy."

Carol tilted her head. Don't get close, but don't be shy? The woman really needed a better speechwriter. Dear gods, where had they found her? A children's camp? *Barney & Friends*? Carol was seriously beginning to rethink that no peeing rule. A little piddle on the carpet might de-chipper Skipper.

The woman clapped her hands loudly enough to startle the sleeping polar bear, which was never a wise move. "All right, people. Let's get those doors open, and good luck!" She bounced off, jumping at the growl coming from Brent. He was cozied up to the small air conditioner set up just for him. It might be forty degrees out, but when Brent was in his polar form, it was practically tropical weather.

Carol suppressed another yawn. A nap sounded rather nice, but the chatter of voices rising as the doors to the House

15

were opened kept her from nodding off. She stared at the now-opened double doors to find a mix of old and young, male and female, and every race coming into the room.

Some of the faces made her gasp as quietly as she could, not wanting to bring attention to herself. There was a freaking *movie star* in the room, one she'd thought was paired up. They must have broken their contract if he was on the hunt again. Next to him was a model who used magic to keep her appearance young and wrinkle-free. She'd probably try to match up with one of the smaller familiars. From the pictures Carol had observed, she preferred pocketbook-sized dogs.

Unfortunately, not one of them made her anima tingle like she'd heard it was supposed to when a sorcerer who might be a match came near her.

Anima had to match to animus and vice versa. Both familiars and mages could sense their opposite in each other, something that drew them together, an indescribable attraction that bound them together. Only time would determine if there was a true match or not. Most were temporary matches, some aspect of personality forcing the pairing apart. And she'd never heard of animus being bound to animus, not even in fantasy stories. She even thought that an animus mage would be turned off by an animus familiar, at least magically.

She sighed and closed her eyes, laying her head on her paws. There was no one here for her, not one who would make her theirs.

Oh well. The thought of following some movie star around sounded boring as hell. They had to stay close for a bit for their magic to mesh, and Carol had dreams she wanted to pursue. Her perfect match would be—

Stacey hopped off Carol's snout, startling her. Carol opened her eyes to find someone holding Stacey with a glowing smile. "You must be mine."

Carol doggie grinned, aware she gave the impression of being a silly pup, but she couldn't help it. The man holding Stacey was cute, a tall, thin man with blond hair and shining blue eyes. He radiated kindness. From the way Stacey was practically dancing in his hand she bet Stacey had found a sorcerer she could potentially bond with long-term.

Across the room, a woman squealed, picking up one of the cat familiars. She was a plump, plain woman with nice eyes and a wide, beautiful smile. Trevor was a sweet guy who hadn't managed to find a long-term bond. Maybe this woman would be the one for him. Carol could only hope so.

The woman petted Trevor, causing the cat familiar to begin purring. "I think we could bond!"

The cat squirmed free, causing the woman to slump. Carol watched, already aware of what the tabby cat would do. Trevor wasn't the type to judge people based on looks alone. Besides, she could hear his purrs. He was definitely into the female.

Trevor's kitty form shivered, changing into a tall, stunning blond man who took hold of the woman's hand. "Your aura is good. I think we can work together."

Thank goodness clothing reappeared when a familiar changed shape or the whole room would be getting an eyeful of Trevor's Willie Wonka and his Everlasting Gobstoppers.

Carol chuffed a laugh before putting her head back down. All around the room, she observed both matches and refusals as familiars found sorcerers and vice versa. Not one sorcerer approached either her, the tiger, or Brent, who was back to snoring lightly in front of his air conditioner. She closed her eyes, prepared to nap once more through the matching process.

"Hmm."

Carol shivered at the deep, masculine voice. There was a slight rasp to it, as if he'd recently gotten over a cold.

"Oh, Mr. Sound, welcome to Familiar House!" Perky Patty was practically gushing all over the...guy who...

Mmm, what was that scent?

Carol opened her eyes.

Holy.

Fuck.

Jonah Sound, younger son of one of the richest men in L.A., had walked into *her* Familiar House, and he was even more attractive in person than he was on the Internet.

She kept her gaze on the dark-haired sorcerer as he wandered the room. His eyes drifted from one familiar to another, but he never stopped his slow stroll, not even when

Perky Patty tried to take his arm and lead him toward the smaller feline familiars.

When he stopped in front of Brent and smiled, Carol thought that maybe her friend had found a sorcerer, but Mr. Sound moved on, shaking his head when Skipper tried to steer him to where the three current owl residents were perched in the rafters.

He stopped in front of the tiger, who stared at him with bored golden eyes. The tiger stood, stretched, and turned his back on Mr. Sound.

Ouch. That had to hurt the man's pride.

If it did, Mr. Sound didn't show it. He merely chuckled again, sending another shiver down Carol's spine. What the hell was going on?

And why was her anima beginning to hum the closer Jonah Sound got to her?

Jonah Sound's gorgeous hazel eyes landed on her. They widened slightly before he smiled. "Well. Hello there, Ms. Wolf."

Carol lifted her head and studied him. Now that he was standing in front of her, she realized he had an absolutely decadent scent. It reminded her of the time she'd walked past a Starbucks that had been placed next to a chocolate shop. She'd practically puddled into a ball of furry goo right then and there, but Stacey had dragged her away before she could make a fool of herself. Well, any more than she already had.

This man smelled just like that, and Carol was having a hard time not licking him to find out if he tasted as good as he smelled.

"What's your name?" Mr. Sound was staring at her, his smile widening when Carol opened her mouth to answer. For a second, she'd forgotten she was still in wolf form and therefore couldn't speak.

"Her name is Carol Voss," Skipper replied, appearing a little confused. Apparently, she'd expected someone as rich and powerful as Mr. Sound to pick a more socially suitable familiar. Predators didn't stroll down Rodeo Drive or ride in limos, at least in Perky Patty's mind.

Carol stood and stretched, making sure her nose was as close to Jonah Sound as she could get without getting smacked for crotch-sniffing.

Hmph. You do something once…

Mr. Sound laughed. "I think she might be the one."

Carol gave him her best toothy grin. She agreed wholeheartedly. She'd never experienced such…longing for another person. Her wolf and her anima were both purring in anticipation of leaving with this man.

Carol was surprised when he sighed happily. "Oh, yes. I think she might do nicely."

"Sir, are you sure?" Skipper glanced between them, apparently dumbfounded.

"If she is, then yes." Mr. Sound turned his gaze back to Skipper.

Carol wasn't sure she liked that, his gaze on another woman, but she had no ground to stand on. At best, it was shaky. They hadn't even spoken yet, let alone begun a true familiar-sorcerer bond. But if what she was sensing was any indication, she and Jonah Sound were about to start one hell of a partnership. She nodded fiercely, giving the go-ahead.

Mr. Sound placed his hand on her head, scratching just behind her ear. It felt so good her eyes crossed. "Start the paperwork."

Carol nearly did a happy dance right there on the ugly floral couch. She had a sorcerer! And not just any sorcerer, but a fucking hot, powerful one. Best of all, Jonah wasn't a man who lived off his family's money. He was a member of the MCU, which made him a badass hottie working in the same field Carol had gotten her degree in. He was absolutely perfect for her. She couldn't have dreamt of a better partner. She did a mental fist-pump and hopped off the sofa, her tail wagging a mile a minute. She couldn't wipe the goofy, toothy grin off her face if she tried.

Score one for the wolf!

Chapter 2

Jonah watched with a sense of satisfaction as the perky blonde woman shuffled away. If the wolf named Carol accepted him as her sorcerer, he'd have a familiar once again. His animus had started to become unstable, his dreams haunted by visions of Terra Noctem—the Night World, the world of the dead. A sorcerer with unstable mana—whether anima or animus—could find his soul drawn into Terra Noctem, or worse. If it went on long enough, he could become a wither, forever hungering for the magic of Terra Mundus. It happened all the time to blood sorcerers if their vile practices weren't stopped in time, as their magic raged and forced the change onto them. The only thing he'd found that would stop a blood sorcerer from killing—and turning—was incarceration in solitary confinement. It was a death sentence either way, as the sorcerer's mana pulled them apart from the inside without a familiar to balance them out. Blood sorcerers rarely lived to old age.

He never wanted to meet one who had. The thought was horrifying.

He was nowhere near that point, thank the gods, but going for a month without a familiar had made him keen to find a new one.

His animus was reaching for her anima already, eager to find the balance that had disappeared when his last familiar refused to renew their contract or deepen their bond. It had happened so many times now Jonah could count his past familiars on both hands and one foot.

Jonah was thirty years old and had gone through eleven partners. He had thought he'd find his perfect familiar by now, but after being rejected so many times, he'd almost given up hope.

Until now.

The wolf was staring at him with a doggie grin, her body small by wolf standards. She had a narrow snout and a black nose. Her golden eyes watched him curiously, but she wasn't pulling away. If anything, she was slowly inching closer, her nostrils flaring as she sniffed at him.

Good. That was an excellent sign. It meant that she—

"Sir?" Ms. Weber glanced between the two of them with an air of concern. "I have the paperwork for you and Ms. Voss to sign if you still want to." She stared at the small poodle who came to sniff at him, smiling. "Of course, there are other familiars who might match better with you." She made it clear she preferred the smaller, less-ferocious familiars with every word and gesture.

Jonah bit back his annoyed sigh. Why Ms. Weber was following him around when there were other people trying to gain her attention was beyond him. He wasn't all that interesting. There was a fucking movie star not that far away from him, trying to get her to acknowledge him, but no. She was fixated on Jonah, on turning him away from Ms. Voss, and he had no idea why.

A wet nose touched his hand. Jonah turned his attention back to Carol, half forgetting that Ms. Weber was even there. Already, a tentative bond was forming between them. He could sense their magics testing each other, another good sign. He could tell her link to Terra Mundus—the human plane of existence—was firm. She'd make an excellent anchor for his magic. "All right. Do you want to shift now or after we get to my home?"

A familiar and sorcerer needed to be close to each other for their magic to mesh properly. If they fully bonded after a year and a day, they could be apart long enough for the familiar to work away from the sorcerer, but that didn't happen often.

Many familiars were given free housing and sustenance by the sorcerer or Familiar House, giving them the freedom to work or not as they saw fit, though most either worked with their sorcerer or chose to be homebodies. It sucked for the familiars, but a familiar could live their entire life without a sorcerer, whereas a sorcerer couldn't survive for long without a familiar. He'd observed—and fought with—the results. It wasn't pretty.

The small poodle shook its head and sneezed, already moving beyond him, but still, Ms. Weber watched it with affection. "Mr. Sound?" Ms. Weber clutched the papers to her chest, her expression hopeful. "Have you changed your mind?"

"No." Jonah snatched the papers from her hands, almost tearing one of the sheets. It was all legalese about how he would pay room and board for the familiar, he wouldn't abuse the familiar, the contract was in effect for blah blah blah. All the rules that had been drilled into him since he was a child, clutching his anima toy and dreaming of a bond that would last his whole life.

"Ms. Voss? Do you want to sign here or at my home?" He'd do whatever his little wolf wished so long as she followed him home.

She edged Ms. Weber away from him with her shoulder. Then she glanced at him and started for the double doors.

Apparently, she was ready to go. Jonah nodded and followed her, opening the front door for her.

"Wait! You haven't signed the paperwork!"

Jonah tried desperately not to fry the woman. She'd been annoying him since the moment he'd arrived, steering him away from his favored type of familiar. He'd have to have a word about her with Patrick Burns, who ran this particular Familiar House. She wasn't supposed to try to influence a match. She was supposed to be there for the well-being of the familiars and to make sure they had what they needed to survive. If she was giving the large predators a hard time, he'd see to it that she was removed from overseeing the meet and greets at the very least.

"We'll be signing at my home." He tried to smile, aware it probably seemed as rigid as it felt. The woman was beginning to exasperate him. There was no law or part of the contract that said it had to be signed in front of witnesses, or even at the House. "Once they're signed, I'll have them couriered back to you immediately."

"But—"

"I believe Ms. Voss is leaving without me." Jonah spun on his heel and walked out, sighing in relief when he was down the steps. Carol was trotting down the street, her tail and head high, practically dancing in a puppyish, endearing way.

Jonah watched her, certain that she was going to be full of sunshine. "My car is this way." He pointed the opposite way that she'd been walking, almost laughing when she lifted her head even higher and trotted past him.

Yup. This one was going to be a handful.

Jonah took the lead, taking Carol to his car and opening the back door. "Once you're human, I'll let you in the front, but for now I think you'll be more comfortable back here."

Carol hopped right in and settled on the blanket Jonah had draped across the back seat for whatever familiar he wound up with. She placed her head on her paws and closed her eyes with a contented sigh.

Huh. That was his blanket. He'd nearly forgotten his appointment and had grabbed the one off his bed without thought. From the way she was nuzzling it, though, she must *really* like his scent.

He found himself curious as he climbed behind the wheel and started his car. Was Carol tiny, like her wolf form indicated, or tall? Were her eyes golden or a different color? Would he like her as much as she seemed to like him?

It didn't take long to arrive. The Sound family kept more than one home, his favorite being the house in Santa Monica. Even in winter, the sun on the water and the sound of the waves soothed him as nothing else could. But those homes belonged to his father. Jonah had his own residence apart from his parents' mansions, a sweet two-story townhouse he'd bought at auction and renovated himself. One his mother couldn't just waltz into and change on a whim whenever it suited her.

For an eagle shifter, she could be very flighty, but his father adored her and wouldn't change a thing about her. Neither would Jonah. She'd proven that predatory familiars were just like everyone else. Their only quirk was they preferred their steaks on the rare side.

Jonah pulled into the garage, hoping Carol would be impressed with his home. The garage opened up onto a stone-tiled foyer. To the right of the garage was his office space, where he spent quite a bit of his time researching magical crimes and their aftermath. The bathroom next to it held a small shower for when he came home covered in bodily fluids. It had happened often enough that the shower stall had become a necessity.

The great room was where he lived and entertained, with a comfortable sectional, a huge television, and all the game consoles he could squeeze into the entertainment center. To the right of the stairs were the kitchen and dining room. The kitchen had French doors leading to a small deck, giving Jonah plenty of room to entertain his family and their familiars or any friends he invited by. Jonah would sit out there sometimes and stare at the city lights when he was weary from another day on the job.

The second floor held three bedrooms, one of which was the master. He'd installed a large clawfoot tub in the master bath, along with a glass-walled shower big enough for two. A vanity sat between two sinks, ready for a woman's makeup should he ever find someone to bond with permanently. The second bedroom he'd set up as a guest room—now Carol's room—and the third was a home gym.

God, he hoped Carol liked his home. He'd sweated blood and tears to make it as comfortable, airy, and livable as possible.

Carol sniffed the air before heading right for his office. She nudged the door open with her snout, glancing around before trotting to the great room and huffing happily at the game consoles. She danced delightedly at the tiny reading nook he'd set up between the great room and the kitchen. It seemed his new familiar liked to read just as much as he did.

Once in the kitchen, she barked at some birds that had dared to perch on the deck railing, sending them fluttering into the mid-morning sky. Her tail started wagging a mile a minute as she watched them fly off. She moved away from the window when the last of the birds disappeared, stopping at the bottom of the stairs and shooting him a questioning glance.

"The bedrooms are upstairs. Would you like the tour before we sign the paperwork?"

Carol nodded eagerly before running up the stairs, tail still wagging.

Jonah followed at a slower pace, grinning as her nails clicked on the hardwood floors. No doubt at some point she'd come running in, skidding across the surface like a goofy dog. She had that sort of aura about her, as if she were part fierce predator, part happy puppy.

He'd done the spare bedroom up almost hotel-like. He hoped she'd add her personal touch to the room, but for now, it was a blank slate, ready for her to make it her own.

The sound of her rummaging around amused him, but he let her be, instead choosing to head back downstairs. He grabbed some soft drinks for them. Not only did they have paperwork to file, but he was dying to find out what his familiar looked like under all that fur and cuteness. He took the drinks to the round dining room table he'd chosen to fit the space. It easily seated six, eight in a pinch.

It wasn't long before she returned, her tongue hanging out of the side of her mouth in a very dog-like way. This was one wolf who seemed to like the comforts of home.

"Can you change? We need to talk." Jonah ignored the way that doggie grin immediately disappeared. "I'd like to meet you in your human form too."

The air around the woman shimmered. A small-boned woman stood before him, her red hair cut in a long, wavy bob. Her big brown eyes were the same gold as her wolf's. She wore a simple T-shirt and jeans, with red canvas sneakers.

If she was over five foot two, he'd eat his wand.

"Hi." She waved warily, her smile shy. "I'm Carol."

Jonah grinned. God, she really was cute as a button, and about the same size. "I'm Jonah." He held out his hand, gripping hers lightly. The threads of their magic twined around their clasped hands, making him gasp at the strength of their connection.

"Wow." Her golden eyes were wide.

"Wow indeed." Jonah took his hand back before he got lost in her anima. This woman could possibly be the one he'd been searching for all these years, someone who could give him not only a familiar bond but a loving relationship. Between the magical bonds and the strong attraction, he was starting to hope for something he'd begun to think was beyond his grasp. "Where have you been all my life?"

She threw her head back and laughed. "The orphanage, then the House."

He scowled. "Orphanage?" *Damn it. Please let it not be what I'm thinking.* Too many parents of large predator shifters familiars abandoned their children, forcing them to live in state-run orphanages before being shipped off to a House for matching once they graduated high school. This wouldn't be the first time he'd matched with an abandoned familiar. His animus was only attracted to the large predators, especially canines and vulpines.

Of course, he could be wrong. Her parents could be dead.

Shrugging, Carol took her seat at the table. "We were a typical case. My brother Sawyer and I were both dropped off when my parents learned we were large predators, not smaller, less-lethal tabbies like our dad."

Guess not. It happened a lot, familiars born different from their parents, either due to a genetic throwback or the magic they carried. He wasn't sure why. Other sorcerers were researching the enigma, but so far, no answer had been found. His mother had once told him that it was the goddess of magic's choice, and why should anyone question it? But Jonah considered it an interesting conundrum that two larger predators were born to a small house cat.

"Dad was a tabby cat, and Mom barely had enough magic to qualify as a sorcerer," Carol continued, her tone nonchalant. "They were afraid they wouldn't be able to contain us if we ran wild. Since our little sister wasn't dropped off, we assume she became a sorcerer, or a tabby like our dad."

Mother of magic, he hated stories like hers. They broke his heart. One child was accepted and loved while the other two were thrown away like garbage. It happened more often than he liked to think. Even other familiars tended to be wary of the larger predators, buying in to the myth that they were as savage as their beast.

Jonah grimaced. "I'm sorry you had to go through that. What is your brother?" She hadn't mentioned that yet, and he found himself curious.

31

She grinned, and this time, it was an expression of pride. "He's a lion." She shrugged again. "I'm sorry too. What sucks the most is I have no idea where they are or even if they're still alive. We never heard from any of them again." She took a sip of the soda he'd poured them. "Mm. It's good."

"Homemade is the best." Jonah leaned back in his chair and studied her. "Do you want to find them?" On principle he was against it, but if it was what she wanted he'd hunt them down.

She paused, carefully placing the glass down on the coaster he'd set out. "My parents? No. My sister, maybe. She'd be eighteen now, I think."

"We can try to find her if that's what you want." Jonah would, whether Carol wished it or not. If the sister was like the parents and wanted nothing to do with her, he'd tell Carol that she was dead rather than subject her to the animosity some people had toward predator familiars.

"I'd like that, but I need to see what my brother wants to do." Carol smiled sweetly, and Jonah found himself drowning in more than just the magic bouncing between them. Those expressive eyes of hers were going to be the death of him.

If this bond didn't work out, Jonah really would eat his wand.

Chapter 3

Carol had decided that for their bond to work, she needed to be as honest with Jonah as possible. No matter how uncomfortable certain aspects of her past made her, she'd come a long way from that frightened, abandoned child. People like Stacey and Brent, as well as her brother, had ensured that she'd grown up knowing she had friends and family who cared for her. The fact that Stacey wasn't a large predator had gone a long way to dismissing some of the resentment she felt toward her parents.

They were the ones with the problem, not her. And someday all of her would believe that, not just most of her. There were times when that child resurfaced, however, times when she wished she were stronger. She just had to pray that Jonah understood.

He had a curious expression on his face when he began speaking again. "I've had familiars who were abandoned before, but I've never asked this. I hope you feel comfortable answering."

Uh-oh. Carol began to tense, wondering what sort of question Jonah had in mind. Would their contract depend on her answer? Her nerves began to fray. They'd talked a lot about her past, but not much about his. There wasn't much she knew about the Sounds beyond what she'd seen on television or on the Internet.

"What was it like growing up in the orphanage?" Jonah leaned on one hand, his elbow on the table. "Did you have a lot of friends?"

That surprised her. She'd expected something else, more along the lines of *how many orphans have you eaten?* Carol picked up the lemonade and took another sip. It was tart and cold, absolutely delicious.

"Not really. Sawyer and I kept to ourselves for the most part. It wasn't until Stacey that the other kids started to talk to us, and we began making friends." Carol would forever be grateful to her too.

"Stacey?" His brows rose, his lips quirking into a gentle smile.

"My BFF, my shopping buddy, and my reason for not eating Skipper today." Carol wrinkled her nose. They really needed to get rid of what's her name before someone—probably Brent—took a swipe at her. Trying to interfere in a match was way against the rules, but it happened sometimes. Since Skipper had shown up, it happened far more often than Carol liked. She'd given her the benefit of the doubt, but three months had passed since Skipper came to work for the House, and she'd tried that bullshit at every matching session. Carol was going to write a strongly worded letter to Patrick, so he had something on file. And she wouldn't sign it *Anonymous.*

"Skipper?" Jonah chuckled.

"The matchmaker Patrick recently hired." She frowned thoughtfully. "Have you met Patrick Burns?"

Jonah nodded. "Yup. He's an old friend."

"Ah." Carol fidgeted with a silver ring she wore on her right hand. "I doubt she'll work there for long. Patrick hates that kind of thing. When he finds out how she tried to influence our match, he's gonna blow a gasket." Carol wanted to be a fly on the wall for that one. Patrick was notoriously protective of his familiars. Perky Patty would soon find her ass handed to her in a very non-perky way.

"I was planning on calling him this afternoon." Jonah shuddered. "She tried to get me to pick a kitty shifter."

"Nothing wrong with the felines unless you're allergic."

He chuckled, his hazel eyes fixed on her. "I'm more of a dog person."

Carol tilted her head, ignoring the way he gazed at her with slow-burning heat. If she focused on that, she'd never be able to speak. "My turn. What was it like growing up rich?"

Jonah glanced around. "Do I seem rich to you?"

"Your family is rich enough to land in the society pages, so yes." Even Carol, who wasn't that interested in the Paris Hiltons of the world, had heard of the Sound family. The Sound family's contributions to familiar rights were legendary in Houses across the world.

"To me, it was normal. When I was a kid, I didn't understand why some of my friends couldn't afford certain things and I could, so I begged my parents to take care of it." Jonah smiled, his expression fond. "My father sat me, my sister, and my brother down one day and told us we were going to start learning about money. Until I was eighteen, I had to account for every penny I spent. I had to earn it, too, doing chores around the house, and when I was sixteen getting a job outside the home. That money was to pay for necessities like gas for my car and clothing, not just partying with my friends."

"Sounds pretty normal so far." Some of the House familiar's families had their kids do the same thing. She was curious what it was like to grow up with parents who cared enough to enforce rules on how their children behaved.

"It was. He wanted us to understand the value of what we had and the good we could do with it if we wanted to." He wrinkled his nose. "He also told us that we'd be poor until we made our own money because we weren't going to live our lives off of what he'd made. We were to go out and make our own livings because he planned on spending his earnings on my mother."

"He sounds like a good man." Carol couldn't imagine living like that. "We had chores, but we didn't get paid for them. It was just part of living there, like part of our room and board. If we wanted anything beyond the necessities, we had to go outside the orphanage and work, but we could only do that once we were sixteen, and only if we kept our grades up." She sighed. "But my brother and I and the other large predators were steered away from working for anyone but the orphanage."

"So, I guess you didn't go on field trips or vacations?"

"Pfft." Carol laughed. Was he crazy? "Vacations don't happen in orphanages. As for field trips, we were schooled at the orphanage, so no, we didn't do those either."

Jonah scowled. "Why no public school?"

She sighed. People just didn't get it sometimes. "Predators, remember? A lot of people, apparently my parents included, think predator familiars are far more dangerous than we really are. They forget that we're still people, even in our shifted form." She shrugged. "Maybe they get that from actual shifters, but we're *familiars*. We don't go feral like some shifters can."

Man, if he scowled any harder his face might stick like that. "You mean the rest of them went to school, but you and your brother didn't?"

What was he expecting, an *Annie*–type happy ending? "Pretty much, yeah."

"What about college?"

College was always an option for familiars, but if they matched with a sorcerer early, it could take them longer to graduate, depending on their match. While another college student would be ideal, it didn't always work out that way, and many familiars had to put college off while they worked with their sorcerer on their careers. "Believe it or not, I've got my degree in law enforcement. I've finished the police academy, too, and was going to start work in about a week." She grinned. "Seems like I'm being transferred already, huh?"

Jonah leaned back in his chair, now completely relaxed. He was smiling sweetly, obviously pleased to hear about her career path. With his next words, she was proven right. "We really are a good match, aren't we?" He winked at her, his expression delighted.

"I think so." Carol yawned. Sometimes their animal halves contributed little quirks to their human halves. For wolves, yawning was one of them. When a canine yawned, it could be from being tired or from nerves. Right now, Carol was beginning to get nervous. Why hadn't he handed over the paperwork?

If she had to go back, tail tucked between her legs, Chipper Skipper would have a field day.

She'd never had such a strong connection to anyone before, not even to her brother. Not to mention, Jonah was very easy on the eyes. His hazel eyes had turned dark, almost deep brown when he'd listened to the story of her childhood. Now it was veering back toward a mix of green and brown. She sensed that if she just studied the color of them, she'd get a handle on all of his moods.

"I'm sorry if I've been intrusive. Do you still want to sign the papers?" He seemed a little less pleased now. His shoulders had stiffened, and the easygoing smile was gone.

Carol smiled. Oh, thank God. "Yes, I do. It's natural to want information about your familiar's past, or so I think. I want to understand you, too, so feel free to ask away. I'll tell you if I don't want to answer. Just do me the same courtesy, and we'll be fine."

"Hmm. You should probably be aware that I can be a bit…" He stared at his hands, his brows furrowed. The brown in his eyes was starting to seep back, overwhelming the green. "Shit. I like keeping my familiar safe. It's one of the reasons I've lost a number of them since I tend to be attracted to predator familiars like yourself."

Her eyes went wide. "Like bubble-wrap, locked-in-my-room safe?" That wouldn't work, not with the goals she had. She needed to be his partner, not his pet.

He snorted out a laugh. "Not quite *that* bad, but most of my familiars have been predators, and they don't take well to having the squishy sorcerer being the one out in front in a battle."

Carol stared at him. "Well, duh. I have teeth and claws and fur that protects my skin. You don't."

His eyebrow rose arrogantly. "But in a sorcerer battle, I have shielding and magic."

Good point. Carol was useless in a magical duel except to keep her sorcerer's magic stable. "I can understand that. In physical battles, I'll take point; in magical ones, you do."

"I have a brown belt in Krav Maga. I can defend myself." Jonah's chin tilted up, his gaze challenging her to say something. No doubt he was very proud of that fact.

She grinned, wide and toothy and totally wolfish. "Good. I don't have to worry about your squishy ass while I'm fighting off bad guys."

He shook his head, his smile begrudgingly amused. "Here, Bad Wolf. Sign the papers." He pushed the paperwork across to her.

Carol practically melted in her chair. Was this man made just for her? "You watch *Dr. Who*?" She bit her lip, just a little bit more interested in her sorcerer. "Name your favorite Doctor."

His brows rose. "David Tennant, who else?"

"Damn. I'm a Matt Smith girl." She stared at the paperwork and tsk'd. "Not sure I can sign these now."

He laughed and handed her the pen. She signed her side, gasping at the unfamiliar tingle from the tattoo on the inside of her left wrist. She glanced at it, smiling at the sight of the word *contracted* under her name and the name of her House. Above them all was Jonah's name, signifying that he was now her contracted sorcerer. She slid the pen and papers over to him. "Is the spare room upstairs for me?" She'd caught whiffs of other types of familiars, some large predators, others not. It would surprise her if it *wasn't* the room she was supposed to use.

Jonah signed. "Of course. You can add any decorations you like. It's pretty plain, so you can add your own touches to it. I want you to make it feel like home."

"Huh." That wasn't the answer she'd expected. "My brother's sorcerer wouldn't allow him to do that. He wasn't supposed to change a thing, even a light bulb."

"Probably because he only planned on a temporary contract. I'm hoping for a long-term one." His gaze was like a physical brand. Her anima reached out to his, finding its match in his animus. She nearly moaned at the sensation filtering down the link between them. His seductive grin sent a craving through her to find out exactly how that wicked mouth tasted. "A *very* long-term one."

Oh, dear God. If he kept gazing at her like that, she might just start humping his leg, and that would be plain old embarrassing. "Is this normal?"

"Is what normal?" He clasped her hand, running his thumb along the back.

"This." She waved her hand between the two of them. "I mean, you're hot, hotter than hot, lava-like, but I never wanted to jump your bones this badly when I spotted you on TV."

His pupils dilated as his hand tightened on hers. "You want to jump my bones?"

She flicked him between the eyes with her finger. "Focus!"

"Ow." He chuckled softly, but he leaned back, releasing her hand. "No, it isn't normal. I've felt attraction for my familiars before, but nothing this strong."

"And this is the strongest bond you've ever experienced, right?" Damn. Double-damn. She didn't want to want him simply because their anima and animus matched up so well. Being forced together by their magic could lead to some very uncomfortable morning-afters.

"It is, but trust me when I tell you my attraction to you has very little to do with the bond that's starting to form and everything to do with what I'm seeing and hearing." Jonah took her hand again, his grip tightening when she tried to pull away. "What can I say? You're just that adorable."

She snarled, allowing fang to show. "I'm not adorable. I'm a fierce predator."

"Yes, dear." He patted her on the head, and she glared at him, eliciting another chuckle. "You're also a fine specimen of womanhood. To put it in your own words"—his voice softened as he leaned in closer—"I want to jump your bones too." He sat back in his seat, apparently pleased with himself.

Carol couldn't answer. She was too busy contemplating whether or not she'd just made a contract with a bigger predator than any she'd ever met before.

From the way his lips curled up, as if he were amused at her inner struggle, she might be right.

Chapter 4

Dear gods, she was magnificent. One moment all feminine need, the next ready to fight him toe to toe as an equal. He'd never met a familiar like her before. Most of them had been arrogant about their abilities and ready to fight anything that dared come near them. Including him.

He'd have to be careful with her. If things didn't work out between them, his heart might not be able to take it. She'd already gained a foothold there, her delicate features and fierce pride striking a chord within him. He'd have to make sure she remained safe from the darker side of his work. If a blood sorcerer got ahold of her, he'd move heaven and hell to get her back.

He was almost afraid of what he'd be willing to do if the bond strengthened. He really would wind up wrapping her in bubble wrap and locking her in a safe room where no one could touch a hair on her head.

Several of his female familiars had left him because of his overprotective streak. Two had been lovers, and when they left, they told him they'd found him and his attentions smothering. The last thing he wanted to do was repeat that mistake, but Carol appeared so frail he couldn't begin to figure out how he'd hold back. No doubt she'd force the issue, and the two would fight, but he'd cross that bridge when he came to it.

Carol was upstairs, in her bedroom, probably figuring how she'd decorate once she moved her things in. Considering her background, he might take her shopping just for the joy of watching her pick out some things that would make the space her own.

Meanwhile, Jonah was in his office, fighting off a raging boner for a woman he'd just met. He would not go upstairs and jump her bones.

He. Would. *Not.*

"Down, boy." Jonah stared out the window at the small garden his mother had created for him. She'd planted a combination of lilac roses, crepe myrtle, and flowering cherry. Under the myrtle was a bench Jonah liked to sit on when he wanted to read outside on a lovely spring night. She'd also set up string lights around the garden, giving it a subtle glow. A small stone patio area with a grill, table, and chairs allowed him to entertain a small group of friends outdoors.

Jonah loved his little garden paradise. He hoped Carol would love it too. He'd have to introduce her to it. He'd also have to take her to the beach house in Santa Monica and let her run on the sand and in the surf in both forms.

How would that slinky little body of hers fill out a bikini?

Jonah groaned. So much for getting his hard-on to disappear.

His cell phone rang, startling him out of his thoughts. It was the ringtone he'd set for the station. "Detective Sound."

"Jonah, it's Miles." Miles was the one who went through the crime calls and determined which seemed to need further investigation by MCU. "We've got a possible blood sorcerer murder for you."

Shit. Talk about throwing Carol into the deep end. "Where?" He jotted down the address.

Fuck, the university?

"It's behind home plate on the softball field," Miles ground out. "The kid was only seventeen, a high school senior checking out the facilities, according to his parents. He'd just contracted with his first familiar."

Jonah drew in a deep breath. These were the cases that bugged him the most. The kids who'd just come into their power were the most vulnerable to blood sorcerers. They barely knew how to defend themselves, but their power was pure candy to the sorcerers who stole it.

"I'm on my way."

Miles hung up without saying goodbye, but that was normal for them. He'd visit Miles when he stopped by the Sherman Oaks PD. They'd be making their way there soon to introduce Carol to his boss and get her familiar badge ready. Eventually, she'd have a full detective's badge, as she'd been through the academy, but she needed to do fieldwork with him before she'd be eligible for that. Her pay would be that of a beat cop until that time came.

He stepped out of his office. "Carol!"

Footsteps came racing down the stairs, and she seemed startled. "Yeah?"

"We have a murder to investigate." Jonah glanced around and patted his pockets. "Where's my wand?"

Carol watched him with a bemused expression as he searched the living room. He could swear that's where he'd put it, but it was nowhere to be found. He didn't technically need it to cast spells, but it helped him to focus. Other sorcerers used stress balls, crystal orbs, or even staves. One sorcerer he'd gone to school with liked to play with a fidget spinner while casting.

"Is that it?" Carol pointed toward the fireplace. Sure enough, his wand was on the mantel.

"Thanks." He tucked it in his pocket, the wand small enough to fit into the palm of his hand. Made of silver and crusted with semi-precious gems, the cool wand meshed perfectly with his magic. "You ready?"

"Are you sure I'm allowed?"

He blinked in surprise. "Of course. Even the familiars I had who weren't cops had to come with me. We can't be far from each other, remember, or the bond won't form properly." And that would be a crying shame.

"Right. Of course." She grimaced. "Let me rephrase that. Will I be allowed to help?"

He had to think about that one. "You were supposed to start work tomorrow, right?"

"Yes."

"Good." That would take care of anyone who questioned why she was there actively helping him instead of just standing around bored, or worse, sickened. "I'm going to have you do simple things like talk to witnesses. If I think you need supervision or if you miss something, I'll be there. Consider it on-the-job training." His captain wouldn't have much of an issue with it, if any. In fact, she'd probably be thrilled to have Carol in her department, and maybe she'd be allowed to stay after the year and a day was up.

He glanced around. "You have everything you need?"

Carol pocketed her phone and shrugged, appearing far calmer than he'd expected. "Not sure what I'll need yet, so let's roll. I'll learn as we go."

He stared at her, surprised at how composed she was. "You'll be observing a dead body in about twenty minutes."

Carol glanced away for a second, her lost expression causing Jonah to start toward her. Perhaps she could remain behind—

"I've witnessed a dead body before." Carol glanced back at him, her lips tight, her eyes closed. "It wasn't pretty, but I handled it then, and I'll handle it now." She opened her eyes and tapped the side of her nose. "Besides, I can be of use to you."

"When did you—"

"When I was around sixteen," Carol interrupted. Her expression was haunted. "I was still in the orphanage. One of the kids was murdered, her body left on the front steps. They caught

47

the fucker who killed her before he got anyone else. It was what made me decide to become a cop. I wanted to catch the assholes who think they can kill with impunity. Honestly, I was hoping I'd be paired with a police officer so I could pursue my dream even during the year and a day period."

He focused more on the murder than her wishes. "Damn. That's young to have caught sight of something like that."

She grimaced. "I wasn't the first on the scene. The grade-schoolers got out earlier than we did."

"Shit." Stories like hers weren't uncommon, unfortunately.

She tilted her head. "So, who's driving, you or me?"

He tossed her the keys. "Have at it."

Her eyes widened in excitement. "Really?"

"Yes, really."

"Whoop!" She threw her hands in the air and danced down the rest of the stairs. "I get to drive, I get to drive," she sang as she raced toward the garage.

Jonah shook his head, laughing. He didn't just want her; he was beginning to like her. She certainly was keeping him on his toes.

It didn't take long to arrive at the location.

Jonah held up his badge when a uniformed officer tried to stop Carol from parking in the lot near the crime scene. "Detective Sound, MCU."

The officer nodded and waved him through.

Jonah loved the badge he'd earned. His designation of Detective: MCU in royal blue lettering was a source of pride. It had taken years to earn that badge, to move from a uniformed officer to a rookie in the Magical Crimes Unit to detective. He hoped never to leave the department. One day, he'd like to take the place of his captain, the sorcerer currently supervising the other detective-sorcerers who worked in the MCU. But if he never made captain, he'd still be proud of the work he did long after he retired.

Jonah stepped out of the car and slammed the door shut. "Stay with me," he said to Carol over the hood. "You don't have your badge yet, so the mark on your wrist is your only ID. Use it if needed. If anyone has any questions, that will point them toward me." He'd make sure she had her own familiar badge soon, allowing her to move around a crime scene without him. Until then, she'd have to show her wrist to any officer who asked.

She nodded and stepped around the hood, keeping close to his side.

The scene had been taped off, but there were still people trying to observe what was going on. Students, teachers, and staff all stared toward the baseball diamond where the body had been found. Several had their phones out, either taking pictures or filming the scene.

He turned to the uniformed officer keeping an eye on the crowd, showing his badge and gesturing for Carol to show her wrist. When the officer nodded, he began his questions. "Who's on scene?"

The officer glanced at his notebook. "Detectives Quentin Wheeler and Vanessa Ridgely, sir."

"Thank you. Who was first on the scene?"

"I was, sir. The call came about an hour ago. When I got here, the body was on home plate, but it was obvious he'd been killed elsewhere."

"What makes you say that?" Jonah pulled out a notepad of his own and began jotting down the detective's words.

"No blood, but he'd been stabbed in the chest repeatedly."

Jonah glanced up from his notepad. "Stabbed?" That wasn't common with blood sorcerers. Could it be a normal homicide dressed to appear like an MCU case? It happened sometimes, especially among those who had a grudge against sorcerers. That kind of attack was usually perpetrated by family members of those who'd been murdered by a blood sorcerer, one who wanted revenge.

Then again, if Miles had called it in, Jonah was going to go with the assumption that there were circumstances that made the dispatcher believe it was a magic-related death.

"Yeah, but around the stab wound were these symbols that blood sorcerers use when they drain a victim of magic." The guy glanced toward the onlookers and lowered his voice. "You know the ones."

Jonah did. They were usually drawn in either blood or some other bodily fluid. "You got pictures?"

"Yes, sir. I'll send them to you right away."

"Thanks." He tilted his head. "Did anything else about the crime scene seem odd to you?"

The officer's brows furrowed. "He appeared...posed."

"Posed how?" That was unusual.

"He had his hands folded over his heart and his legs together like he was in a casket." The officer shrugged. "Sick bastard put a white lily in his hands."

Jonah made a note of that. He'd have to make sure the officer's description matched the scene, but that first impression could be a clue that wound up solving the case. "Interesting. Done any interviews yet?"

The officer shook his head. "Nope. Wheeler and Ridgely insisted on doing that."

"Thanks." Jonah made a note of it and closed his notebook. "I'll need your notes as well, asap."

"Yes, sir." The officer turned back to the crowd, and Jonah made his way to the police tape. "All right, people. Move along. The body's already gone, nothing to see here."

Jonah turned around sharply. "What did you say?"

"Shit," Carol muttered under her breath. She was glancing around, obviously upset at Jonah's angry tone. She even tried stepping slightly in front of him, but he waved her back. She couldn't take point on this, not yet, not until she'd earned her detective's badge. A familiar badge only gave you so much power on the force.

"Uh, the body's gone?" The officer gulped, his eyes wide and terrified.

"Who ordered that?" Jonah was going to fry whoever had moved the body before he got there. How the hell was he supposed to do his job if his victim had been removed? There was no coroner's van, meaning the body had to have been taken before Miles even contacted him.

"Wheeler and Ridgely, Detective Sound." The man glanced at Carol, probably using her expression as a barometer of Jonah's mood. He shrank back. "I'm sorry, but there wasn't anything I could do."

Jonah gritted his teeth. Shit. A pissing match between Homicide and MCU was *so* not what he needed right now. "Thank you again, Officer."

The officer smiled wanly and returned to his post, probably grateful he didn't have to deal with Jonah any further.

Jonah would deal with Wheeler and Ridgely once he found out how the victim had died. If it was his case, he'd have to talk to their captain. Depending on what he might have found, they could have destroyed vital evidence.

Christ, he hoped someone took pictures of the crime scene. He might be able to use those to help piece things together. With the rookie way they'd removed the vic before MCU showed up, anything was possible.

If it was their case, he'd have to eat some crow. But from the sensation of lingering magic in the area, he doubted he'd be shitting feathers anytime soon.

Chapter 5

Carol sniffed, wrinkling her nose at the odor of stale bodies, rotting flesh, old blood, and magic. Strong magic. Wrong-smelling, foul, and filled with the coppery scent of blood, it almost overpowered the sweaty smells of an athletic field. The closer they got to home plate, the stronger the smell became. "This is definitely an MCU case, Jonah."

He nodded brusquely. Even she understood that you didn't move the body until the CSI guys had gone over the scene with a fine-toothed comb. She doubted they'd had the time to do more than park their van, so why had the detectives released the body to the coroner?

The soft hum of voices caught her attention. She touched Jonah's arm to get his attention. "Over there."

"I see them." He diverted their path to the dugout, where a man and a woman were standing over a much younger man. The young man was slumped on the bench, his hands clenched between his knees, his hair covering his face. One of the officers was pointing at him while the other wrote in a notebook.

"They think he did it?" She could scent the animal on the man. She'd known a few of that species in her time. The poor familiar wouldn't hurt a fly unless someone were trying to infringe on his territory. She highly doubted that was the case here. He'd be more likely to go after a romantic partner or someone who was bullying his sorcerer. "He's a fucking cockatiel."

Jonah stopped in his tracks. "Why is that important?"

She stared at him. "Predators are considered dangerous for a reason, Jonah. We're more aggressive than the prey species, more likely to hurt or even kill in anger, though it's rare. A cockatiel familiar, however, likes nothing better than hanging out with his friends, singing and whistling, and eating seeds. The only time they get aggressive is when their territory is under attack, and he'd consider his sorcerer as part of that territory."

He blinked, seemingly stunned. "Just like wild cockatiels?"

She'd thought he was well versed in how close familiars were with their beasts, but apparently not. "And pet cockatiels." She shook her head. "They get scared easily too. A cockatiel rarely kills. It's just not in them. They're herbivores. They don't have that killer instinct a predator species would have."

His shoulders relaxed. "Then we need to inform the fine detectives that they need to back the fuck away. You think he was the sorcerer's familiar?"

Carol shrugged. "He's the right age, and the cops are talking to him. I'd say yes."

Jonah began walking forward once more. "I'll deal with the detectives. You find out what you can from the familiar. He's more likely to talk to you if he's been…rigorously questioned."

"Gotcha." Carol strode beside him, ready to defend her sorcerer should the two detectives become hostile.

"Detectives?" Jonah's voice was cold. His legs were apart, his hands clenched at his sides. It looked like he was ready for battle, but why? Jonah could kick both their asses, unless one of them was also a sorcerer. She sniffed, but neither of them carried that special scent that indicated mana resided within them.

Carol caught a clue as the two turned around, wearing equal expressions of annoyance and anger. Neither of them seemed to notice her at his side, but considering they were detectives she doubted they hadn't caught sight of her. They were just ignoring her, focusing on the bigger fish in their little pond. There must be friction between Homicide and MCU. She slid closer to Jonah, watching the two detectives warily.

"I'm Detective Jonah Sound, MCU, and this is my familiar, Carol Voss." Carol turned over her wrist as Jonah held up his shield. "I'm here to investigate the murder."

"This isn't an MCU case," Detective Wheeler growled.

"I beg to differ." Carol held her ground as the two detectives turned their glares on her. Jonah was right, and she could back him up. "I'm a wolf familiar. I can smell the magic all over this field."

Detective Wheeler backed up a step, distrust and fear stamped on his features. Detective Ridgely stiffened, her hand drifting toward her sidearm.

Carol backed up a step. Apparently, the two detectives feared predator familiars. Unfortunately, there was always the chance for violence, but rarely was the familiar the one who initiated it.

"Of course, you can smell it," Detective Ridgely replied snidely. "This college has magical classes. You can probably smell it everywhere."

Carol shook her head, keeping her movements slow and easy. She didn't want to spook them any more than she already had. "I'm sorry, but the magic I'm concerned about is concentrated over by home plate, and it's almost definitely blood magic." Her teachers in the academy had used a tool that could imitate the scents of certain types of magic. This one was impossible to forget. In fact, she found it slightly nauseating, but she wasn't going to tell them that. She focused on Jonah, who was scowling fiercely at the two detectives. "I think the last of his magic was bled away there."

"I'll cast some spells and see what I can come up with." Jonah turned to the detectives, who were appearing less annoyed and more concerned, probably for themselves. They had to be aware that if this was an MCU case, their actions had jeopardized the investigation.

"This is our case," Detective Ridgely said with far less venom than her earlier statement. She'd relaxed slightly, but her gaze remained glued to Carol as if Carol would jump her at any moment. "MCU can't just waltz in here and steal it."

Jonah shook his head. "I'm sorry, but facts are facts." He crossed his arms over his chest, apparently ready to stand his ground.

"He was stabbed to death, and it was made to appear to be an MCU case," Wheeler added, glaring at Carol. His fear was palpable, in his stance, his expression, even his scent, bitter and venomous.

Jonah moved, putting himself between Wheeler and Carol. "My familiar isn't a threat, Detectives."

Carol growled, just low enough that only Jonah could hear it. She didn't like that he'd put himself in potential danger, but she held her place. In this battle, as an MCU detective, he had far more power than she did.

Jonah remained where he was. Either he hadn't heard her, or he was ignoring her. "I'm afraid not. I'll need the vic's familiar to talk to mine while I go over the crime scene."

The two detectives glanced at each other, their expressions inscrutable. Ridgely finally replied, her tone uncertain. "The sniffer didn't detect anything."

Sniffers were magic detectors built for those without magic of their own. Most police, firemen, and rescue personnel were trained in their use, but that didn't mean they were infallible.

Carol snorted disgustedly. She'd learned all about sniffers in the academy and how they were supposed to be used by detectives without delicate noses like hers. "Because you didn't read it properly. There's ambient magic here, so you just

58

stopped at that reading instead of allowing the sniffer time to work."

The detectives seemed thoroughly aggravated once more, possibly because she'd dared to speak up. "The sniffers should have picked up any kind of magic if it was concentrated," Detective Wheeler grumbled. He seemed a little more at ease now that Jonah stood between them.

Carol tapped the side of her nose. "Well, *this* sniffer will go talk to the poor familiar of our victim while you guys hash the rest of this out."

She didn't bother waiting for a response. She took a step around the flabbergasted detectives, squaring herself in front of the cockatiel familiar and blocking their view of him.

"Hi." In deference to his nature, she kept her tone friendly. "What's your name?"

The guy was visibly shaking, his arms trembling so violently she was afraid she'd manage to break his bones. "Ronnie. Ronnie Stewart."

Carol smiled, hoping to put the poor guy at ease. "I'm Carol Voss. I work with that guy." She pointed over her shoulder with her thumb at Jonah. "I'm sorry, but I have to ask you some questions. Is that okay?

"Yeah. Sure." Ronnie glanced up at her through the fall of his hair. "But I'm not sure if I can be of any help."

"It's okay. We'll do this as slow as you need, all right?" Ronnie nodded once more, so Carol began asking her questions. "Can you tell me what you saw?"

Ronnie shook his head. "I was in class when I felt him die." He shuddered. "Louis was my best friend. We were going to stay bonded forever."

Shit. He would have suffered from the bond snapping the moment his sorcerer died. "The pain must have been terrible." Carol took a seat next to him and pulled out a small recorder. She didn't have a notebook. She preferred to have words as they were spoken rather than short notes. She'd used the same recorder in college. She'd transfer the file to her laptop when she was home.

For a moment, she jolted. Home was no longer her House. Home was now back at Jonah's place, in a comfortable room that was as sterile as a hotel room.

"It was," Ronnie replied, shivering. If he'd been in cockatiel form his crest would have been completely raised, his feathers flat against his body, the signs of an upset, scared, or startled cockatiel.

"Can you tell me when you sensed his death?" Carol glanced toward Jonah. He was walking away from the two detectives, heading for home plate and some numbered evidence identification markers. He'd exchanged his notebook for his wand. His magic pulsed along their bond as he began to channel their combined energy.

"Around six last night." He wiped away a tear. "I tried to tell the campus police that something was wrong with Louis, but they didn't listen to me."

"Ugh. This is exactly why I wanted to go into law enforcement," Carol muttered. Sorcerers were always listened to; familiars, rarely. "Can you tell me his full name? The boys in blue didn't bother telling me."

He sniffled and nodded. "Louis Reeves."

"Thank you." She glanced over and caught sight of Wheeler and Ridgely talking to each other. Their hands were flying and their expressions absolutely furious as they glanced between her and Jonah. She did her best to ignore them, but it was hard when they both kept turning to glare at her. "So, you tried to talk to campus police. What happened when they brushed you off?"

"I called the police." He shook his head. "They said they couldn't search for him until he'd been missing for forty-eight hours because he's an adult."

"The laws need to be changed where familiars are concerned." Far too often they were treated as extensions of their sorcerer only when it was convenient. The law was still ambiguous where the sensations fed through a familiar-sorcerer bond were concerned. A landmark case against familiar bond sensations was the rape of a woman by a sorcerer. The familiar attempted to report it to the police even though he wasn't present. He'd been aware of the attack through their bond. The police failed to respond until after the woman managed to escape her attacker and get to a police station. The courts had stated that, while the familiar had done the right thing by trying to turn his sorcerer in, without corroborating evidence, the police couldn't act on the "feelings" of a familiar.

Carol hoped someday to help change that law. "Did you try calling him?"

"It went straight to voicemail." Ronnie bit his lip. "I tried to find him using our bond, but it was gone. There was nothing to follow."

"Which meant waiting for him to be found." Carol rubbed his shoulder. "I'm sorry for your loss."

"Thank you." He was folded in on himself, his arms wrapped tightly around his middle. "I just wish I'd felt something before he died. I might have been able to find him, save him."

"Yeah." She touched his left wrist, and he flipped it over, showing her the *available* written in magic letters. "This sucks rocks."

He gave a bitter chuckle. "You said it."

She stood and grabbed her recorder. "Can you think of anything else you think I or the police should know?"

He stared up at her, his head tilted at an almost boneless angle. It was always a little freaky when bird familiars did that. "Tell those two to go to hell for me."

She nodded. "I will."

The poor bastard had a right to be angry. The laws were written by humans, the majority race. Humans just didn't understand how the contract worked between familiars and sorcerers. Hell, they were responsible for the Burning Times, where humans, dimens, shifters, merfolk, and all sorts were burned at the stake simply for being different. The ensuing years had shown that the majority of magical folk, both native to Terra Mundus and interdimensional, just wanted to live their lives in peace. Interdimensional beings, aka dimens, weren't that different from their human counterparts.

Mostly. The jury was still out on infernal beings, the *real* demons, that walked the earth. The denizens of Terra Infernum could be a bit malicious at times.

Carol headed toward Jonah, who was kneeling by home plate and one of the evidence cones. She stopped and crouched next to him. "He says he became aware that the vic had died at six last night. Despite the fact that he reported it to campus security, no one would investigate his whereabouts because the law involving familiar-sorcerer bonds sucks." She sighed. "I taped the interview; you can listen to it and find out if I missed anything."

"Good work." Jonah held out his hand, a square piece of paper in it. "Here. Give him my card. Tell him to contact me if he or any of his friends find themselves in similar circumstances."

"Got it." She went to Ronnie and delivered Jonah's message.

Ronnie stared at her. It seemed he couldn't believe Jonah. His glance at the two homicide detectives explained why. "Do you believe him?"

She glanced back at Jonah, who was talking once more to the two homicide detectives. Man, he was *pissed.* She made a judgment based on what she'd observed of him combined with his family's reputation for fairness. "Yup."

Ronnie slipped the card in his pocket without another word.

Chapter 6

Jonah pulled away from the campus, heading to the coroner's office. Dealing with xenophobes like Wheeler and Ridgely happened far more than they should. There were laws preventing people from discrimination against larger predators, but people would forever view them as different, frightening. Only vampires faced more prejudice than shifters and familiars who happened to be large.

Jonah and Carol arrived at the coroner's late Saturday afternoon. He was starving, ready to go eat, but his window of time to speak to the coroner was slim. He doubted Paul would have more than a rudimentary cause of death for him, but it would give him a start.

At least there was a Jack in the Box across the street. He could almost taste their spicy sriracha burger.

"What was at home plate?" Carol stepped out of the car into the hot July sun.

Carol's question pulled his mind away from the thought of Oreo shakes. "Not much, unfortunately. A footprint, which should be molded by now, a candy wrapper that will hopefully give either DNA or fingerprints, and a cheap vape pen." He had high hopes for the vape pen. It should be a good source of DNA, plus they might be able to trace the pen to a specific store. They might even be able to trace the vape liquid.

65

That was if it even belonged to the bad guy. A lot of times what was picked up was only trash, something left behind by someone else, but it still needed to be investigated and either verified as evidence or eliminated. He'd hate to be the guy who failed to catch a killer because he thought a gum wrapper was insignificant.

"What did your spell reveal?"

"Dark magic was definitely present. I found blood magic residue, but there was something else there, something dark." Jonah shook his head. "I'm not sure what it was, but it made the hairs on the back of my neck stand on end."

"That can't be good."

"No, it's not. Worse, I might know where I've sensed it before."

"Terra Noctem?" Carol shivered and rubbed her arms.

He wasn't surprised that she'd paled. Terra Noctem was not a place he wanted to fuck around with.

None of the planes other than Terra Mundus were designed for anyone but their own denizens and Travelers, those who could travel through the other planes without harm. As far as magical science could tell, there were ten planes in total, Terra Mundus—the realm of humans—and Terra Noctem being two of them. The belief was that, somehow, Terra Mundus had been created from each of the other nine, allowing the denizens of the other planes to live, or at least move about comfortably there.

"Yes." Jonah wasn't about to speculate more than that. He needed to focus on the body and what Paul had to say about it. Once he'd done that, he'd consider what he'd experienced at home plate.

Carol was staring at the Mission–style brick building where all bodies were taken to be autopsied. "I'm surprised we can get in on a Saturday."

"I had to call ahead. I took care of it while you were talking to the crowd, searching for witnesses." He'd tasked her with working with one of the uniformed officers, giving her the chance to learn from him while Jonah called Paul. At the end, the uniform had given Jonah a discreet thumbs-up.

Carol brushed her hair aside as the wind blew it against her cheek. "No one noticed the body getting dumped, so that was a dead end."

Jonah walked up the broad steps of the ME-Coroner's building. "Here's hoping Paul has found something already."

The coroner's office was located on the grounds of the LAC+USC Medical Center within the Forensic Science Center. Paul Lofland, MD-M, was the doctor in charge of magic-related deaths in L.A. County. His familiar and spouse was Debbie Miller-Lofland. A bloodhound who helped him in his work, she had a master's in forensic science and a bachelor's in magical studies. She was a huge help in identifying rare magical substances used in murders, suicides, and unintentional deaths.

Jonah led Carol up the steps and to the third floor, where Paul's office was. He knocked once on the door and opened it, not waiting for a response.

Paul's secretary wasn't present, but Debbie was. She was at the secretary's desk, rummaging through the drawers.

"Looking for something?" Jonah grinned when Debbie jumped with a yip.

"Jesus, Jonah." Debbie put her hand over her heart. "You suck."

"Only when asked nicely." He winked, his grin widening when Debbie chucked a pen at him. He bent down and picked it up, almost jumping himself when a hand brushed over his backside.

"Who's your friend?" Debbie sounded amused.

Jonah straightened, pen clutched in his hand. His face was a bit red not only from bending over but from that soft touch to his ass. Had she meant to do that, or was it an accident due to proximity?

"Carol Voss, my new familiar. Carol, this is Debbie Miller-Lofland, the wife of the coroner and an expert in deadly magical substances."

Carol's expression was far too innocent to be real. Maybe her hand brushing his ass hadn't been an accident at all. One could hope.

"Nice to meet you." Carol stepped forward and held out her hand.

"You too." Debbie met her and took her hand, widening her eyes in amusement. "You keeping Jonah in his place?"

Carol chuckled. "We only met today, but I'm working on it."

"Debbie?" Paul came out of his office, frowning at his spouse, only to stop when Jonah waved hello. "Oh, hey, Jonah. Right on time."

"You could have told me he was coming," Debbie muttered, glaring at her husband.

Paul shook his head. "I did, but you were too busy muttering about Sally to pay any attention." He tilted his head. "Why did you think we were here on a Saturday anyway?"

Debbie sniffed. Her head snapped around to Carol. "Oh. You're a wolf."

"Yup, and I understand you're a bloodhound." Carol tapped her nose. "Gotta be a pain down in the morgue, right?"

"Ugh, you have *no* idea." Debbie put her arm through Carol's and led her into Paul's office. "The crispy critters are the *worst*. I always crave barbecue afterward."

Paul got out of the women's way, allowing them into his office. "Nice. Debbie could use more friends."

"Carol too."

"We'd better get in there before they start plotting something," Paul whispered. He gestured for Jonah to follow him.

Jonah entered the office to find the women going through some papers on Paul's desk. "What are you hunting at?"

Debbie glanced up. "Come take a look. I think you'll find it interesting."

Carol's expression was grave, her face pale. "I think the pictures tell the tale." She gestured toward one in particular that gave Jonah pause.

In the picture, their victim lay with his hands crossed over his chest in a funereal pose. He was lying in the dirt, home plate under his head, his legs closed. His shoelaces had been tied in such a way that his feet remained close together. Between his hands was a white lily. Around the stab wounds under the corpse's hands, almost invisible thanks to everything blocking them, were dimenic runes, ancient writing used by interdimensional beings.

"What the fuck?" He picked the picture up, examining the runes closely. "Something's off about these."

"Here, this gives you a better view." Paul handed him a different picture. This time the man was lying on a steel gurney, his head propped up on a small pillow designed for use in autopsies. The stab wounds were much clearer, angry red and deep enough in some spots to show bone. He could tell it was a blade with only a single edge from one of the stab wounds. One part was thicker, with a flat edge, almost triangular in shape. They were clustered, almost as if someone were aiming for a bull's-eye. Around the wounds were runes, much clearer now that the blood had been washed away. The separated skin of the stabs made it impossible to read the ones in the area of the stabbings.

"These runes are just dimenic language, not magical," Jonah muttered.

"Eat at Joe's, basically." Carol stared at the picture in her own hand, another autopsy shot. "It looks like someone typed a phrase into Google Translate and just wrote what the program told him to."

"What does it say?" Jonah wasn't great at reading dimenic languages, but he could recognize what was magical and what wasn't. They were two distinctly different alphabets, much like Japanese had kanji, hiragana, and katakana.

"'To enter a friend.'" Carol rolled her eyes. "I wasn't kidding when I said it sounded like Google Translate."

"What the fuck does that mean?" Jonah couldn't figure out what the killer had wanted to say. Was it sexual, or meant to hint at possession?

"I have no idea." Paul shrugged. "I'm sending a copy to someone who speaks different dimenic languages to see if they can figure it out."

"Good idea." Jonah pointed to the wound. "Is that the cause of death?"

"No, it was definitely mana draining. The stabbing was post-mortem." Paul pointed to the edges of the wound. "There's no antemortem bleeding. The flesh isn't red. This was done after he died, not before."

"Why stab him after the fact?" Jonah frowned at the picture, trying to put the pieces together in his mind.

"To obliterate the rest of the runes?" Carol asked, frowning at her own picture.

Jonah smiled at her. "That's a great guess." He brought up a mental picture of the scene. "I think I saw surveillance cameras overseeing the field. If we can get pictures of him before the stabbing, perhaps we can find out what they were trying to hide."

"Whatever runes they used would have to be drawn in ink or somehow made at least semi-permanent. Otherwise, they could have simply washed it away." Debbie, scowling at her own picture of the body, grunted. "I can't make anything out though. Whoever it was, they were thorough."

"I may not be able to tell you what was under the stab wounds, but I can tell you this. Once the victim was dying, their mana was definitely drained, but not completely. That's the other unusual thing about this. The rest of his mana was drained post-mortem." Paul gestured to the stack of papers. "This wasn't a vamp murder. There aren't any signs of bite marks on the body. There was a lump on the back of his head, though, which makes me think he was attacked first with a blunt object, probably knocking him unconscious, then he was killed via magical drain."

Hmm. Jonah stared at the vic, trying to check everything at once but unable to focus on anything but those runes. "So, the perp didn't want him to suffer?"

Paul shrugged. "Or they wanted him subdued and unable to fight back."

Carol stared at the wound, pointing at the jagged edges. "What kind of knife was used?"

"Serrated, probably about six inches long. The pattern reminds me of a steak knife." Paul put the picture down. "You're definitely searching for a blood sorcerer. Until I open him up or get a tox screen, there's not much more I can tell you."

"Knocking him out first means that they didn't want a struggle with him. Could be the sorcerer is someone who's physically impaired," Carol muttered.

"It's a definite possibility." Jonah made a note to check for those with disabilities at the college. "I hate these fuckers," he muttered. Those idiots out there who thought sorcerers were enslaved by their familiars, or that having a familiar made you weak were stupid. Most gave in to the need for a familiar before becoming blood sorcerers, thank the goddess.

"But why wasn't Mr. Reeves drained completely, all at once?" That baffled him. That was what usually happened.

"Could the sorcerer have been interrupted before his work was complete, then finished draining him when he had the chance?" Debbie's tone was clinically curious. Not surprising, since she often assisted Paul.

"That might explain why Mr. Reeves wasn't drained completely before death," Carol replied. "The sorcerer couldn't finish the job."

"Then why drain the rest? Why take the risk? He had enough from the initial drainage, right? Unless…" Jonah examined the picture. There had to be more to be found in the image than what he'd discovered so far. "A wither?" A creature born of a dead blood sorcerer, withers haunted the spaces of Terra Noctem like infernal serial killers. They hungered always for their lost mana, sucking their victims dry before moving on. A dying baby sorcerer with no defenses would be a tasty little appetizer for one of them.

Other, darker things haunted Terra Noctem, things he prayed weren't coming through the veil to this side. Things that would suck the life and magic out of someone without batting an eye. "I want status updates the moment you find out anything."

"Don't you always?" Paul replied.

Jonah picked up the page with the clearest picture of the runes. "Can I take this?"

"Sure, I printed all these out for you. We've got them saved elsewhere." Debbie yawned and gathered the pictures into a large envelope, handing them over to Jonah when done. "By the way, is anyone else hungry?"

Jonah's stomach grumbled right on cue. "Oh, god, yes. Jack in the Box?"

Carol spun on her heel and strode toward the door. "Let's go. I love their shakes."

Jonah followed her. "A woman after my own heart. You two coming?" he called back to Paul and Debbie.

Two sets of footsteps ran after them. Soon, Jonah found himself sinking his teeth into his burger. "Mm. That is so goddamn good."

The four of them ate, enjoying some quiet, non-work talk before Jonah and Carol had to leave. Debbie and Carol made plans to get together over the weekend, making Jonah and Paul smile indulgently.

Apparently, Debbie and Carol shared a passion for someplace called Sephora? Whatever that was. He'd walked the mall and seen it, mostly from a distance. Wasn't it some sort of makeup store? From the way the women gazed at each other, Jonah could tell that Carol and Debbie were going to be fast friends.

Good. Anything that bound sweet Carol more tightly to him had his utmost approval.

Chapter 7

Carol hadn't been to the station before, so she found the place fascinating. The steps leading up to the double glass doors were concrete, the railings metal. The building was modern in style, with rows of concrete parallel to rows of darkened windows.

Jonah held open one of the doors, letting Carol step through first. She sniffed the air, getting whiffs of gun oil, metal, fear, and sweat, along with the usual people of an office building. The quiet hum of electricity was occasionally overwritten by the sound of voices, some distant and indistinct, others closer, the words clear as a bell.

The front desk was dark, the walls an off-white. The floors were a bland off-white tile.

"Morning, Detective." The young officer manning the front desk smiled at Jonah. "New partner?"

"Morning, Bob. This is Carol Voss, my new familiar. Carol, this is Officer Robert Simpson."

Carol nodded her greeting, holding up her wrist to the officer, showing Jonah's name inked into her skin. "Nice to meet you."

"Are Detectives Wheeler and Ridgely back yet?" Jonah stood by the front desk and tapped on the countertop with his fingers as Officer Simpson covertly checked out her chest. Since her T-shirt was plain, he wasn't reading anything printed on it.

"Yup. They're probably expecting you. You're working that university murder, right?" Officer Bob was talking with Jonah but still checking out Carol's boobs.

Guh. Men. "My eyes are up here, stud." She pointed to her peepers with two fingers, watching as Officer Bob's cheeks slowly turned red.

Jonah slowly shook his head. "I wouldn't mess with my familiar if I were you." His voice had a chill to it that hadn't been there previously. "Not unless you want to know how tasty frogs find flies."

The guy pulled back, his cheeks paling much faster than they'd reddened. "Oh. Yes, sir." His wan smile was half-hearted. "Sorry, sir."

Carol smiled. Jonah had used his magic rather than her teeth as the threat. That went a long way to making her feel like he wouldn't use her as a threat in the future. It also made her wonder if he worried over whether or not she could protect herself.

She'd have to wait and see. Once she had her visitor's badge, she followed Jonah into the interior of the station.

"C'mon, Homicide is on the second floor." He scowled at the visitor's badge like it personally offended him. He touched it, lifting it gently away from her chest. The light brush of his fingers against her sent a tingle down her spine. "We'll get you an F-class badge as soon as possible. Once you've completed your training with me, I'll have you listed as my official partner."

She swallowed, trying to keep her nerves at bay. The light in his gaze was ferociously possessive, as if he'd already begun to bond with her on a deeper level than the simple year and a day contract. "I'd like that."

An F-class badge, or familiar's badge, was only temporary. She'd need to earn her detective's badge or wind up working the beat once the year and a day were up.

He smiled secretively, dropped the visitor's badge, and began leading her to the stairs and up to Homicide.

Jonah stalked down the hallway to the office of the lieutenant who was running Homicide. He knocked politely on the door, his face an expressionless mask. Carol straightened her shoulders, wishing she'd worn something a little more presentable than her T-shirt, jeans, and canvas sneakers.

"Come in," a deep voice bellowed.

Jonah opened the door. "It's me."

"Shit." The man behind the desk scowled. "If this is about Wheeler and Ridgely—"

"It is," Jonah interrupted smoothly.

The big man sighed, running fingers through his dark hair. "Jonah, Wheeler and Ridgely acted appropriately. From the information they'd gathered, it appeared to be a routine homicide, not an MCU case."

Jonah shook his head, taking one of the two seats in front of the lieutenant's desk. "Ralph, we both know that this was a pissing contest, pure and simple. I found them badgering the poor kid's familiar. They didn't believe him when he said he felt his sorcerer die."

"They were questioning a suspect." The lieutenant scowled at her. Apparently, the detectives had not only complained about Jonah, they'd given their boss an earful about her as well.

She was proven right when the lieutenant's scowl deepened. "And she's too new to be at a murder investigation."

So, he was going to go with that route? That wouldn't work at all.

Jonah snorted disgustedly. "You know the rules on sorcerer familiar bonds, Ralph. She stays with me." Jonah matched the lieutenant's scowl. "At least she's been through the academy. Hell, she was supposed to start the week after I found her. She'll be an asset, not a liability, especially with a wolf's nose."

The lieutenant seemed a little more interested in her when he heard of her species. "Wolf shifter, huh?"

She wanted to hunch her shoulders under his scrutiny. This man ran an entire department. She was just a rookie. He could end her career before it even started. Still... "Wolf *familiar*, sir. There's a difference."

"Oh, I'm aware of that." The lieutenant shot Jonah a vaguely amused look. "His mother has been very insistent on the differences between the two."

"Oh." She relaxed. Her status as a wolf wouldn't be a problem, at least not with this man.

She glanced at his nameplate, curious as to who those two yahoos reported to. She almost laughed as she read his name. *Lieutenant Ralph Kramden?* "Pow, zoom! Straight to the moon!" She clapped her hand over her mouth. "Oh my god, I'm so sorry."

How could she have quoted *The Honeymooners* at a police lieutenant? Her career might be over before it even started if he got mad at her for it.

Thankfully, he seemed to take it well. Lieutenant Kramden's reluctant grin made him almost attractive. "Yeah, like I've never heard *that* one before. And the quote actually is 'One of these days, pow! Right in the kisser.'"

Carol frowned. She could have sworn she was right. "He never said the moon bit?"

Lieutenant Kramden rolled his eyes. "He would say 'bang zoom' and 'you're going to the moon,' but not together." Lieutenant Kramden shook his head. "Can we get back to the case?"

"Yeah, sorry." Carol's shoulders slumped. She was *so* embarrassed she just wanted to get out of there as fast as possible.

Jonah coughed into his fist. She could smell his amusement, light and crisp like lemonade. "We've confirmed that this murder was magical in nature. The runes on his chest were a ruse, but the body definitely had been drained of its magic."

"You sure?"

Carol touched the tip of her nose. "Positive. And both the coroner and the coroner's wife, Debbie, agreed with me. The scent is unmistakable." She gagged slightly just remembering it.

He sighed, long and low, his shoulders slumping. He sat back in his chair. "The sniffer didn't detect anything."

Carol grunted, but before she could answer Jonah did. "Those things don't always work. You need familiars on the force with good noses, like Carol."

Lieutenant Kramden shot her an assessing glance. "Perhaps, but tell that to the city council. They want to cut the number of officers we have now, not add to them."

Jonah grunted. "Volunteers? Familiars who want to get into law enforcement could work as interns, learning the different scents of a crime scene."

"But their testimony isn't always admitted. Judges aren't always open to the idea of new evidentiary procedures." Kramden held up his hand. "I agree with you. I wish the sniffers worked the way they're supposed to, but they don't. I'll be complaining to the city myself. For now, though, give my people a break. They were working with what they had."

Jonah nodded, his lips tight. The corner of his right eye twitched. "I'll do that." He glanced at his watch and grimaced. "We need to go report to my boss. I have to introduce Carol to her."

"First day on the job?" Kramden stood and offered his hand. "Welcome aboard, Ms. Voss."

"Thanks." She shook his hand and didn't even try to match his grip. She'd learned early at the orphanage not to show too much of her strength. If she did, the kids would cry wolf.

Literally.

"Get out of here, Jonah. I have work to do." Kramden waved them away with a grin that belied the grumpy tone of voice.

"Yeah, yeah. You love it when I stop by." Jonah flipped Kramden the bird.

The two must be friendlier than Carol had first thought. She'd remember that for the future.

Carol followed Jonah, her departure much more subdued than his. He was calling out hellos here and there, but he didn't stop to introduce her. Instead, he headed to the stairway once more. "Our department is one floor above Homicide. Some of us work with them on murder cases involving sorcerers, while others work other sorts of magical crimes."

"Like vampires taking blood without the permission of the donor?" She kept up with him easily despite the fact that he was almost a foot taller than she was.

"Exactly." Jonah grabbed her hand and threaded their fingers together. He kept her at his side as they walked through the new department. She couldn't keep the smile off her face as she tightened her grip on him.

She could scent the magic on this floor, and it soothed her wolf. Her anima reacted as well, swelling at the sensation of so many sorcerers in one area.

"Down, girl. No touching." Jonah tugged her close, putting his arm around her shoulder. He whispered in her ear, making her shiver with more than the sensation of his breath tickling her. "You're *my* familiar. I'm not letting any of these guys poach you."

She trembled, unable to do anything else but respond to the possessive tone. The man wouldn't allow her anima to touch anyone in the room other than him. She found that ridiculously hot. She licked her lips, a small whimper making it past her control.

Jonah's arm tightened around her shoulder, but it was the only sign he gave that he'd caught the embarrassing sound. "C'mon. You'll like our boss. Her name's Anne Ford, and she's one tough-ass broad."

"I heard that!" A tall, broad-shouldered woman came toward them with a determined stride. Her hair was short and platinum blonde, her eyes pale blue. She wore a gray suit with a pale blue shirt underneath and shiny black boots, the type that were good for running in. "You must be Carol, right?" She was smiling, her hand held out as she approached them, her whole demeanor open. "You poor baby, stuck with a grouch like him."

"Hey!" Jonah's tone was affectionate. "Carol, this is Captain Anne Ford. She runs the Magical Crimes Division of the LAPD. Anne, this is Carol Voss, my new familiar."

She preened a little at the pride in his voice when he introduced her, not that she'd admit it. "Hi, nice to meet you."

Her hand was taken in a firm, no-nonsense grip. Anne didn't try and prove she was stronger than Carol. She already knew she was. "Nice to meet you too." She let go of Carol's hand and glanced at Jonah. "Jonah, I want you to work the university case while I show your familiar around." She frowned at the visitor's badge Carol wore. "We need to get you an F-class badge pronto." Jonah sputtered behind them as Anne whisked her away. "More importantly, let me show you where the coffee machine is."

Carol grinned and fell into step with the captain, visions of hot coffee dancing in her head. "I like how you think."

Chapter 8

Jonah was watching Carol as she familiarized herself with the workspace she'd been assigned. She twirled in her seat, looking as happy as a child in a sandbox.

"This is awesome," she whispered, smiling so wide he could practically see her molars.

"Excited about being on the job?" He remembered when he'd first started. Putting on the uniform had filled him with both a sense of pride and trepidation. He was putting his life on the line for the good of the community. While most cops retired safely, some did not. Add in the fact that being a rookie naturally meant making mistakes, and he'd been a basket case for about a week.

"Big time," she replied. She put her hands on her desk, her expression becoming more serious. "Time to inspect the desk." She wrinkled her nose. "I'm smelling something a little funky, and a little...chocolatey?"

Jonah had cleaned the desk out himself. "Are you sure? I thought I got rid of all the trash." His last familiar, the hedgehog, had loved snacking and kept herself well supplied.

She tapped the side of her nose, making him chuckle.

"Okay. You do that, I'm going to—" Jonah's phone rang. It was Lieutenant Kramden. "Answer the phone, apparently. Excuse me."

"Go right ahead. Let me know if it's about our case."
She shivered, once more that excited child. "*Our* case."

Jonah was smiling almost as widely as she was. He'd
had familiars excited about the job before, but never to the
extent that Carol was. He answered the phone, feeling good
about his coming day. "Sound here."

"Jonah. How is Carol settling in?"

"Really well. She's met my captain, and now she's
settling in at her desk."

"Good. That's good." Ralph coughed. "I'm glad to hear
that."

Something was up. Ralph sounded so uncomfortable,
so flat-toned that Jonah began to worry. "Is something wrong?"

That got Carol's attention, but he waved her back to her
exploration of the desk, hoping that Ralph wasn't about to say
what Jonah was afraid he would.

"Listen, there's no easy way to say this, but it's been
brought to my attention that you're a little…overprotective of
your familiar." Ralph's voice was apologetic, almost
sympathetic.

"What are you talking about?" Jonah leaned back in his
chair, frowning. He had no idea what the fuck Ralph meant,
other than Wheeler and Ridgely must be behind it.

"Well, Wheeler pointed out that you seemed to think
that you were being…"

Damn, he was right. "Wheeler backed away from my familiar like she had the plague, Ralph. All because he heard she was a wolf."

Ralph sighed. "Wheeler's an ass, okay? But if he goes to Internal Affairs and bitches about you being too cozy with your familiar, it could mean your badge."

Jonah blinked in shock. "What the hell, man? He's just pissed because he got kicked off this case."

"Maybe, maybe not. Wheeler's known to have some issues with shifters, especially the predators, and Ridgely is backing him up."

Fuck. "God damn it," he muttered, running his fingers through his hair. Wheeler and Ridgely were seasoned detectives. They could easily give Carol a hard time. As a familiar, even though she'd been through the academy, she simply didn't have the pull that two homicide detectives would. Add in the fact that she was a wolf and there were those who would want her gone no matter what they had to do to achieve it. "There's a zero-tolerance policy against just this sort of thing, Ralph."

"And if you didn't have a history of dating some of your familiars, it wouldn't be an issue. At least, that's where I think this is going to go with them."

"You and I both know how effective it," Ralph replied. "Remember when they implemented the zero-tolerance policy against LGBTQ+ bullying? One guy died because backup never arrived."

Jonah shuddered. He'd been in college when the cops responsible for the gay officer's death had been found not guilty on a number of charges. His mother had been furious, his father quietly fuming. Jonah had overheard them discussing the same thing happening to a familiar or shifter officer someday.

They'd been right. A lion shifter had been shot by his partner when the man shifted for the first time in front of him. He'd thought he was about to be eaten.

The lion had just wanted his partner to be comfortable around him, including his shifter side.

The shifter had wound up losing his job due to the disabling shot, and the cop who'd shot him had been put on paid leave while the matter was investigated. He'd ultimately been reinstated, with no charges filed. It had been deemed justifiable fear for his life.

"Listen, Jonah. Whatever you do, don't give them any ammunition. Neither of us wants to deal with the headaches, especially if IA is given the idea that you're banging your subordinate."

Jonah did his best to keep his anger from his expression, but when Carol sent him a questioning look, he realized he must have failed. He shook his head at her and tried to smile, but she still seemed concerned. "If you hear anything, would you give me a head's up? Carol and I *have* to be close for our magic to mesh together properly."

"And you've always liked the cute ones."

Jonah kept his mouth shut. There was no way he could deny Ralph's accusation. He'd take a cute, funny girl over a traffic-stopping beauty any day of the week.

"I'm sorry about this, Jonah. I'm just watching out for you, kid."

"I understand."

Ralph had been a homicide detective when Jonah had been promoted to the MCU. He'd helped walk Jonah through his first case and had been there more than once when Jonah had broken bonds with a familiar. If anyone was allowed to call him kid, it was Ralph.

"The last thing I want this city to do is lose a good cop like you."

"Thanks, man." Jonah had no intention of not pursuing a possible relationship with Carol, but he didn't want to lose his job either.

"You also don't want her filing sexual harassment charges."

That thought sent cold shivers down Jonah's spine. The possibility hadn't even occurred to him. Carol had seemed receptive to his mild advances so far, but perhaps he should put the brakes on and move a little more slowly. "I'll keep that in mind."

"Is she there?" Ralph spoke so softly Jonah could barely hear him.

"Yes." He glanced at Carol to see her going through her desk with a determined expression. He had no idea what she was looking for, but she was sure adorable doing it. Her brows were furrowed, her nose crinkled. When she held up an old chocolate wrapper and gagged, he silently laughed.

"Shit. Think she heard us?"

Wolf hearing. He'd completely forgotten about that. "Not sure, but I don't think so." She was so busy rooting around in the desk that he doubted she was paying attention to anything beyond it.

"Good." Ralph sounded relieved. "Because if the two of you get together, there's a good chance she'll be transferred out of your department after the year and a day. Hell, there's a good chance of that anyway, since she doesn't have the years in to be an MCU detective yet."

Jonah was aware of that possibility. You didn't have to be a mage or familiar to work in the MCU, just like you didn't have to work in MCU if you were a sorcerer or familiar. She could go to Ralph's department, she could work Vice, she could be anything she wanted within the LAPD.

He just hoped she chose the MCU and remained his partner.

"I'll keep feelers out on Wheeler and Ridgely. Just watch your back, okay?"

"I will. Thanks, Ralph."

"You're welcome." Ralph hung up without saying goodbye. It was his way. He'd said his piece, and now he was off to his next task.

"I wouldn't do that, you know." Carol's soft voice broke through the burgeoning gloom of his thoughts. "What's between us stays between us."

Jonah glanced at her to find her giving him a stern glare.

"But, FYI, if you ever touched me in a way I didn't want, I'd bite your hand off." She gnashed her teeth at him, her canines appearing remarkably pointed in her human mouth.

He nodded, not at all certain if he was being reassured or threatened. Probably both. He tried not to smile back. Even with her teeth bared, she was just too cute. "Understood, ma'am."

"Good!" She sat back with a big grin, her canines shrinking back to normal. "Coffee. Now. Let's go."

Jonah stood, shaking his head in amusement. Like she hadn't known that after less than an hour in the precinct. What the hell, he could use a cup. He gestured away from their desks toward the common corridor. "Follow me, my lady."

It had started raining almost as soon as they got home. Jonah had cooked a quick meal of soup and grilled cheese, afraid they'd both fall asleep before eating. They'd had a long day, with the murder and their newly formed bond draining them both.

"This is good," Carol muttered, drinking the last of her soup. She blinked and yawned. A gust of wind blew the rain against the windows, rattling them, and she jumped slightly. "I'm glad we got here before the weather got bad."

There was a severe thunderstorm warning in effect, but it hadn't hit by the time they were done eating. Thunderstorms in L.A. were so rare it was like finding a unicorn dancing in the middle of city hall. "It's supposed to get worse before it gets better. We might lose power."

"I hope not." She stretched, her T-shirt tightening against her breasts. He had to glance away before she found him gaping at her more obviously than Officer Bob. She smiled tiredly. "I have plans to cuddle up with a good book tonight."

Jonah had never enjoyed simply observing another person so much. Her face was so expressive, showing so many different emotions that he had to wonder what she was thinking. When he'd mentioned the possibility of a thunderstorm, she'd paled slightly before controlling her expression. She must not like storms, but unless she mentioned it herself, he'd keep his curiosity to himself.

He yawned, hiding it behind his fist. They were both tired, having spent longer at the station than he'd planned. He'd wound up introducing Carol to all of his coworkers and their familiars. She'd charmed them all, asking about families and offering assistance on cases as needed. She wasn't the only predator in the room, but she was the only wolf, and wolves were notorious for their sense of smell.

Jonah stood as the first rumble of thunder sounded. "I'm going to watch the storm." He couldn't pass this light show up, not when it was so uncommon. "Sure you don't want to join me?"

Carol, once again pale, shook her head. "Um, no, I think I'll just hit the sack and read. I've got a bit of a headache, so I think I'll just try and sleep." She stood and smiled shyly. "Good night, Jonah."

"Good night." He got up, gathering the dishes. "Wait. You want some aspirin?"

She shook her head. "No, I think I'll be okay." She shuffled her feet, appearing more and more awkward the longer she stood there. "Good night."

He watched until she was gone, rounding the corner to the bedrooms. Something was definitely wrong. She'd practically skittered up the steps. If she'd been in wolf form, her tail would have been tucked between her legs. He checked along their bond but got nothing. Their anima and animus were continuing to weave together, leaving little spaces where emotions leaked through, but right now all he could sense was weariness.

Sometimes a bond wound so tightly that the sorcerer and familiar could communicate telepathically. Jonah hoped that would happen with him and Carol. Already his home seemed sunnier because of her presence.

Jonah sat in one if the chairs by the window, almost bouncing in his seat like a little kid. Before too long, a split-second spark lit the night sky, the lightning so brilliant it was dazzling, even inside the house.

Jonah grinned, admiring the rage of mother nature, when a small whimper made him turn around, but no one was there. "Carol?" The thunder roared in response, but his familiar's voice was silent.

Jonah went up the stairs, listening for that whimper. Lightning flashed, backlighting the staircase. He could perceive to the end of the hall in the brief flashes of light, but no wolf bounded out of Carol's room to greet him.

Another whimper came after the boom of the thunder shook the house. This time, the fear along their bond was so strong he staggered from the force of it.

Shit. He'd been right. Carol was afraid of lightning storms.

Jonah raced to her room and threw open the door, expecting to find Carol huddled under the sheets. They were depressingly flat against the mattress. His pretty little wolf was missing.

"Carol?" He stepped into her room warily, wondering if she was in wolf form or not. She wouldn't hurt him on purpose, but he didn't want to startle her nonetheless. A terrified wolf could do a lot of damage without meaning to. "Where are you?"

A small hand waved out from the closet. "In here."

He opened the closet door, sliding it until it was flush with the other one. "Oh, Carol."

She was on the floor, pressed as far into the back corner as she could go. She was covered in the blanket from the bed, only her eyes and nose visible. Even her feet were covered.

She winced when another lightning strike lit the bedroom. "Jonah?" The terror in her voice shook him, bringing out every single one of his protective instincts.

This would *not* do. Jonah could almost taste her fear. He reached into the closet and picked up his terrified familiar, keeping a tight hold on her as he strode out of her room and back downstairs. He settled her on the sofa, growling slightly when she immediately crowded into the corner. "I'm going to make you tea, then we'll sit here until the storm passes. Okay?"

She nodded but didn't answer, her gaze glued to the windows.

Poor baby. Jonah made the tea as quickly as he could, adding honey and milk to it, something his mother always did to soothe him when he couldn't sleep. He carried the mug back to Carol, who hadn't moved a single hair from where he'd left her.

He set the mug on the coffee table and sat down. Reaching for her, he murmured nonsense words until she was firmly ensconced on his lap. He kept her wrapped in her blanket for the extra security she seemed to need. He kept his arms were firmly around her, hoping the combination of cuddles and his scent would calm both her and her wolf. "Think you can drink some of your tea, sweetheart?"

Carol reached for the mug, her hand slipping through the blanket's folds, barely moving it. She drank some, sighing happily, her body relaxing into his. "Mm. It's good. Thank you."

"No problem. Have you always been afraid of thunderstorms?" He couldn't imagine his brave little wolf shuddering under blankets, but here she was, breaking his heart with every soft cry. She'd faced her first crime scene without flinching. Witnessing her reduced to a whimpering mess made him want to kill something.

She shook her head. "It was fine when I was little, but—" She jumped as lightning flashed.

He could tell that strike was pretty close because the thunder sounded almost immediately. Carol buried her face against his neck. She was trembling so hard he was afraid she'd drop the tea. He took the mug and—careful not to move her too much—placed it back on the coffee table.

"Tell me, but don't move."

He was hoping his scent would keep her calm. He began rubbing her back, keeping his strokes gentle. Tugging on their connection, he weaved a barrier around them, one that dampened both sound and light without eliminating them. If it eased her even the tiniest bit, it would be worth the expenditure of energy.

Carol immediately reacted, loosening her death grip on the blanket. "Um. When I was about nine, one of the girls who hated my brother and I locked us out of the orphanage during a thunderstorm. It's one of the reasons we both moved to California. No thunderstorms, or maybe one a year at best."

Jesus.

"We were out there for hours and couldn't find a place to hide. Sawyer, my brother, knocked on the doors, the windows, everywhere he could think of to get attention, but no one answered him. We didn't find out until later that the girl who'd locked us out got everyone else to play musical chairs in the upstairs playroom. Between the stereo and the storm, no one could hear us."

Jonah tightened his hold on her. "What happened next?" She needed to get it all out. Even if she never got over her fear, he wanted her aware that someone was more than willing to hold her during a storm.

"My brother and I huddled against the house. He kept his arms around me like he could protect me if lightning struck us. Eventually, the headmistress realized we weren't there and went searching for us. When she couldn't find us, she finally went outside and found us soaked to the bone and exhausted. She took us in and yelled at us for staying outside in the rain."

Jonah growled. Fuck that woman, and fuck the little bitch who'd traumatized his familiar. If he ever met them, he'd be on trial for murder soon afterward.

Carol laughed. "Not bad, sorcerer. You almost sounded like a wolf."

He wasn't surprised. He wanted to hunt down both of them and rip their throats out. "Who told her the truth?"

Carol grabbed hold of his shirt and held tight, creasing the fabric. "Sawyer did. I was too busy sobbing and trying to hide under the table, but Mrs. Johnson wouldn't let me." She smiled against his neck. "He was *pissed*. He yelled so loud he rivaled the thunder."

97

"Good for him." Jonah would have done the same thing. "I can't wait to meet him."

She took a deep breath. "When Mrs. Johnson found out what happened, she called the girl into the room."

"Did she at least let you get changed out of your wet clothing?"

Carol snorted in disgust, which was really ticklish against his neck. He held as still as he could, considering his neck was now tingling. "Of course not."

"Of course not," he echoed sadly. She'd been neglected and abused by a system set in place to protect her. He *really* had to have a talk with the head of the familiar orphanages about making some changes. Maybe he'd get his parents and his sister in on it. His mother loved her causes, especially when it came to familiar rights.

"The girl lied about what she did, and she would have gotten away with it if someone hadn't spoken up. One of the boys noticed what she did, but he was too afraid of her to defy her and let us back in. But at least he told the truth when Mrs. Johnson asked the others who was lying."

"Good for him."

"Yeah." She jolted again as thunder rumbled through the room. "Uh, she was transferred a week later to a different facility because everyone knew she'd do it again in a heartbeat, even Mrs. Johnson. She wasn't sorry at all." Carol gasped as thunder rattled the house.

Damn storm. "Shh. I'm here. The lightning won't get you. I'm a badass sorcerer, remember?"

She snorted again, this time in amusement. "What are you gonna do, oh Sorcerer Supreme?"

He put his finger to her lips. "Shh! Don't call me that. It's copyrighted."

This time her laughter was open, light, a beautiful sound he wanted more of in the future.

"Seriously, woman. You want me to get sued?" He ignored the tightening of her muscles when lighting struck. This time the thunder didn't sound until after he'd counted to five.

Good. That meant the storm was starting to move on.

He kept watch over her as she continued to sip her tea, the two of them settled into a comfortable silence. Whenever the lightning struck or thunder sounded, she'd turn her face into his neck and just breathe.

He closed his eyes, loving her in his arms. "Next time you're scared, I want you to come to me, no matter what time of day or night it is. Okay?"

It took a long moment before she answered, so long he was afraid she'd fallen asleep. "Okay, Jonah. Okay."

He smiled and held her until the storm was over.

Chapter 10

It was a beautiful day out, the rain-washed sky so blue Carol had to smile. As much as she hated thunderstorms, the smell of damp soil and the blue of the sky was always a pleasure for her.

"Focus, Carol."

She turned away from the window to where Jonah sat. Well, *sat* might be the wrong word. Jonah was hovering about three feet off the floor, his legs crossed over one another. A ball of light surrounded him, glowing with faint magical symbols. He was meshing their magic, testing their bonds to figure out where they needed to be sturdier. Carol was supposed to be doing the same but had gotten distracted by the beautiful view outside the windows.

Carol shivered as his magic wrapped tighter around her, practically stroking her skin. "Mm." Her anima reached out, shoring up his animus, amplifying it and filling in any gaps that existed. It was how it was supposed to be, one of them being what the other needed. Her innate magic, the power that allowed her to shift into a wolf, meshed seamlessly with his. Where his was a golden glow, hers was more amber, closer to the color of her eyes as a wolf. As they swirled together, the ball surrounding him began to resemble a beautiful marble. Striations of amber infused the gold and shadowed the runes, giving them a three-dimensional effect. The colors enchanted Carol, calling to her, calming her. A peace she'd never experienced before filled her, as if she'd finally found a place where her soul could rest in utter safety.

Her wolf grumbled in contentment, curling up inside her as it acknowledged that Jonah was the stronger of the two. The sensation that they were protected from all harm so long as Jonah was there was so strong she relaxed into it, allowing her anima to flow freely. The marble around Jonah brightened as the amber and gold began to mesh even closer, the edges of the colors blurring together, darkening the gold as the amber lightened.

She noted the color change absently, her mind wandering as thoughts of Jonah filled her mind. The realization that Jonah was her alpha, the only one she'd bare her belly to, almost shattered the sphere.

Her anima spiraled out of control, sending the blended colors back to separate swirls.

"Concentrate," Jonah muttered, shoring up the weak spots that had appeared, shouldering her part of the magic while Carol scrambled to correct her mistake.

At least she hadn't broken the connection completely, but Jesus. The thought of Jonah stroking her belly, and points in between, made her shudder with desire, once again distracting her from the task at hand.

She'd forgotten how closely they'd meshed until Jonah's eyes went wide. Their intertwined magic must have taken her desire and transmitted it to Jonah. His expression changed, his eyes becoming heavy-lidded, his skin flushing. "What were you thinking of just now?"

Carol's cheeks heated. She bet she was the color of a cooked lobster. She cleared her throat, fidgeting with her hands. "Nothing."

He shook himself and stood, the marbled bubble popping with an audible sound. "Carol."

"Jonah." Wow. She could smell his desire, musky and strong, filling the room. She stood and took a step back as he stalked toward her. She cleared her throat, aware that she'd just become prey. "Aren't we supposed to be practicing magic?"

"Hmm. I bet together we could find some practical uses for it." His skin still glistened with sweat, amplifying his aroma to the point where the idea of baring her throat to him became less about submission and about more fuck-me-now. "What do you think?"

"Eep," she squeaked, backing up farther. She'd never withdrawn her anima, so their magic was more closely entwined than it usually was. Now, beyond their mingled fragrance beginning to fill the room, his desire caressed her senses through their link.

He snickered, still stalking her. "Oh, sweetheart. Our magic *really* wants to join."

Carol's back hit the wall next to one of the windows. "Maybe they can go out for coffee? Pastries, even?"

"Coffee." His head tilted, the gesture almost wolf-like. "You mean like a first date?"

She nodded furiously. She might want him in more ways than one, but she wasn't someone who went tail up that easily.

Maybe.

God, he was hot. Her palms were beginning to sweat, and the lump in her throat was the size of a boulder. Her heart was racing at his nearness, his scent overwhelming her senses. And the way their magic blended had her panting like a dog in heat.

Crap. Would she be able to resist him if he made a move on her? She wasn't sure, but maybe he'd go with her request.

He stopped when there was barely a half an inch between them. If she took a deep breath, her breasts would be pressed up against his chest. "Do you trust me?"

She blinked. Did she? After last night, when he'd held her throughout the storm and offered her not only comfort but protection, she did. Not as much as she trusted her brother, but that was all right. Trust took time to build, and he was off to a great start laying the foundation of their relationship.

"Yes."

"Good." He cupped the back of her head and kissed her.

His lips were softer than she'd thought they would be. His magic caressed her as the kiss deepened. Jonah tasted her languidly, touching her as if she were precious, as if they had all day to do nothing but slowly sink into each other.

She'd never been kissed with such care. He cradled her body against his own, his hand on her hip, gently pulling her closer. Their magic coiled around them, giving her goose bumps. She couldn't stop herself from wrapping her arms around his neck, moaning into his mouth as the kiss heated.

It wasn't until her breath was coming in gasps that he lifted his mouth from hers. He didn't go far though. He rested his forehead against hers, their noses brushing together, their breath mingling. He was breathing just as hard as she was.

"Fuck." He closed his eyes and shuddered against her.

"Not on the first date," she muttered, trying desperately to stop herself from throwing him on the ground and mounting him like a polo pony.

He chuckled, the sound rough and husky. "Yes, dear." He kissed the tip of her nose, then surprised the hell out of her when he hugged her tight. Their magic slowly began to separate while they stood there just holding each other. Her breathing evened out, her body going lax against his. "I'm sorry. I couldn't stop myself." He quivered, shuddering in her arms. "The magic between us is stronger than I'd thought."

"In more ways than one," she muttered, trying to calm her racing heart.

"You'll tell me if I ever go too far, right?" His eyes closed, his expression close to pain. "I never want you to feel I've pushed you into something you don't want."

She pushed his hair away from his forehead. "I have some pretty big teeth, Jonah. If I want you to stop, believe me, I can stop you." She took a deep breath, the heat of the moment finally leaving her veins. "I'm hungry."

Jonah gave her one last squeeze. "Want some coffee? Maybe pastries?"

She snickered, aware he was referring to her offer to date. "I'd love some."

He let her go, his movements reluctant, his expression the same. He sighed as he stepped away from her. "You're so tempting, but I promise I'll be good until you tell me I can be bad."

Her brows rose. "I'm almost afraid to find out how bad you can be."

He smirked. "I can't wait to show you." He took her hand and tugged her after him. "C'mon. Let's get that coffee, then we can get back to work."

She whined in the back of her throat. "Do we have to?"

"Honestly? I think we can get our magic to blend even more." He sat her down at the kitchen table, kissing the back of her hand before letting her go. He walked to the coffee maker and began running a pot of the blessed brown liquid. They'd found out their first morning together that neither of them functioned well without coffee. "This was our first attempt at doing magic, so let's find out how far we can take it."

"If it blends any tighter it'll get pregnant."

He almost dropped the tin of coffee. She watched as he fumbled it onto the counter before he turned and stared at her.

"What?" She tried to appear innocent but wasn't sure how well she was pulling it off. *Think fluffy bunny. I'm just hopping through, trying not to get eaten.*

It must have worked because after a moment he shook his head and turned back to the coffee maker. "Evil woman."

She kept her amusement to herself as she watched him make the coffee. When he placed the steaming mug in front of her, she took a sip, moaning at the taste. "God, I needed that." She licked her lips to catch a drop of the yummy goodness that had tried to escape its fate.

He grunted, staring at her mouth as he took his seat.

"Something wrong, Detective?" She licked the edge of the mug, aware that she was playing with fire.

Jonah cleared his throat. "Nope." He took a sip of his coffee, but his gaze was still glued to her lips.

Carol smiled and took another sip. "So, Mr. Sound, tell me a little more about yourself."

He chuckled, his gaze finally leaving her lips. He sat back in his chair. "Like what? We've done the family thing already."

She tilted her head. "What made you decide to become a cop?"

"My family has always been giving back to the community in one way or another. My maternal grandfather was a cop, and he used to tell me stories about all the people he'd helped." Jonah put the mug back on the table and folded his hands over his stomach, his pose utterly relaxed. "He took me to the precinct a few times, and the cops there talked to me like I was one of them." He smiled sweetly. "My mother was *so* pissed about that. She wanted me to be a lawyer or a doctor or, hell, a baker, anything but a cop. She didn't want me playing with guns."

"But you decided the best use of your talents was finding the bad guys and putting them in the hoosegow."

"Hoosegow?" He shook his head, grinning at her fondly. "Where do you come up with this stuff?"

She shrugged. "Internet." She sipped her coffee as he sputtered out a laugh.

"I can't wait for you to meet my family." His grin became lazy, sensuous. "They're gonna love you."

Now it was her turn to choke on her coffee. "Um. I've never met anyone's parents before." Including her own.

"Trust me. They're going to want to adopt you." Jonah's easy smile turned into a frown. "I'd better talk them out of that. I'm not into incest."

Carol shuddered. "Dear God." She sipped her coffee again. She'd have to meet Mr. and Mrs. Sound if she was planning on bonding with Jonah long-term. The thought terrified her.

What was she supposed to do with parents?

Jonah's hand covered hers. "You'll be fine. I have every faith in you."

It was good that one of them did, because Carol wasn't so sure she'd survive leaving Jonah if the Sounds decided they didn't like her. After all, what could a throwaway child offer their son beside herself?

Chapter 10

A week later, Jonah couldn't believe how relaxed he was around Carol. He'd had familiars in the past who'd made living with them so miserable he'd almost rented them apartments rather than have them in his home but couldn't because of the distance restrictions on early bonds. Just because magic might mesh didn't mean the people did. While some could be as far away as fifty yards, others he'd tried to bond with had to be within twenty. That didn't allow for much wiggle room when it came to housing his familiars, let alone working with them.

But Carol, she fit in ways he was having a hard time defining. He already loved watching her hum as she did the dishes. She'd offered since he'd made breakfast, arguing that while she lived there, they should share the chores. He leaned back in his chair, checking out her ass and hoping she wouldn't catch him.

"So, I want to head back to the college and confirm whether or not they have any surveillance cameras facing the area where the body was dumped." They'd been working other cases during the week and had been forced to let this one drop while they awaited the tox reports. MCU, just like any other department, didn't work like they did on TV and in movies. They often had more than one case on their plates. In Jonah's case, they had three other magic-related crimes they were trying to solve.

The murder had made the papers, and the public wanted answers. So far, Jonah had nothing for them, so he let Captain Ford handle the press while he went over his and Carol's notes.

Nothing had turned up on the radar for their victim. He got good grades, about a 3.0 average, and had several friends. He was friendly, outgoing, and so far, had no enemies that Jonah could find.

The kid was practically a saint.

She glanced back at him over her shoulder, and he quickly raised his eyes. He was pretty sure she'd caught him, though, because her expression was mildly amused. "Sounds like a good idea. I'd check the rest of the cameras as well. Maybe he was murdered on campus, and the cameras caught something."

"Not a bad idea. We should also stop off at the station. They should have your familiar badge ready."

"I'll need to take a photo for the employee badge, right?"

"The one that lets you in the building?" She nodded, and Jonah continued. "Yeah. We can take care of that tomorrow though. Your police badge should be ready for you at the front desk."

"Huh. They work fast." Carol put the last mug in the dishwasher and washed her hands.

"Familiar badges are always fast-tracked so that the sorcerer doesn't have to explain why someone who isn't necessarily a cop is allowed onto a crime scene. We've had issues with newbies giving familiars grief, so they have the F-Class badge within a few days of familiar registration. Your normal badge will be issued once the year and a day are up and you get your assignment." Hopefully, she'd be allowed to remain by his side, but he somehow doubted it. With the warning Ralph had given him, she'd probably wind up working as a rookie uniform just like everyone else.

Carol shrugged. "Works for me." She started the dishwasher and headed for the front door, where she'd left her shoes. "Ready to go?"

He needed to take her clothes shopping. Her wardrobe so far consisted of nothing but some T-shirts and tank tops, worn jeans, and canvas sneakers. He'd been startled at the small suitcase that had been delivered to his residence a week ago. She needed to be pampered, and he was just the man to do that. First things first though. "Ready."

They made their way to the LAPD building. Carol's badge was waiting for her at the front desk, but no police-issued weapon. Until she received her official assignment on the force as a cop instead of just a familiar, she wasn't allowed to carry a police-issued firearm. Even when after she became a cop, as a large predator, it was considered optional by the higher-ups. Their theory was that, if necessary, she could shift to defend herself. Jonah believed it had more to do with budget concerns than anything else.

Jonah didn't consider it a sidearm optional. If necessary, he'd teach her how to shoot. The more weapons she had at her disposal, the better.

While she waited for her badge, Jonah called the college. He was passed around from line to line until he was connected with the secretary of the provost, Dr. Hill. "Hello, my name is Jonah Sound, and I'm a detective with the LAPD's magical crimes unit." He rattled off his badge number. "I'd like to speak to Dean Hill about viewing any videos of the crime that occurred there a week ago."

The secretary cleared her throat. "Of course, Officer. When do you think you'll be here?"

He glanced at Carol and noticed that Officer Bob had taken over the front desk. "In about thirty minutes."

"I'll inform Dean Hill. She'll make the arrangements with our head of security, Chief Rivers, and his boss, Dean Anthony."

"Thank you." Jonah said his goodbyes and hung up.

Officer Bob cleared his throat. "Hey, Carol." The moment he'd spotted Carol, his gaze had gone to her breasts.

He'd definitely teach her how to fire a gun himself. No one else was going to help her but him. Especially Officer Bob.

Maybe he'd teach her on a Bob-shaped target.

"Hey, Bob. Bye, Bob." She waved goodbye as she hung the badge from the chain lanyard he'd given her. He'd had each of his familiars use the chain, and she kept sniffing at it and wrinkling her nose. "Why does this smell like hedgehog?"

Jonah chuckled as he led the way back out of the station. "Joan. She was a cutie, but we didn't mesh properly, so she moved on."

Carol stared at him, her lips curling back in a snarl.

Jonah risked his hand, patting her on the shoulder. "Don't worry, she's married with a kid on the way. Her sorcerer is named Julia." Just like that, the snarl disappeared, a chagrined expression replacing it. "We'll go to a cop store and pick up something you like, okay?"

"I want one of those that has my ID in it as well as the badge." She scowled. "And make it faux leather, not the real stuff." She stopped sniffing at the lanyard and focused on the street ahead of them, the scowl disappearing quickly.

Jonah smiled. He could just picture what she'd pick out if left to her own devices. "They don't sell pink sparkly ones."

The scowl returned. "Asshole."

"Or leopard print." He ducked quickly. "Don't claw the driver!" He huffed at her as he readjusted himself in his seat. "That's bad. Bad dog."

She whined at him, the canine sound odd coming from that cute little face.

"No. No biscuit for you." Jonah chuckled as she slid down in her seat with a whimper.

The rest of the ride to the college was uneventful, the silence only broken by the static-y sound of the police scanner.

He'd already called in where they were headed, informing Miles that they were working the university case. It was standard procedure, one he was going to teach Carol. As shotgun, she'd be calling Miles in the future when they were in the car. He'd have to make sure to introduce her to him as soon as possible.

He hoped the dean he needed to speak to was not only available but accommodating. Jonah didn't want to have to get a subpoena to view the tapes. Since the body had been found on campus, he doubted the dean would have an issue, but he hadn't dealt with her before.

Sometimes colleges could be dicey when it came to cooperating with non-campus police, citing the privacy of their students and staff. Vice especially would complain about how colleges would clam up when it came to student drug use. Robbery-Homicide Division, or RHD, had often run afoul of administration, especially when it came to investigating sexual assault cases. One detective had complained about one of the state's largest colleges cock-blocking him on three rape cases. He'd been forced to get a court order to get the college administration to cooperate with him.

It was frustrating, but it was part of the job they'd all signed on to do.

He parked in visitor parking in front of the administration building. Carol got out, her expression all business, her shoulders back and her hair blowing in the slight, ocean-scented breeze. He smiled as he followed her, his eyes once again drawn to the sway of her hips.

114

She had no idea how beautiful she was. One of the best things about her was that she didn't notice or didn't care about the hungry gazes that landed on her. Jonah wanted to gut every man who had nasty thoughts about her.

How had he come to want her so much in such a short time? Was it the magic between them, or how adorable she was? Remembering the trusting way in which she'd curled up in his lap during last week's thunderstorm, he was pretty sure he understood exactly why he'd grown so fond of her.

Not one of his previous familiars had ever made him want to keep them forever, even the ones who'd gone from friends to lovers. She'd understood his need to protect and had given him the gift of allowing him to do just that. Despite being a wolf, she'd permitted him to protect her without once complaining about how she could take care of herself. If they could find the balance between her wolf and his instincts…

"Can I help you?" Jonah noticed a woman walking toward Carol, a professional smile on her face. "Admissions is one building over."

"No, I'm not here for admissions." Carol pointed to Jonah and then her badge. "We're here to speak to the dean."

Jonah nodded to the woman, who was busy shaking Carol's hand. "Detective Jonah Sound, LAPD. This is my familiar, Carol Voss. We're investigating the murder that occurred here on—"

"Oh no, Detective," the woman interrupted, shaking her head. "The murder didn't occur here."

Shit. Official stance at the ready, willing to fuck with his investigation. "And you are?"

"Laura Butler. I'm Dean Anthony's secretary." She took his hand, still smiling that professional, fake smile. "It's a pleasure to meet you."

Jonah smiled back, giving her the same fake expression that was on her face. Shit. Did the university decide to send his secretary to deflect them? It wouldn't be the first time a secretary had been sent to "help" the investigation, and he doubted it would be the last. "We need to speak to the dean about surveying the security camera tapes from the night of the murder." He flipped open a notepad, pretending to check something. "I'll also need a list of every sorcerer who was on campus at the time of death."

Ms. Butler winced. "I'm not certain that's possible, Detective. We're very protective of our students and staff here. Perhaps you should—"

"Is there a problem, Ms. Butler?" A female voice broke through Ms. Butler's spiel, startling the secretary.

She jumped, whirling around to face the speaker. "Dean Hill. I wasn't aware you were here today." Ms. Butler's composure was rattled.

Interesting.

Dean Hill's pale blonde brows rose. "It's Monday morning, Ms. Butler. Where else would I be?" Her grass-green gaze rested on Jonah after quickly passing over Carol. "Detective Sound, right? I'm Dean Arlayna Hill, head of this university." She glanced dismissively at Ms. Butler. "That will be all, Ms. Butler."

The woman sputtered for a moment before walking off with a stiff nod of farewell to the dean.

Dean Hill shook her head, revealing slightly pointed ears. She must be a half-elf. Full elves could only hide their ears with elaborately styled hair, scarves, or hats. "I'm sorry about that. Dean Anthony and I are having a slight disagreement on some things. I'm afraid it's spilled out onto campus security." She gestured toward the door. "Come, I'll show you where our security setup is. I'm sure you have questions for me as well."

Dean Hill walked them back out of the building and down a pathway to another brick building not far from the administrative building. "Dean Anthony is the dean of students, whereas I run the school itself. I can understand his desire to protect them, but I'd rather find out if we have a murderer in our midst or if some asshole just used our baseball field as a dumping ground."

Jonah held open the door of the building for the two women, accepting the quiet thanks of the dean. Carol stood by the door once inside, staying close to Jonah's side.

"Let me introduce you to Larry, our security expert. He should be able to bring up the videos you need." The dean took them up a set of stairs to an office. The nameplate said Laurence Rivers, Chief of Police.

Jonah kept quiet as the dean knocked on the door. While he didn't always care for campus police, he understood

117

that the majority of them truly cared for the safety of the students. Having their hands tied by bureaucracy couldn't help their situation, especially in a situation such as this.

"Come in!" a voice bellowed from behind the door, deep and cheerful.

Dean Hill opened the door. "Larry, I've got two LAPD officers here to talk to you about the murder."

A large man stood from behind a maple desk, his shoulders practically spanning the width of the doorway. "Jonah Sound, huh?"

Jonah tilted his head. "Do I know you?"

"Nope, but I've heard of you. Your mother heads one of my favorite charities." Chief Rivers waved his hand. "Come in, come in. You want to view the security cam footage, am I right?"

Jonah allowed Carol to enter first. "Yes, that's exactly right." Jonah put his hand on Carol's shoulder. "This is my familiar, Carol Voss."

"Ms. Voss." Chief Rivers held out a beefy hand. "Welcome to our humble campus."

"Thank you, Chief Rivers." Carol smiled and shook the proffered hand. "I look forward to working with you."

"We'll need a list of professors and students, those with magic, who would have been on campus the day of the murder." He didn't say anything about how the body hadn't been completely drained. They'd decided to hold back that choice little tidbit, at least for now. It was SOP on murder cases. You always held something back, something only the murderer would know.

Chief Rivers sighed, his shoulders slumping. "Of course. We can do that, but it will take time. I've been working on it, but things have been a little more tense around here. I haven't had time to go through the videos yet, so do you want to go through them first?"

Jonah nodded. The last thing he wanted to do was antagonize someone who had the ability to aid in their investigation in such a large way. Chief Rivers had information that Jonah didn't. "Thanks. Your cooperation means a great deal to us."

"Not a problem. I want this fucker caught before he kills another student." Chief Rivers rubbed a hand wearily over his face. "To be honest, the kids are scared shitless, and it's leading to people asking for escorts around campus at night or calling us to look into things they're finding suspicious."

"Like what?" Jonah was hoping at least one of those students had given a good lead to the chief.

"People they haven't seen before hanging around a dorm room, which turned out to be visiting friends of one of the residents. Another call was about a woman seen somewhere near the athletic field. Turned out to be one of our secretaries, out jogging because she was going out with her boyfriend after work and wouldn't have time to get her exercise in otherwise." Chief Rivers shrugged. "Simple stuff like that. I'll get you the notes of the officers who responded, but I doubt you'll find anything linking these calls to the crime."

"Thank you." Jonah sat in front of the desk. "Now, let's get this asshole."

With Carol's quiet agreement and Dean Hill's silent assent, the four of them got to work.

Chapter 11

Carol's eyes fluttered shut as the video rolled on and on *and on*. Dear gods, was it ever going to end? Students entered, students left, faculty stopped to chat; lather, rinse, repeat.

Someone nudged her shoulder, and she jolted upright. "I'm awake."

"Uh-huh." Jonah's voice was low, amused. "Watch monitor three."

She turned her gaze, only to find Chief Rivers fast asleep, his mouth open as his head rested firmly against the back of his chair. They'd been at this for hours now, and none of them had spotted a damn thing. The most exciting thing she'd caught was a view of a guy checking out another guy's ass.

Carol scooted over and began watching monitor three as instructed. "Mother of magic, I need coffee."

"We all need coffee," Jonah muttered, his gaze still glued to his own monitor.

"Jesus God, yes." Dean Hill's eyes were wide as she also stared blindly at a monitor. "Get some for me while you're at it. Light sugar, no cream, please."

"I thought elves didn't believe in Jesus," Carol muttered, frowning when she thought she spotted the victim's familiar walk past the baseball field.

"They do if they're half-elves raised by a minister." Dean Hill yawned and shook her head. "Seriously, make with the caffeine already."

Carol pointed to the monitor. "Watch this then."

Dean Hill grumbled but let Carol past. Jonah didn't say a word, just kept his eyes on his monitor. He was making the rest of them look bad.

Either that, or he'd mastered the art of sleeping with his eyes open.

Luckily, Chief Rivers had a one-cup coffee maker in his office, so all Carol had to do was insert pods and press some buttons. Soon, three steaming mugs were in her hands. She gave a lightly sugared one to Dean Hill, a black one to Jonah, and kept the third sweat and creamy one for herself, then managed to crawl back over Dean Hill—without spilling a drop of either her coffee's or the dean's—and began watching her monitor once more.

Students occasionally crossed the field, some lone, some in groups. It was confusing the hell out of her, unless… "Where are the dorms?"

"Um." Dean Hill rifled through some papers until she grabbed a campus map. "Here, see? You go past the quad, down toward the sports fields—"

"Sports fields?" Carol paused her video so she could stare incredulously at the dean. "Seriously?"

Dean Hill grimaced. "Yeah, I probably should have mentioned that."

"Ya think?" Carol sighed and turned back to her video. "We need the names of these kids so we can question them, find out if they saw or sensed anything out of the ordinary."

"Sorry." Dean Hill grimaced. "I didn't even think of it."

Jonah grunted, the sound irritated, but his gaze remained on the screen in front of him.

"So, every student goes past the sports fields to get to their dorms." Carol leaned back in her chair and groaned. "We're never gonna find this asshole. It's a blood sorcerer smorgasbord out there."

"We'll find him. It has to be…I mean… What the fuck?" Dean Hill paused her video, then squinted at the screen. "What's that?"

Carol rolled closer so she could observe the monitor over the dean's shoulder. "What?"

Carol sucked in a shocked breath. The creature on the screen was bipedal, its skin black and wrinkled, sagging in places like the biceps and thighs. Its eyes were eerily white and sunken in the flesh of its face. Its nose was gone, its lips thin over stained teeth.

Shit, shit, shit. A fucking wither? What was a wither doing on this side of the veil?

Carol reached behind her and tried to get Jonah's attention. "Jonah. Oh, God, Jonah?"

"Hmm?" Jonah was soon there, his face close to hers as he stared at the screen. "Fuck." He took hold of Carol's chair and moved her out of his way. He crouched next to the dean and stared at the creature with a hard, angry expression. "A wither."

"Oh, shit." The dean shivered. "It's like it's staring at me."

Jonah turned off the monitor with a pissed expression. "It may have been."

"What?" The horrified screech of the dean almost woke Chief Rivers. He muttered something in his sleep, moving restlessly before he settled back down.

"Someone had to have summoned it, right?" It was the only way she could think of that a wither would be on Terra Mundus.

"Wonderful." The dean scrubbed her face. "So, we have a dimen murderer?"

"Not likely. Withers leave a very noticeable mark on their victims, a black splotch over the heart where they suck the mana out of their victims." Jonah stared at the blank screen. "No, this one must have been under the control of a blood sorcerer. A powerful one."

"Why a powerful one?" Carol was shivering for some reason, unable to sit still, her hackles rising.

Jonah's hands were clenched on the desk, his jaw tight. "Only a powerful blood sorcerer can control a wither and have it do his or her bidding. They'd have to feed it power, or it would devour them instead."

"What's going on in here?" A man stood in the doorway, staring at them curiously. He was about five-foot-nine with short, thinning brown hair and puppy-dog brown eyes. His skin was almost vampire pale and slightly sallow. His suit did not complement his thin frame. The shoulders of his tan tweed jacket were too broad, making his head appear too small. The golden color of the shirt he wore underneath only emphasized the yellow undertones of his skin. He wore jeans a size too small, causing him to appear as if he had a beer gut.

"Dean Anthony, these are the detectives assigned to the case of that poor Reeves boy," Dean Hill answered, her tone full of authority. "Detective Sound, Ms. Voss, this is Dean Anthony. He's in charge of—"

Carol started to growl, her wolf on full alert. The compulsion to shift had never been so strong before. The urge to shove Jonah behind her, to guard him from whatever was driving her wolf mad, was so powerful she reached out to him. She grabbed his arm, trying to tug him behind her.

Jonah stopped staring at Dean Anthony and turned his attention to Carol. "What's wrong?"

Dean Hill stood, her gaze glued to the doorway. "Something's coming."

Dean Anthony backed out of the doorway, his gaze glued to the slowly flickering lights in the hallway.

Carol was surprised that the dean caught on so quickly, but maybe her elven genes were giving her the same heebies that Carol had. Her wolf was snarling, snapping, eager to be released.

Carol wasn't one to ignore her instincts, not since she'd been locked outside in that fucking thunderstorm. Her wolf had been howling that something wasn't right, but she'd listened to someone she shouldn't have and had regretted it ever since.

Never again.

Carol shifted, slipping under the shoved-together desks to stand guard in front of the door. Whatever was coming would have to go through her to get to Jonah. She crouched, snarling, ready to attack.

If what Jonah said was true, then odds were good it would be the wither.

The hall lights began to sputter sporadically, fluctuating between extra bright and completely out so rapidly she had to narrow her eyes or be blinded. Energy crackled along her skin, raising the hairs on the back of her neck even higher. An alien hunger crawled along her spine, making her gag in horror.

Whatever was coming wanted Jonah. It would settle for her, but its primary target was the sorcerer filled with animus.

Carol waited until the first hint of darkness filled the doorway. She lunged, biting hard into leathery flesh, bone snapping as the creature shrieked in pain.

She did her best not to vomit at the vile taste of the thing. It was like biting into a really dried-out pepper. The skin gave easily, but it was so dry, so parched, with none of the juices you'd expect when biting into flesh. No blood flowed, no flavors burst on her tongue to tell her she'd actually bitten anything. Only the impression of skin, muscle, and bone.

It was *so* weird.

From behind her came a multi-tonal voice chanting. Dean Hill must be using the unique magic of the elves. Usually, their power was nature-based, focused on healing and growth, a remnant from their original dimension, Terra Dryadalis.

But when it came to creatures that did not belong in this world, their magic could be a powerful tool, forcing dimens to return to their original dimension. Strong elves could force dimens back to their own dimension using their solid connection to Dryadalis to fuel their magic. The elves claimed the magic came from when there was a war between Dryadalis and Terra Aether, the plane of air.

No matter where it came from, it was useful as hell.

Carol shook her head viciously as the wither tried to back away. She wound up taking a chunk of its calf. The creature shrieked, the pitch so high she wasn't certain the others could even perceive it.

She spat out the dried flesh and advanced on the creature, trying to ignore the flashing lights. They made it harder to track the wither, possibly a defense mechanism against visual tracking. It seemed to flash in between the lights, appearing in the shadows and dark spots in the hallway. Behind her, the computer monitors were beginning to flash, too, making her wonder if the wither was using those shadows to teleport as well.

If so, Jonah was in more danger than she'd thought.

Which was why she growled at him when he stepped into the hallway, standing next to her with his hands raised. A spate of words left his lips, words that twisted weirdly in her gut.

No one but a sorcerer could speak the language that now poured from Jonah. It came with the magic, an instinctual knowledge similar to Carol's bond with her wolf, a language that was simply there when a sorcerer called upon his magic. Deep and resonant, his voice calmed her despite her best efforts to remain vigilant. She focused on blending their magic, steadying the golden light that surrounded him until it was a steady glow that counteracted the flashing overhead lights.

Their magic combined, wrapping around them both in an embrace that made them stronger than they'd ever been. Their renewed energy pushed into her muscles, her eyesight becoming sharper, her nose twitching with new scents that filled the hallway. Cinnamon and allspice mingled with the horrific scent of the wither, the former beginning to overcome the latter. Soon all she could smell was pumpkin spice—the scent of Jonah's magic.

The hallway was filled with light, banishing the shadows and dark spots. The sputtering lights were now nothing more than an annoyance, giving the wither no place to hide from Carol's next attack.

The wither screeched in anger, moving away from them so swiftly that Carol lost sight of it before she'd taken a step. The scent of it began to fade.

"It's gone back to Noctem." The magic that surrounded her dulled, faded until their normal connection returned. He'd doused their magic to a small candle instead of the bonfire it had been.

She snorted in disgust and turned her back on the hallway, trotting back into Chief Rivers's office. Dean Hill was crouched next to the piece of wither Carol had spat onto the floor, still chanting in that multi-tonal voice unique to the elven race.

"It's gone. Why is she still chanting?" Chief Rivers seemed confused as the dean continued her spell.

"She needs to finish the spell. If she doesn't, the creature will return for its body part. It will be drawn here despite any demands its master might make." Jonah answered Rivers, all the while petting Carol's head and scratching behind her ears.

She lowered her head so he wasn't touching her anymore. She was pissed at him, damn it, and no wonderful ear scritches were going to get her to forgive him.

"Yes, you're a big bad wolf, but there was no way in hell I was leaving you alone out there." Jonah chuckled, scratching behind her other ear.

She refused to allow her leg to twitch. Absolutely no…

Damn it. Her leg bounced, giving her away.

"You're so cute when you're sulking."

Carol turned her back on him and sat.

Jonah made kissy sounds. "Aw, c'mon, precious. I've got a biscuit for you."

She glared at him. She was going to bury his ass in the yard for that one.

Chief Rivers chose that moment to pop his head over his desk. His eyes were wide, his skin pale. "What the hell just happened?"

Carol sighed and laid her head on her paws. Let Jonah explain this one. Her furry ass was taking a nap.

Chapter 12

Man, Carol was cute when she was sulking, but there was no way she could think that he'd have left her alone to face the wither. He couldn't hurt a wither directly. It would just absorb his magic, creating a link between them, but there were ways he could help in the fight. The only way to use his magic against a wither was peripherally, like making light.

He had no idea how much Carol had learned about withers. Had she been aware that his power was limited against the creature? Was that why she'd been angry when he'd appeared beside her? If so, he'd be pleased beyond words, but her protective instincts would be both a blessing and a curse. A blessing, because she'd be his first line of defense against creatures like the wither.

A curse, because he'd rather die than allow her to face an enemy alone.

Dean Anthony was glaring at Chief Rivers. "Where the hell were you when our lives were in danger?" He began to chew Chief Rivers out for his cowardice, and Chief Rivers didn't bother defending himself. He simply replied with things like "Yes, boss" and a lot of sorries. Dean Anthony was pale and shaking, probably taking his fear out on the chief. There hadn't been a damn thing Chief Rivers could have done to the wither other than annoy it. He'd done the right thing in allowing Jonah and Carol to deal with it.

"Stop chewing him out," Jonah said as the tirade continued. "He couldn't have helped us, not with this."

Dean Hill cleared her throat. She'd finished banishing the piece of flesh, sending it to Terra Noctem. She was pale and swaying, even seated on the ground. "The detective is right, Frank. Knock it off."

Dean Anthony huffed and puffed, but thankfully, he didn't continue.

"So. A wither." Dean Hill leaned back against the desk, staring out into the hallway. "We're dealing with a blood sorcerer, then, one strong enough to summon a wither."

"But how did it know we were watching it on tape?" The confusion in Chief Rivers's voice was echoed in his expression.

"Withers can do that. They can sense when they're being watched, even if it's on a week-old tape, and react to it. Especially if one of those watching has magic." Jonah had no sympathy for withers or blood sorcerers. Blood sorcerers had options other than killing others for power. The stronger the blood sorcerer, the more likely he or she would become a wither, eternally hungering for something they no longer had. They had nothing but their unending hunger and a cunning that had gotten more than one unwary sorcerer killed.

"That eliminates all of my students," Dean Hill continued. "None of them would have the control to summon a wither. That comes with time and practice as well as raw talent." She turned to Chief Rivers. "Get me a list of every professional sorcerer who was on campus that day, both those who are part of the college and those who are not."

"Got it." Some of Chief Rivers's color had come back, but his hands were still shaking. He began typing on his computer, his brow furrowed in concentration. "It'll take me a bit, though, probably a week. There were a number of sorcerers on and off campus during that time that I'll need to identify, including those who were visiting their kids or here for guest lectures. I want to make sure it's complete and correct before I send it to you."

"Can you email me the list once it's done?" Jonah nudged a napping Carol with his toe. "We should get going, find out what else we can dig up on this."

"Not a problem." Dean Hill blew out a breath. Her eyes were still glowing green with power, but it was slowly fading. "Add me to the list, Rivers."

Jonah's brows rose. "I doubt you'd use a wither, Dean Hill." The thought of an elf using a wither was laughable. Not only did they despise them, their magic didn't trigger the hunger of a wither. Elves didn't need familiars, as they didn't use mana, but ley lines, the energy of the earth itself. Withers simply couldn't devour that type of magic. Even if they *could*, it would be like drinking from a magical fire hose rather than dining on steak.

The magic of the elves was tied to the earth in ways Jonah didn't understand. Jonah had some theories on that, but he'd leave the theoretical stuff to his sister, Lessa.

The dean straightened her spine, looking much better. Her color was slowly returning. "Every sorcerer should be listed and eliminated. If you want to strike me off immediately you can, but remember, I'm half-human. It's entirely possible I have sorcerer powers beyond my elfin ones."

"And telling me to investigate you would make me less likely to do so." He nodded. "All right. I appreciate your willingness to put your neck on the chopping block."

"The blood sorcerer killed one of my students." The green glow in her eyes brightened for a moment. "I want him or her *dead*."

And that was very un-elf-like. Elves didn't believe in a death penalty. They believed that everyone, even the worst offenders, could be redeemed with enough time and education.

"Do the same for me, Chief." Dean Anthony held out his hand. "I'm sorry we weren't introduced under better circumstances, detective. I'm Dean Anthony." He shot Dean Hill an admonishing look. "One of the things I'm in charge of is campus security. Chief Rivers reports to me."

Jonah shook the dean's hand. "Detective Sound, MCU. This is my familiar, Carol Voss."

"Arrange a time to come and talk to me, please." Dean Anthony's handshake was firm, almost too firm. This was a man who wanted others to be aware that he was the one in charge. "I want to do everything I can to assist in the investigation."

"Thank you, sir, I appreciate that." Jonah smiled the agreeable smile he broke out for people he had to question. It wasn't overly friendly, but it couldn't be called cold either. His mother had taught him very well how to fake pleasantries. "Should we go through your secretary or call you directly?"

"Call me directly. The fewer people involved in this, the better."

Jonah was far less sympathetic than elves. "I agree." He nudged Carol once more. She grumbled and climbed to her feet, yawning and stretching. "You have a good nap, princess?"

She wagged her tail and yipped, causing everyone but Jonah to chuckle.

Jonah rolled his eyes. "Change. We're heading out."

Carol shifted, the process fascinating Jonah as always. She shimmered, light flowing around her wolf body, brightening until it was near blinding. The light moved from all fours to upright, finally dimming and extinguishing. In the afterglow stood the woman who'd managed to push almost all of his buttons in a matter of days. She grinned at him, cheeky as hell. "Where to, boss?"

He turned his gaze on Dean Hill. "I also need a copy of that video with the wither on it." He glanced at Carol, ready to explain his seemingly insane request. "There's a safe room at the precinct where the wither can't come no matter how often we watch the video." He returned his attention once more to Dean Hill. "We'll take care of it and follow any leads it shows."

Withers could sense things that others couldn't, like someone watching it on a fucking video. He should have taken precautions against such a thing, but he hadn't thought they'd be facing a dimen instead of a human. Damn it. Carol had him distracted with the adorable way she'd tried desperately not to nod off while watching the videos.

Carol poked him on the shoulder, her brow furrowed. "What if it shows us nothing?"

"Then at least we can close that line of inquiry." He bit his lip, thinking hard. "The wither might decide to come after us no matter what precautions we take, in which case we'll be forced to stay at one of the precinct's safe houses."

Dean Hill raised her hand. "There's another option if it comes for you."

That offer wasn't going to go over well with either his bosses or his familiar. "No. We can take care of this. I'm not putting the elves in danger." There were enclaves of elves all over the city, each one defended from outsiders, including humans. To enter an elven enclave was a high honor, one very few humans had experienced.

"We can guard you in ways humans can't," she replied softly.

"I appreciate the offer, I really do." Jonah smiled softly. He really liked her. "But you're a civilian."

Dean Hill gestured toward Carol. "So is your familiar. She hasn't gone to the police academy yet."

"Yet." Carol's voice was so cold he had to check out her expression.

If that glare had been turned on him, he would have backed away immediately, fearful that she'd attack at any moment. Something about the way the dean had spoken, or something he'd said or done, had caused his familiar to turn on the dean. He'd have to ensure that Carol didn't try and take a bite out of the elven woman.

The paperwork on that sort of thing was exhausting.

Jonah turned back to the dean, eager to set his familiar's mind at ease. "She's my partner, officially and unofficially." He ignored the way the dean's eyes widened, too intent on keeping Carol calm. "Can you copy that video for me?" He reached into his pocket and pulled out a small USB drive. It had a carved symbol in it for protection, one Jonah charged while he held it out. It would keep the wither from sensing the video on the drive.

The dean took the drive, her fingers brushing against his. Carol growled again, but Jonah leaned toward her, whispering in her ear. "Shh."

Carol huffed. "I'll be in the hall." She stomped out the door, her expression thunderous.

What. The. Fuck?

"I think she's jealous." The dean winked at him as she put the drive into the USB slot and began copying the file.

"Why?" Jonah was confused. He had no romantic intentions toward the dean. She didn't make his cock hard the way Carol did. Carol should be able to scent his lack of interest. The dean was attractive but not his type.

He preferred cute, growly women who curled up in his lap and trusted him to protect them from big, bad thunderstorms.

"She senses that you like me, maybe?" The dean's smile was wicked. She winked at him.

Oh, shit. "As a person, not… I mean, you're good-looking and all, but…" Jonah was rarely flustered, but right now, he was tired and ruffled.

The dean's chuckle was just as evil as her smile had been. "Tell *her* that."

Jonah gazed out the door to find Carol pacing the hall. "Almost done," he called out, hoping he sounded calm. The dean's quiet chuckle didn't help.

"Good." She continued to pace, her gaze going over and over again to the lights. "I want out of here."

"I don't blame you." He stepped into the hall, halting her progress. "Was that your first encounter with a wither?"

She nodded, the anger that had been there earlier giving way to disquiet. "How often do you face those things?"

"More often than I like, but less often than you'd imagine." Jonah pulled her close, hugging her, trying to comfort her. He rubbed her back, breathing in her scent. She smelled of earth and sky and running, clean water, all things he loved. "I'll protect you, I swear it."

She stiffened and pulled away. "Understand something right now. I'll be the one protecting you, Jonah."

The determination in her gaze, the way she stared him right in the eye, made his cock twitch. God, she was one sexy little wolf.

He couldn't let her announcement go unchallenged, however. "I don't think so." He held tight as she tried to pull all the way out of his arms. "I mean it, Carol."

"Perhaps the two of you could protect each other." The sound of the dean's voice startled Jonah. He'd been so intent on his familiar that, for a moment, he'd forgotten that anyone else was there.

The dean held out the USB drive, barely holding it with her fingertips. Jonah took it with a muffled thanks. "I appreciate your help."

The dean glanced behind her to where Chief Rivers sat, watching them quietly. She turned back to them, nodding. Softly, she replied, "We appreciate what you're doing. If those other detectives had their way, an innocent familiar would now be in jail. I'd have lost two of my students."

Jonah finally released Carol but remained close to her. "We'll get out of your hair. Contact us directly if anything else happens." He gave the dean his card.

She took it, careful not to touch him. "It was a pleasure meeting both of you. Remember, if the wither becomes more than the police can handle—"

"We'll be fine," Carol replied firmly, shutting the door once and for all on the dean's offer of help.

The dean nodded farewell and returned to Chief Rivers's office, closing the door behind her.

Carol sniffed, tilting her chin in defiance as she walked away.

Jonah shook his head. He had the notion that whatever had set Carol off had nothing to do with the dean and everything to do with being afraid of the wither. He'd have to make sure she was safe, no matter what happened.

Nothing, *nothing* would happen to Jonah's brave little familiar.

Chapter 13

Carol slipped inside the precinct behind Jonah. "I could fill out paperwork while you watch the video. I still need to get my employee pass and all of my employment stuff done, like health care plans and vision." Please say yes, please?

"No can do." Jonah nodded to the officer manning the front desk. This time it wasn't Officer Bob, but a female who kept her gaze to herself when it came to Carol's chest. "I need your perfect eyesight in case I miss something."

"What makes you think it's perfect?" She squinted at him, hoping he'd believe the lie that her vision was wonky. "Maybe I have trouble seeing." She blinked rapidly and wiped at her eyes.

He chuckled. "Where are your glasses? Or your contact lens stuff?"

Damn it. She was caught. The last thing she wanted to do was glimpse the wither again, but for Jonah, she'd bite the bullet and do what she could. However, that didn't mean she had to stop a pout from making her lips droop. "Fine. I guess I can fill it out tonight."

He grinned back at her, the expression filled with affection. "That's my girl."

Carol's cheeks heated. *My girl.* She was beginning to wish she was exactly that. Jonah was strong, protective, funny, and hot as hell. He was the complete package, all wrapped up in a police uniform. How was she supposed to resist *that*?

Jonah took her to a room with magical symbols on the door, along the jam, and even on the knob. They weren't taking any chances with anything like a wither getting into the precinct. Any dimens working as cops would avoid this place like the plague.

The door closed quietly behind her. Carol shivered as she scanned the room. Her wolf whimpered quietly, wanting out.

"Your wolf doesn't like the room because, technically, she's an interdimensional being." Jonah's expression was sympathetic. "However, you live in a willing, symbiotic relationship with her, so the wards allow her, and therefore you, in."

Carol frowned. Maybe she was wrong, and dimen cops could come in. "What about the dimens who work on the force? Can they come in here and view things like the wither?"

Jonah shook his head, confirming her previous thought. "Nope. I already told you, remember? It's something they have to deal with whenever they come across this kind of thing, so they're usually paired with someone who can come into one of the warded rooms without problems."

"Huh. Guess that works, but then you can't have your partner's eyes helping you."

"It's a problem, but there's no way around it." Jonah began fiddling with the computer. "Turn out the lights, will you?"

Carol did so, then took a seat beside Jonah and stared at the setup. The actual computer was set on the floor, hooked up to a seventeen-inch monitor. There was a large, flat-screen TV across the room attached to the wall. A cord came from the side of the TV and ran to the computer. "Dual monitors?"

"Yes." Jonah opened the file in his email and began playing the video Dean Hill had sent. "Makes it easier to view details you might miss otherwise on the smaller monitor." Jonah watched the screen intently.

Carol did as well, but focusing on the screen was more difficult than she'd thought when Jonah took hold of her hand. All she could sense was the warmth of his skin on hers. In the confined space, his scent filled her nostrils, distracting her even further.

"There." Jonah let go to pause the video. The wither was in the corner of the screen, glancing behind it. "Let's slow this down. Maybe we can find something we missed before." Jonah started it up again but slowed down significantly.

The wither was just as ugly and frightening as it had been in real life. Worst of all, it began to batter against her senses, seeking her out but unable to find her behind the shielded door. "Can you feel that too?"

"Yeah." Jonah sounded calm, almost serene. "Don't worry. It can't locate us here."

She took a deep breath and tried to dismiss the sensation of something searching for her. It was unnerving, to say the least, but Jonah's composed attitude went a long way to keeping her and her wolf from bolting out the door.

The wither was pulling something as it moved farther into view. She watched in horror as the body of the victim was dragged along. The wither was using the victim's arm to tug it along, causing the body to leave behind deep grooves in the sandy earth of the baseball field. "How the fuck did the wither get the body to the field without anyone catching it?"

Jonah bit his lip before replying. "Only a Traveler can survive that."

"Traveler? The sorcerers who can cross dimensions?" Carol whistled softly. "I've heard of them, but never met one."

"Not surprising. I've only ever met one. They're incredibly rare." He pointed to the victim, pausing the video once more. "Do you see that?"

"What?" Carol squinted at whatever Jonah was pointing at.

Jonah stepped in front of the television and put his finger right next to the victim's chest. "That."

Carol stood and stepped closer to the TV. She stared at the victim, tilting her head as she stared at the edges of a rune…a magical one, not the symbols she'd read before. With the way the body was twisted, she could only glimpse a little bit of it. "The knife was used to get rid of that rune."

"Exactly." Jonah pulled out his tablet as he started the video once more. She watched as he scribbled down what they could see of it.

144

The body turned on-screen, and Carol stifled a gasp. Oh, shit. "The rune…" Carol thought she recognized it, but she didn't want to say anything until she was certain. Besides, part of it was still obscured by the way the victim's body was leaning and the arm the wither was using to pull the victim along.

"What about it?" Jonah's tone was absent as he continued to scribble.

"I think…" Carol shivered as she considered the ramifications of that particular rune being etched into someone's skin. "No, wait. I need to observe more of it before I can be sure."

He headed back to the computer to start the video once more. Still moving slowly, the video continued as the wither dragged the victim to home plate.

"Stop." Carol held up her hand as the video froze. She stared at the rune, shivering. A cold chill traveled down her spine. "Damn it. I was right."

"What is it?" Jonah once more stood at her side, staring at the rune with an intent expression.

She studied the image of a tightly coiled snake burned into Louis Reeves's flesh. "The serpent of Apophis, aka Apep." Carol closed her eyes and tried to remember her Egyptian mythology. Mythology was her second love after the law. She'd almost chosen to become a magical anthropologist, studying magical mythology connected to different religions around the world, but the puzzle-solving aspect of police work had won out in the end. "Apep is the ancient Egyptian spirit of evil, darkness, and destruction."

"Oh?" Jonah pulled up a web browser and began typing Apep into the search engine.

Before a page loaded, Carol continued. "He's the arch-enemy of the sun god, Ra, and would attack him at the end of every day or the beginning of the new one, trying to stop him from ascending into the heavens."

"Why?" Jonah was studying one of the pages he'd found.

"Ra is the bringer of light, so he's the one that upholds Ma'at, or order, Apep's opposite. That makes Ra his mortal enemy." She closed her eyes and went over everything she could remember. "It's said Apep's roar can shake the earth, so those who worship Egyptian gods claim he's the source of thunder and earthquakes, and that he's also the reason for eclipses as he temporarily overcomes Ra."

"Can he be stopped?" Jonah sounded worried now.

Carol could understand that. No one wanted to mess with gods. They tended to be a bit tetchy if you moved against their priests, but Apep was supposed to be one of the gods that *wasn't* worshipped. "He can't be killed, only temporarily overpowered."

"Priests?"

She shook her head. "No one worships him because they are terrified of him. You have to always put other gods with his image or symbol to make sure he's contained, but it's always temporary."

"So why would Apep's serpent be on our victim's flesh? And without some other image to protect him?" Jonah studied the marking, probably seeking something embedded in the image that would make her interpretation invalid.

"I have no idea. We can send your sketch to an expert, right?" Carol clenched her hands. If she was right about what had happened to Louis Reeves, then his death hadn't been torture enough for the killer. They'd wanted him to suffer in the afterlife as well. There was a margin of error, always, but the story of Apep had always fascinated and horrified her.

"My sister can take a look at them. Lessa's an expert on runic and dimenic symbols and languages."

"This is bad, Jonah. It means that if I'm right, even his soul is gone. He won't go to the afterlife or be reborn because his soul has been fed to Apep."

If he was a follower of the ancient Egyptian gods, this was the worst fate anyone could bestow upon him. Hell, if the rune-maker was a follower, then…Reeves was truly fucked, no matter how you looked at it.

"A sacrifice, then?" Jonah scowled at the screen.

"Sacrifice the soul and keep the magic?" Carol tried to figure out the riddle. "Is that why he wasn't drained completely?"

"Enough magic to send him to a soul eater, using the rune as a portal?" Jonah ran his finger across the head of the snake. "If we're right…"

"We'll find more of them. More victims to feed to the perpetrator's god. It's just a matter of when." Carol blew out a breath. This… Jesus, they *had* to stop anyone else from being a sacrifice. "More students, or others?"

"Impossible to tell, other than students can be easy targets. They don't have the same control over their magic that older sorcerers have, so fighting back is harder for them."

"Louis Reeves didn't even get that chance. He was hit from behind, dazed or knocked out." Carol shook her head. "His familiar will be devastated when he finds out. They'll never meet again, in this life or another." She bit her lip, wondering what she would do if something like this ever happened to Jonah.

She couldn't even begin to imagine it. Already, the bond was so strong that if something happened to Jonah, she'd want to follow him into the afterlife.

Was it always like this? If so, how could a familiar walk away from a sorcerer who matched them, ever? Or was their bond different?

Jonah pulled out his phone. "I have to call Dean Hill. It seems we've got some sort of ritual going on. If you're right, there will be at least three more murders. We need to keep a close eye on the baseball field until this fucker is caught."

Carol listened silently as Jonah made the call. He explained the situation and told the dean that the police would be there for the students. She couldn't make out Dean Hill's reply, but the soft smile on Jonah's face pissed her off. She held back a snarl, turning away from Jonah to stalk over to the computer. She started the video once more, still in slow motion, watching carefully as the wither stabbed the student's body over and over until the serpent symbol was gone.

It was possible that the stabbing was done not only to hide the symbol, but also to make the murder look like a homicide case. If Wheeler and Ridgely had kept the case, there would be no chance of solving it.

Once that was done, it posed the body, placing the lily in its hands. It waved a hand, dispersing the trail the body had left as he'd dragged it through the sand to home plate. Finished, it disappeared from sight, leaving no trace that it had ever been there.

All of the evidence collected at the scene, like the cheap vape pipe, was useless. The killer hadn't been anywhere near the dumpsite. They'd need to call the CSI guys before the city wasted any more money on useless tests.

She stopped the video and glanced up, to find Jonah watching the TV. His phone was no longer in his hand. He spoke absently, his gaze glued to the dead body. "If we can track where the wither came from, we could find the blood sorcerer."

Carol shook her head. "It's a dimen. There's only a few ways to track one of them."

Jonah glanced at her over his shoulder. "Then perhaps it's time we spoke to one."

"Huh? You're friends with a dimen?" Carol had met some pretty...intense dimens during her time at college. Somehow, she couldn't picture even one of them who'd be willing to help them.

"Mm-hm." Jonah rubbed his hands together, his expression evil. "And I can't wait for you to meet her."

Chapter 14

Jonah pulled the car to a stop in front of a familiar adobe house. He'd spent quite a lot of his life there, playing video games, practicing magic, and just getting into trouble with one of his best friends in the world. "We're here."

Carol glanced up from her iPad and stared out the window. "Huh. Not what I expected."

"You were thinking brimstone pathways and fire-filled windows?" He got out of the car, watching as Carol also got out. Her gaze never once left the house.

"Nah, not quite. I was thinking more Stepford wife, with a picket fence, and two-point-five children. You know, *really* scary. Not hippie central."

Jonah gazed at the house again, trying to view it through Carol's eyes. True, there were a number of hand-made wind chimes strung around the house and several strands of colored lights in the trees that Rose loved to turn on every night. And the hand-made stepping stones were shaped like sunflowers. There was an overabundance of plants, lots colorful furniture on the front patio… Okay. Carol was right. It was kind of hippie-ish and really cluttered. "If you think that now, wait until you see the inside."

Carol shivered. "I can't wait."

He strolled around the car and took hold of Carol's elbow. "C'mon. Rose probably has tea and cookies waiting for us."

Carol gaped at him. "Isn't that how children get lured into an oven?"

Was she serious? "Does this house look edible to you, Gretel?" Jonah shook his head over Carol's obvious unease. He had to reassure her that Rose was mostly harmless. "Seriously, you're the big bad here, not Rose, okay?"

Carol sniffed and immediately sneezed. She peered around, confused, and sniffed again. A third time she sneezed, her curls bouncing with the force of it. "What's that?"

"Rose." Jonah knocked on the wooden door using the wrought iron knocker.

Within moments, the sounds of pounding feet reached his ears. He braced himself for the onslaught, aware of what was coming.

The door swung open, and Rose Wright came tumbling out and into his arms. "Jonah!"

Carol snarled, then sneezed again. "'Scuse me." She rubbed her nose, taking a step back.

"Jonah, who's your friend?" Rose didn't bother gazing at Carol. She'd been down this road with him before. Her dark brown hair was soft against his chin. "Another familiar?"

"Her name is Carol Voss, and she makes my magic sing." Jonah stepped out of Rose's embrace to find his friend ogling Carol.

"Really?" Rose drawled. Her hands went to her ample hips. Like most earth elementals, Rose tended toward what she lovingly called "goddess size." That never once stopped her from wearing whatever she pleased.

Today, she was in skin-tight jeans, a halter tunic in an eye-searing fuchsia, and sandals covered in multicolored bits of plastic meant to mimic gems. Her toenails were painted in an iridescent shade of pink, but the nails on her hands were bare. She'd told him once that nail polish didn't stand up to the amount of digging and crafting she did on a daily basis, so she colored her toes instead.

"Come in, come in. I've just made a batch of chocolate chip cookies." Rose surprised him by grabbing hold of Carol's arm with a gleeful expression that terrified him. "I bet we're going to be really good friends."

Carol was pulled into the house, staggering behind Rose with a pleading backward glance.

Jonah, amused by Carol's uncertainty, followed the women, closing the door behind him. Rose's two small dogs, Hermes and Hera, greeted him with yippy barks and waggling bodies. He took a moment to pet the small bundles of happy fur before heading for Rose's kitchen.

Carol was sitting at the concrete and colored stone table that Rose had made one day when she was bored out of her gourd, she said. She did some of her best work then. The colorful, seemingly random pattern was actually a magical ward, keeping Rose's home safe. A plate of cookies and a teapot sat on the table, with steaming cups of tea at each place setting.

Rose was sitting across from Carol, her chin on her hands. "So, you're a wolf?"

Carol nodded, apparently dazzled by the affable Rose. Jonah took the seat beside her and glared at Rose, aware of how curious she'd be about his new familiar and how little brain to mouth filter she had. "Have you been hounding my familiar, Rosie?"

The earth dimen seemed offended by the hated childhood nickname, but the twinkle in her eye told the truth. Rose was thoroughly enjoying herself. "Of course not, Joanie."

Jonah winced. He deserved that for calling her Rosie. She'd told him more than once how much she despised being called Rosie. He was always compelled to tweak her tail only to have it bite him in the ass. "Please don't call me Joanie. I swear I'll be good."

Rose smiled sweetly and turned back to Carol. "Jonah and I have been friends since we were toddlers." She shot Jonah a smirk that scared the crap out of him. "When he was six, he used to—"

"Can you follow a wither to its master?" There was no way Jonah was going to allow her to tell Carol *that* story. Hell. No.

Rose blinked. "What?" She bit absently into a cookie, quietly pushing one into Carol's hand. "Eat up, dear. You're way too skinny."

Carol nibbled on the cookie, still apparently shell-shocked.

"Can. You. Follow. A. Wither. To. Its. Master." Jonah pounded each word into Rose, waiting for her reply. If he let her, she'd talk their ears off before allowing them to get to the reason for their visit.

Rose pouted. "And here I'd hoped you'd come to visit for friendly reasons." She sat back and shook her head. "No. I. Can't." She then turned back to Carol. "When he was six, he used to pee in his mother's petunias. She never did figure out why they kept dying."

Carol giggled, choking on her cookie.

Jonah shut his eyes in pain. "Dear gods, woman."

"What?" Rose sounded both smug and innocent.

"I haven't met his mother yet."

Jonah opened his eyes at Carol's words. She sounded shy, and her cheeks were bright red. "You want to, right?"

Her eyes went wide, and so did her smile. "Yes?"

Hmm. She seemed both interested and terrified at the thought of meeting his family. "Then I guess it's a good thing we're going to my parents' place for dinner Friday night."

She made a sound that to his dying day he'd swear was an *eep*. "Oh. That's good." She shoved the whole cookie in her mouth and began to chew.

"They're good people." Rose winked. "You'll like them."

Jonah sighed. He'd take the attention away from Carol and allow her to regain her composure. Otherwise, she'd just start shoving cookies in her mouth till she either choked again or exploded. "Rose. Why can't you track the wither?"

"For one thing, which wither would I follow?" Rose shrugged. "Without something that's a part of it in some way I can't track it. And"—she held up her hand when Jonah went to interrupt—"because the wither was once human, the realm created for them is off-limits to those of us of purely otherworldly blood. To follow him to his master, first I'd have to follow him through the realms. I'd lose him before I ever got to the master." She picked up another cookie and handed it to Carol. "There's just no way I can go there."

Carol had finally managed to swallow the first cookie. "Wait. I don't understand. Why can't you follow it?"

Rose sighed. "I'm a full-blooded earth dimen. My parents were from the earth realm, making them earth giants, if you will. I can travel to my realm and track someone there with the right spells. I can even go to some of the other realms, but there are those that are closed to me, such as the water realm or the realm of hellfire."

"Okay, I get the water realm. You'd literally become mud." Carol nibbled her third cookie. "But why the realm of the withers? Why is that closed?"

"She'd need human blood to enter Terra Noctem, and she has none." Jonah rubbed his eyes. "Damn it. I hadn't thought of that."

"Created by the gods or the hands of man, it doesn't matter one little bit. I'm confined by my nature, just as the wither is." Rose sat back with her teacup cradled in her hands. "I don't make the rules. Hell, I'm not certain why we're allowed here but not, say, the wither's realm."

"Because it's a place of punishment?" Carol tilted her head in her dog-like way. He imagined her nose twitching as if she'd caught a scent.

"Terra Noctem isn't inherently bad, but it isn't good either," Jonah replied. A lot of people, even those educated in magic, made the mistake of thinking that Terra Noctem was a place of evil. "It is, however, human-oriented. It's where lost souls, ghosts, poltergeists, withers, shadow men, and wraiths live, all of it covered in ectoplasmic mist. I've caught rumors of animal spirits living there as well, but I'm not sure if that's true or not."

"Exactly." Rose sipped her tea. "And since I'm neither animal nor human, Terra Noctem is closed to me."

"Following the wither isn't a path we can take without paying a price I'm not willing to even consider." The thought of contacting a realm walker or a necromancer made him shiver with dread. His animus might contact Terra Noctem, but Jonah couldn't imagine actually *visiting* the place.

The people who did were either super courageous or crazy. Probably both.

He grabbed another cookie. Hell, he might as well enjoy the visit with his old friend. "By the way, Rose is *totally* in love with me."

Carol's head snapped to him, a snarl forming on her lips.

Rose rolled her eyes. "When I was five, dickhead. Then I learned what you were really like when you popped Tommy Leary on the nose for no reason whatsoever." Rose sniffed in disgust.

There'd been a good reason for it, but he'd never tell Rose what Tommy Leary had said about her to deserve that punch. Rose was as close to him as a sister, and Tommy Leary had been—and still was—a douche. "Yeah, I was a total bad boy when I was young."

"I can believe that." Carol sat forward and gave Rose a sweet, sugary smile. "Tell me more."

Rose laughed deeply, that wonderful belly laugh Jonah had come to love. Rose was as much a sister to him as Lessa was. Watching Carol enjoy their talk was worth the humiliation that was about to be heaped upon his head. "I'd be delighted."

Or not. Jonah shoved the cookie in his mouth and prepared to be mortified.

Chapter 15

Carol was still giggling off and on as Jonah drove them to a restaurant. He had the grumpiest expression on his face, but every now and then his lips would twitch, and she'd catch him trying to stop a laugh with a cough.

Once she got over her initial jealousy of Rose, she'd found the other woman entertaining as hell. The stories of Jonah's childhood had made him sound like one tiny hellraiser. The one where he was taking a bath, only to empty a wastebasket to use it to "bail out the leaky boat," had her holding her sides. Rose had enacted Jonah's mother's reaction, making Jonah cover his head in response. Apparently, the words "Go to your room" had never terrified him more.

Jonah had winced through most of the stories, his cheeks heating in embarrassment as Rose's stories had gotten more and more enjoyable, at least for the women.

The cookies had been really good too.

"Can we visit her again?" Carol batted her lashes at Jonah, trying not to laugh again at his disgruntled face.

"No." Jonah pulled into the parking lot of a popular steak house. "She might start telling stories about when I was a teenager."

Carol got out of the car, smiling broadly. "Then we definitely need to go."

Jonah got out, but he was no longer paying attention to her. Instead, he was scowling at his phone.

Carol's amusement immediately fled. "What's wrong?"

Jonah muttered something evil-sounding under his breath that she didn't recognize. "Rose is going to be at dinner on Friday."

Carol bit her lip to stop herself from laughing. "Does your mother like her?"

"My mom adores her." Jonah offered his arm, and Carol took it. "Rose helped set up her garden."

"Did she help with yours?" Carol opened the door to the restaurant before Jonah could do so.

"Nope. Rose was busy with her business by then. My mom and I did mine." Jonah was grumbling again, but he strode ahead of her to where the hostess stand was. "Sound, party of two." Jonah led her to the benches along the wall. He had one of those flasher things restaurants gave out. He handed it to her and pulled out his phone. "I need to send Paul a text about the serpent symbol we found on the victim."

Carol nodded and sat patiently, waiting for their flasher to go off.

Jonah took a deep breath and let it out softly. "Paul's worried about the combination of dimenic runes and the serpent symbol."

Carol shook her head. "Trust me, the dimenic runes were nonsense. The serpent was the important one."

This was one of those teaching moments he'd been expecting. "My gut says you're right, but it's better to be thorough than miss something. Neither one of us wants to get our asses chewed out by the boss lady, trust me." When she nodded her understanding, he continued, "We can have my sister take a look at them. She's an expert on this kind of thing, and she'll be discreet." Jonah took back the flasher and grabbed her hand, folding their fingers together. "We'll get him, don't worry."

"I'm not." Carol squeezed his hand, hoping to show her support. Jonah's determination was almost visible, like a cloak that surrounded him. She had to figure out a way to break him out of his funk. "Speaking of sisters, did you really glue your sister's pigtails to her pillow?"

Jonah shot her a horrified glance. "I would never do something like that. No matter how many of my cookies she stole, the little brat."

"You're an evil man." Carol patted his hand. "I like that about you."

He huffed out a laugh. "I like you too. I'm glad you and Rose are getting along." He seemed a little more relaxed as he crossed his ankle over his knee. "And my mother is going to love you too."

Too? It was a little soon for the two of them to be sharing words of love, so he must be talking about Rose. "I think I'll invite Rose and Debbie out for a girls' day of shopping."

"Have fun. Oh, by the way, I forgot to tell you. You have an account, automatically set up the moment you became my familiar. I'll get you all of the necessary checkbooks and credit cards associated with it as soon as we get home."

She blinked. "How? When did you…? There's no way it got set up in my name that fast." It was what, a week since they signed their contract? They'd been busy setting her up as his familiar as well as chasing down leads on several cases. Besides, didn't he need her signature for all of that stuff?

He kissed the back of her hand. "It's done, so don't worry about it."

Jonah really was magic. "So… I can go shopping?"

"Yup. In fact, I insist on it." Jonah grinned. "You'll need to pick up some work clothing. Debbie can help with that if you're unsure of what to pick up."

"I'd appreciate her help." Carol's mind was racing with possibilities, but until she had a handle on her new financial situation, she couldn't really plan much. "When does the department pay me?"

"We get paid every other week, so you'll get your first check in two weeks." Jonah frowned slightly, biting his lip. He seemed to do that whenever he was thinking. "Yeah, two weeks. They hold one check back."

"Huh." She made a disappointed face. "Guess I have to wait to go shopping."

"Nope, you can—" At that moment, the flasher went off, and Jonah tugged her to her feet. "Let's go eat. I'm starving."

"Oh, hell yes." She'd been smelling steak the entire time they'd been talking and was having a hard time swallowing her drool.

They were led to their seats and given their menus. With a cursory glance, she decided on her dinner—the medallions and loaded mashed potatoes, with her favorite brown ale. Jonah picked the T-bone with red wine, and they agreed to share a cheese plate appetizer.

When the drinks came, Carol took a sip and sighed in satisfaction. "Mm, that's good."

Jonah was watching her, his gaze heating up. "Glad you like it. I'll have to stock some of that in the fridge."

"Have you ever tasted this before? It's a local brewer, really good." Carol held out her glass.

Jonah took it, turned it to where her lips had been, and took a sip. He licked a drop off of the glass before handing it back. "It is good."

It was almost as good as if his tongue had touched her lips. She cleared her throat, her hand shaking as she put the glass down. "Jonah?"

"Hmm?" Jonah nodded at the waitress as she placed the cheese plate in front of them. "That looks good, thank you."

Carol picked up a piece of cheddar, hoping she'd managed to hide the way she was reacting to his simple yet sensuous action. "Tell me about your previous familiars." She wanted to understand what had gone wrong with the others and what had been right.

She couldn't understand how anyone would want to leave Jonah. The man was so perfect for her that she never wanted to go without his magic sliding across her skin.

"Mm." Jonah leaned back, absently toying with his glass. "My first familiar was a guy I was in class with. We both knew it was temporary. More a convenience for both of us while my magic matured and he waited for a good match. It lasted a year and a day."

Okay, that made sense. A lot of young mages and familiars did just as Jonah and his friend had. "Were any of them as close to you as I am?" Her eyes went wide as she realized what she'd said. "Magically, I mean." Crap. She had the uncanny knack of embarrassing herself around this powerful man.

Jonah shook his head, his gaze boring into her, heating her from the inside out. "Hell. No." Letting go of the glass, he took her hand in his. His thumb stroked over her knuckles, their magic tingling along the path he stroked. "I told you before that I was lovers with two of them, but again, it wasn't like this." He picked up her hand and kissed her knuckles, sending shivers up her arm and straight to her heart, which began to pound in response.

Her anima began to react to him, reaching out to form that deeper connection they'd been practicing with surprising ease.

"You think we'll be lovers?" Her voice came out husky, almost silent. She wanted that so badly her body ached, yet they'd only known each other a week.

The smile he gave her bordered on sinister. "If I have anything to say about it, you'll be dessert." He licked his lips as his gaze drifted to her chest. "You have no idea how badly I want to taste you."

Carol clenched her free hand, only then remembering the piece of cheddar she'd picked up. "Oops."

Jonah sat back with a soft laugh. "Let's eat, go home, and…talk. About things."

Her gaze was wicked as she licked her lips. "Whatever comes up, huh?"

This time it was Jonah whose voice came out husky. "You bet."

Carol blew out a breath and picked up her beer. "Here's to interesting conversations."

Jonah clinked his glass against hers. "Amen."

Chapter 16

Jonah's hands were shaking as he drove home. He wanted to bury them in her soft curls and tug while he devoured her mouth. Just the thought of her lips swollen from his kisses had him almost pulling over. He wasn't sure he could make the drive home without kissing her at least once.

Her anima had been stroking him all night, a fur-like sensation, warm and soft and driving him insane. From her expression, she was experiencing something similar. Her cheeks were flushed, her pupils dilated. She kept playing with her hands, her fingers dancing across each other.

"Light's green," she muttered, staring straight out the windshield.

He tore his gaze away from her and began driving again. "Sorry. I'm... You're a hell of a distraction." He couldn't tell her that his dick was so hard he was pretty sure he had zipper marks on it despite wearing boxers.

She glanced at his lap, her cheeks flaming bright red before she turned to stare out the window. "I guess. I've never gotten a reaction to my presence quite like yours though."

Just the fact that she understood what she was noticing made him growly. Whose dick had she been eyeing?

She rolled her eyes. "Are *you* a virgin?" When he shook his head, she smiled. "I promise not to be jealous over your past love life if you promise me the same."

166

Damn it, that one was going to be harder than his dick. "If I meet any of them, I promise nothing."

She thought about that for a moment. "Deal."

"And stop growling at Dean Hill. I have no interest in anyone other than a certain redheaded wolf, okay?" He put his hand on her knee and stroked her leg gently. He carefully did not go above mid-thigh, not wanting to go where he wasn't invited.

She didn't push his hand away, a good sign for their coming night. "If she flirts with you, I promise nothing."

He bit back a laugh at the low growl in her voice. He firmed his grip on her thigh. "Promise not to bite unless she touches me in any way that's not professional or friendly, okay?"

"Hmm." Carol's gaze had gone wolf-gold. Her anima wrapped around him, cocooning him. "I'll think about it."

It was the best he was going to get.

He pulled into his garage and turned off the car. He kept his eyes on the steering wheel, unsure of how she'd react to the question burning through him. "I want you." When she didn't answer, he continued. "If you say no, I will go to my room, take the world's coldest shower, climb into bed, and go to sleep with no hard feelings. I never want you to think you need to—"

Carol's lips came down on his, halting any further speech.

Jonah wasn't going to ask again. He considered this kiss consent.

He was proven right when she lifted her lips from his. "Take me to bed, Mr. Sound."

"My pleasure." He started to get out of the car and was immediately halted by his seat belt. "Damn it."

She was laughing as she hit the button, freeing him from his nylon prison. He felt like an idiot, but how could he resist her shy smile or the way she tugged insistently on his hands?

He crawled out after her, all thoughts gone as he allowed her to pull him into the house. She smiled over her shoulder, sending his heart racing a mile a minute. They ascended the stairs in silence, anticipation riding him hard. His cock throbbed behind his zipper as she reached for the doorknob and entered his bedroom.

She stopped in the middle, turning to him, her gaze uncertain. She bit her lip, looking everywhere but at him.

Jonah smiled, taking her into his arms. "I'm not doing going to do anything you don't want me to, remember?"

She finally looked at him, her hands pressed against his chest, her fingers digging into his shirt. One strawberry curl got caught in her lashes as she blinked up at him. "I know." She kissed his chin. "Don't worry, okay?"

Don't worry? That sounded more like she was concerned for his sake rather than her own.

Instead of answering, he kissed her, gently at first, soft and sweet, barely breaching her lips. Desire rode him hard, but he held out against it, gentling her against him until she was no longer clinging to his shirt but curled around him, her arms around his neck and her body against his. Jonah opened one eye to make sure the path to the bed was clear, then began walking her toward it. Not once did he remove his lips from hers, even as he eased her down, pushing her back until her legs dangled over the edge and her back was to the mattress. "Scoot up."

She did as told, her face flushed and her movements jerky. When her head hit the pillow, she sighed. "Your scent is all over the place." Her words were slurred, almost as if she were drugged.

Jonah didn't care. All he wanted was to taste her, to see her skin against his sheets. He pulled at her T-shirt, kissing her until she lifted her arms and allowed him to remove it. He lapped at the tops of her breasts, salt and warmth and Carol mingling on his tongue. He caressed her stomach, tracing her warm skin with his fingertips.

Her bra was in the way. He wanted to taste her nipples, suck on them until she writhed beneath him. He lifted it up, pushing it toward her chin, releasing her to his hungry gaze.

"Wait." She sat up just enough to undo the hooks, allowing the bra to fall free. "Go ahead." Her voice was breathless, her gaze glued to him.

He couldn't resist her invitation. He drew her into his mouth, sucking at her nipple until her fingers dug into his scalp.

"Oh, God, Jonah. More." Her legs spread, cradling him between them as he moved to the other nipple.

She moaned, rubbing against him, their pants in the way of what he wanted. He reached for her zipper, tugging and pulling until he could reach his hand inside to find her soft curls and the wet nub begging for his attention.

Carol exploded beneath him in a frenzy of movement. She pushed her pants and underwear down her legs, shoving them forcefully off her and almost kneeing him in the balls in the process.

Jonah moved with her, keeping his fingers buried in her pussy and his lips on her breast until she cried out, coming for the first time. Her body froze before she bucked, almost throwing him off as her orgasm swamped her.

He wasn't leaving it at that. She needed to come at least twice more before he'd be done with her. He began to lick down her middle, ready to taste her pussy, when she dug her fingers into his hair again.

"In me. Now." Her voice was guttural now, her eyes the color of her wolf's.

Jonah nodded and released his prick, not even bothering to undress. She smiled up at him, teeth sharp, fangs on full display as he eased into her hot warmth.

Now it was Jonah's time to groan as he was surrounded in the tight, hot fist of her body. She arched against him, drawing him deeper, her body undulating as he began to fuck her in slow, steady strokes.

"Jesus." Her claws were scratching him, the small bite of pain egging him on. From her fierce gaze, he understood that the wolf would take over if he didn't give her what she wanted.

Jonah sped up, fucking her with intent, their bodies slapping together as he kissed her again. She wrapped her legs around his waist, her heels digging into the top of his ass. He took hold of her hands and forced them down to either side of her head, showing the wolf who was in control. He kept his gaze on hers as they fucked, trying his best to prove that he was a worthy mate.

Carol's eyes flickered then changed back, the beautiful hazel color making him slow for a moment. This must have been what she'd been worried about, that her wolf might take over and hurt him.

To show her he wasn't concerned, he kept his hands wrapped around her wrists even as he sped up the pace, making sure that he kept watching her. He wanted to see the exact moment she came, wanted it burned into his memory to take out on nights when they couldn't be together. If he was right, if she was going to be his, those nights would be few and far between.

If he was wrong…

Jonah grimaced. If he was wrong, he was in deep shit, because if Carol wasn't perfect for him than he'd never find the one.

"What's wrong?" Carol tried to free her hand, the dazed look receding as if she'd guessed that he was having troubled thoughts.

"Nothing. Just thinking about how perfect you are."

Her already pink cheeks turned bright red. "Jonah!" The second syllable of his name ended on a gasp as he took her nipple into his mouth once more.

He needed to experience her tightening around him, her muscles spasming as he fucked her. Already she was clenching her hands, her mouth opened wide as she panted for him. He picked up the pace, almost at the point of no return.

Carol cried out once more, her body stiff as her pussy clamped down on him rhythmically. She was coming, and she was stunning in her ecstasy. Just watching her pushed him into his own orgasm, his limbs shuddering as he came undone.

When his vision cleared, he realized he'd collapsed on top of her. Her fists were banging against his shoulder. He lifted up, breathing hard, to hear her gasp.

"Sorry." He fell to the side, half asleep already. He put his hand on her bare stomach, smiling when she put her hand over his.

"Couldn't breathe." She giggled, and the sensation of her moving under his hand again made his cock twitch. "You're heavy, Mr. Sound."

"No, I'm not. You're just teeny." He yawned, pulling her close. "Gotta cuddle."

"You need to get out of your clothes first." Fabric moved against his skin as she took his clothing off until he was left in nothing but her scent. "Now we can cuddle."

"Mm." Jonah smiled as he closed his eyes, content to have his familiar by his side.

Chapter 17

Three days after their visit to Rose, they received an answer from their Egyptologist, Dr. Ramsey. Dean Hill had been kind enough to give him the name, a friend of hers who was working in a different university close by. In her email, she'd confirmed Carol's guess that the symbol was that of Apep and had expressed extreme concern over the fact that there was no accompanying god represented to subdue Apep.

Jonah was worried as well. If someone was feeding a god of evil someone's soul, nothing good could come of it. There was a hellacious amount of power in a soul. Feeding it to a god of destruction could only lead to ruin.

"I doubt we'll find out anything new on the toxicology report." Carol spoke softly from her seat across from him. Jonah had a partner's desk in his office, designed for two people to work together face to face. It was the best setup for himself and a cop familiar, but Carol was the first one he'd worked with who was genuinely pleased by it. Others had wanted their own desks to clutter up without having to deal with his paperwork in their space. Carol had simply sat and begun picking things up, examining them, then putting them where she decided they belonged.

She was a first in a lot of ways.

"I agree." Jonah stretched. He'd been at his desk for over an hour, going over the Egyptologist's notes. "You read the report from Dr. Ramirez?"

Carol nodded. "Yeah, and I'm not that happy about it." She peeked around her monitor at him. "I mean, human sacrifice is bad enough, but sacrificing the soul?" She shuddered hard. "I'm inclined to agree with my wolf. This fucker needs killin'."

"Don't eat the bad guy, he'll give you indigestion," Jonah replied absently. "Did you read the note about Apep being the, uh…" He scrolled through the email. "The serpent of rebirth?"

"Serpents and snakes shed their skin, so ancient people often associated them with rebirth," Carol replied.

Jonah's work cell phone rang. He answered quickly, hoping it wasn't another victim. "Detective Sound."

Miles's tone was grim. "Jonah, we've got another one."

"Fuck." So much for hope. He ran his fingers through his hair, then gestured for Carol to get up. "Where?"

"The college. Same place, except first base this time and the victim is carrying a— What kind of flower did the caller say?" Miles yelled to someone in the distance, then said, "Yeah, a white gladiolus."

Jonah frowned. "The last one had a lily in his hands."

"Yeah, well, apparently this vic wanted a different flower." Miles hung up with a curt farewell.

"Huh." Jonah followed Carol out of his office and into the garage. "This victim is different. Same field, but on first base and carrying a gladiolus."

"First base?" Carol frowned. "Hmm…"

"What?" Jonah was willing to listen to any hunches Carol had. So far, she'd had better luck figuring things out than he did, and he was a seasoned professional.

"There's got to be something significant about the flowers. Otherwise, why place them in the victim's hands?" Carol slipped into the passenger seat and put on her seat belt.

He'd come to the same conclusion. "I agree. We'll call Rose and ask her opinion. She knows her flowers." Jonah pulled out of the garage and headed for the college, where no doubt onlookers, gawkers, and police had already gathered. He pressed a button on his cell. "Call Rose." He handed Carol the phone as it started to ring. "Here, talk so I can drive."

Carol put the phone to her ear. "Hello, Rose? It's Carol. We need some help." Carol nodded in response to something Rose said. "Yeah, we do owe you. I was going to ask you, Debbie, and my friend Stacey to go out for lunch and some shopping soon." Carol smiled. "I look forward to it, but first, what can you tell me about lilies and gladiolus?"

Jonah could make out Rose's voice, but not the actual words. Carol uh-huh'd and occasionally murmured something until she finally said, "Both flowers were found on the victims of the college murders."

Jonah winced. That was privileged information, something that hadn't been handed to the press.

"Oh, yeah, keep that on the down-low. We don't want anyone to know about it. It's one of the ways we can use to identify the killer."

Jonah was nearing the college, so he tried to signal for Carol to finish up her conversation.

"Okay." Carol seemed to get the message because she wound down the call just as they reached the parking lot. "Yeah, I'll see you tomorrow. Bye." She handed Jonah back his phone. "Well, she said lilies represent restored innocence after death while gladiolus represent strength of character, sincerity, and integrity. Both are often found in funeral arrangements."

Jonah frowned as he parked the car in the athletic field's parking lot. Already, there was a small crowd with uniformed officers keeping them back. "Maybe our perp knew the victims, and this was his way to show some remorse. That puts professors even higher on our suspect list." Jonah got out. "We need a list of classes our victims took together. It's a good bet that it's someone familiar with them and their schedules."

"We also need a list of their families and friends of their families. It's possible the connection is there somewhere. If so, the baseball field could be a convenient dump site rather than part of the ritual." Carol joined him as he walked toward the crime scene. "Think we'll find the same pattern of wounds?"

"It would be strange if we didn't." This was seeming more and more like some sort of ritual, but what would the final phase be? Someone on the pitcher's mound? Would they start finding bodies in the outfield?

"Detective Sound?" One of the uniforms left the throng of onlookers and came toward them. "This way, sir." He led them around the crowd and toward the baseball field. "The victim's name is Sara Miller, age eighteen, taking magical studies here. She lived off-campus since her family is in the area."

"So that's different from Reeves," Carol murmured.

"The body's been left, and we're retrieving the video footage from Dean Hill. She's right over there, consoling the person who found the body." The uniform gestured toward Dean Hill, then headed back to the crowd.

"Which do you want? Dean Hill or the body?" Jonah was already glancing toward the corpse.

"I'll talk to the witness, you go over the body. Meet you in a few." Carol walked off, already pulling her little recorder out of her purse.

Jonah began walking toward the body. Hopefully, he'd find more evidence this time than he had around the nonexistent one last time. At least he'd gotten to this one before Frick and Frack had a chance to show up and wave their collective dicks around. A lot of cops still thought of him as an entitled rich boy, but Jonah had worked damn hard to get where he was, and he wasn't about to let anyone step all over his crime scenes.

"Detective." A different homicide detective, neither Wheeler or Ridgely, nodded a greeting to him. His features were

Asian, probably Japanese or Korean. His guess was confirmed when the man introduced himself. "I'm Ian Matsumoto. I just transferred into Homicide from Vice. I'm now the detective working this case."

"Nice to meet you. I'm Jonah Sound." Jonah held out his hand.

Matsumoto's grip was firm as they shook. Matsumoto then glanced down at the victim and sighed. "This is fucked up. Number two, right? Same bat time, same bat place?"

"Pretty much, yeah." Jonah glanced down.

The victim was female, a neatly dressed blonde, lying on the ground with her head resting on first base like it was a soft pillow. Her were hands folded across her chest and holding a white gladiolus. Her shoelaces had been tied together to keep her legs closed. The skirt of her dress was carefully arranged, making it seem like the killer had tried to make it appear as if she were floating on water instead of bleeding on sand.

There was no pool of blood near the body, no drag marks, nothing to indicate that she hadn't just laid down and died. There were no wrappers or cheap vape pen either. Nothing that would indicate anyone other than the wither and the victim had ever been there. "Did someone clean the crime scene?"

Matsumoto shook his head. "Nah, the area was cleaned because there was supposed to be a game here today. They found the body about an hour ago when the team captain arrived to check that everything was ready." Matsumoto gestured toward where Carol was questioning a young man in workout gear. "Poor guy got the shock of his life."

"He a sorcerer?" It was a long shot, but best to check.

"Nope. The vic was though." Matsumoto gazed at the notebook in his hand. "Sara Miller's mother is going to identify the body, but since her student ID was on her, including picture, it's pretty safe to assume she's the victim."

Jonah carefully knelt next to the victim, trying to detect if a serpent had been burned into her chest. "These runes, they're the same ones that we observed on the other victim." He pointed toward Ms. Miller's chest. "On Mr. Reeves, we found the symbol of Apep right where the stab wounds were. This was the work of the same person." Every instinct he had was screaming at him. From the depths of the wounds to the posed body and loss of mana, there could be no doubt that they were hunting a single perpetrator.

"The what of who?" Matsumoto shook his head. "If I'm going to be on this task force they're talking of setting up, I really need to bone up on magical runes," he muttered.

"Huh?" Jonah shot him a startled glance. Were they finally listening to his constant complaints?

"Someone didn't read his emails." Matsumoto smiled, the expression friendly. "My boss wants to set up a task force with your boss so that there are so-called 'regular' detectives permanently assigned to the MCU." He'd done finger-quotes when he said regular. "This way, we avoid the kind of situation you had with my buddies in Homicide."

Jonah nodded, almost sagging in relief. He'd been hounding Anne for something like this to happen. Thank the gods of magic, it seemed his nagging had paid off. "It would be nice not to be fighting the other divisions all the time."

"Yeah." Matsumoto scratched his ear. "I've been informed that MCU is trading someone to Vice."

That was a surprise. As far as he understood, not many sorcerers participated in drug smuggling, prostitution, gun-running, or illegal gambling. Then again, he'd never had to work those cases either. Maybe there were those out there who used their powers to help mobsters run their organizations.

The more he thought about it, the stupider he felt for not realizing that was more than likely the case. "Why haven't they come to us before?"

Matsumoto shrugged. "Whose balls are bigger, of course. It's still a boys' club, yeah? What's that saying? No matter how powerful the sorcerer—"

"A bullet to the back of the head will stop him cold." Jonah shook off the thought of other departments finally using the MCU's detectives. He hoped that someday, the division between MCU and the rest of the departments would disappear, but it would take time. "We have info on how the body got here."

"We?" Matsumoto glanced once more at Carol. "Your familiar?"

"Yeah." Jonah glanced across the field toward Carol, who was striding toward them. The man she'd been interviewing was in the dugout, his head in his hands. "Hope you like wolves."

"Oh yeah. Wolves rock." Matsumoto cocked his head. "Does she have a sister?"

Jonah laughed. He was certain they were going to get along just fine.

Chapter 18

Carol and Jonah arrived at the coroner's office that afternoon, having spoken to everyone on the scene. The poor guy who'd found the body had been so traumatized that he had to go to the hospital to be sedated. It seemed that he'd been in a class with the victim, though they'd never spoken to each other. Still, it had scared the hell out of him that someone so close to him had been murdered.

Carol could understand. If someone from her House had been the victim, she would have had issues as well, even if it was Perky Patty.

"The body should be here by now, but Paul probably hasn't had a chance to go over it." Jonah had been quiet until they arrived at the coroner's office. She figured he was also going over the crime scene in his head, just like she was.

"Once we have the video feed from the CCTV cameras, we should be able to find out if the serpent was on her chest." Jonah parked and turned off the car, turning to her. His expression was serious. "What did you get from the baseball guy?"

Carol shook her head. "Not much that was useful, I'm afraid. Before he went to the hospital, he told me she was in one of his classes, with Professor…" She pulled out her small recorder and put it to her ear, listening intently. "Right, Professor Ballenger." She turned off the recorder and rifled through the emails on her tablet PC, pulling up the list of university employees Dean Hill had sent them. "Professor Elroy Ballenger, teaches herbology."

"Herbology, huh?" Jonah scratched his chin. "Check if Reeves had herbology this semester or the one before."

"We don't have a complete list yet, but I'll see if that's one of the ones we've gotten. If not, I can contact Dean Hill and ask her to expedite Ballenger's class lists." Carol put her tablet away, tucking her recorder next to it. She'd transcribe the recordings to the computer once she got home.

She noticed the stares as they made their way through the building to Paul's office. She *really* needed to get some work clothing now that she had the money to do so. She'd gotten confirmation from Debbie and Rose for the coming weekend shopping spree. Stacey hadn't gotten back to her yet, but Stacey was also busy getting used to her new sorcerer. They could go for a week or two without talking to each other, then squabble like the closest siblings once they were together again. It would be a shame not to introduce Stacey to her new friends right away, but she wanted Stacey to form a strong bond and find the sorcerer she could best work with, maybe even love. Hopefully, her latest match would be just that.

She glanced at Jonah, her mind no longer on the case. His broad back and narrow waist were defined by the powder-blue shirt he wore. His black belted slacks hugged his ass, and he'd worn a tie today—basic black with gray diamonds. From his appearance, you'd never think his parents were multi-millionaires.

Jonah might have a bigger house than most, but other than that he lived simply. He vacuumed his own carpet, scrubbed his own toilet, and cooked his own meals. She found she admired him a lot more than she'd thought she would. He might be on the society pages from time to time thanks to his family, but other than that he was just like any other person.

It made her far more comfortable than she would have been if he'd lived in some fancy mansion with servants doing his bidding.

"I'm betting there was a little bit of mana left within our vic, just like the last one, and that it was sucked away after death."

Carol brought her attention back to the subject at hand. "That would match with our theory, yeah." She had to stop staring at his ass and focus on their murder victim. Ass viewing could take place after work.

Jonah bent over to pick up a piece of paper off the floor.

Or during work. That was good too.

"Hey, Debbie, does this belong to you?" Jonah held out the piece of paper, smiling whimsically at Paul's wife.

Debbie was standing in front of the secretary's desk, her arms akimbo, a scowl on her face. She was staring down at a pretty woman who was currently touching up her lipstick.

The stench of the secretary's perfume stung Carol's delicate nose, making her sneeze. She could only imagine how torturous it was for Debbie to smell it day in and day out. No wonder she was scowling.

"Yeah, thanks." She turned to Jonah and took the piece of paper, glancing over it. Her expression tightened as she read. "Hmm." She turned to the secretary, her scowl returning. "Why was this on the floor? I asked you to file this an hour ago."

The woman shrugged nonchalantly, but there was a nasty gleam in her eye. "I have no idea." She reached out for the paper, her dark brows rising when Debbie held on to it. "Mrs. Lofland?"

Debbie's teeth were visibly grinding as she handed over the piece of paper. "Please make sure that this time it's filed properly, in a cabinet." Her tone was so sugary, Carol was afraid she'd get cavities.

"Yes, Mrs. Lofland." The woman stood and headed for the corridor.

"I hate that woman," Debbie muttered under her breath. She turned to Carol and Jonah with a strained smile. "Let me guess. You're here for our latest blood sorcerer vic?"

"Yup." Carol leaned in close to Debbie. "What's with her?"

"She's a bitch who thinks the only person she needs to listen to is Paul, despite the fact that I outrank her." Debbie turned on her heel and led the way into Paul's office. "Think you could eat her for me?"

"Nah. I never eat things that smell that bad." Carol nodded a greeting to Paul, who was seated at his desk. "Hey, Mr. Reaper."

Paul, appearing stunned, laughed. "I haven't heard that one before." He stood, holding a file folder. "I can guess why you guys are here. C'mon, I'll explain what I've got so far. Just remember, it's not much, just an initial assessment."

Jonah and Carol followed Paul into the autopsy room where Sara Miller lay. Her head was propped up on a special pillow, her body covered by a white sheet. Underneath, she was naked, her skin pale and gray from death. "Got an estimate on time of death yet?" Jonah asked, his gaze glued to the victim.

"From the lividity, the rigor mortis, and core temp, I'd say…" Paul checked something in his file folder. "Between ten p.m. and two a.m. last night. Wherever she was, I think she was inside. There were no signs of insect activity, at least on an outward examination."

Jonah nodded. "Right. Was there a blow to the back of the head?"

"Right around the same area as the last one." He gently turned the victim's head so that they could all observe the raised, bleeding cut peeking through her hair. "There wasn't this jagged cut on the last victim's head, however. The murderer switched weapons."

"And flowers," Carol added.

"We did find some signs of branding around the stab wounds, just like you suspected." Paul pointed to a tiny dark spot on the victim's chest. "When you view the video…"

"We'll find the symbol of Apep." Carol shuddered.

"I think so." Paul returned the victim's head to its original position. "I'll have a slightly better time of death once I do the full autopsy." He lifted her hand, turning it slightly. "I did notice something under her nails. I've sent it to the lab for analysis. It might be skin, or it could just be dirt."

"She might have managed to scratch her attacker?" Carol glanced at the body. "But that doesn't make sense, unless…"

"She woke up during the ceremony and managed to scratch him." Jonah wrote something in his notebook. "Which means she might have seen his face too."

Carol winced. "Please tell me we're not calling in a necromancer."

"We're not calling in a necromancer," Jonah replied absently. "There isn't enough mana left in the body."

Necromancers weren't zombie creators, like some feared. They simply were able to use the link between body and soul to call upon the departed. But without residual mana in the body, the link was irretrievably broken. Most bodies lost their mana within a week of death, meaning necromancers were in high demand with those who wished to contact the departed. Some people simply wanted to say goodbye to a loved one, others wanted the keys to treasure, and still others, like Jonah, used necromancers to solve murders.

"Wait. Something here is different." Debbie pointed to the dimenic runes circling the stab wounds. "Gimme a sec."

Carol read as best she could the runes Debbie had pointed out. "She's right. This isn't just Eat at Joe's like Reeves. I think this has a signature embedded in it."

"Huh?" Jonah leaned in closer. "Are you sure?"

Carol nodded. "We'd need to send it to an expert to be sure, but yeah." She glanced at Jonah, only to find him pulling out his phone, probably to take pictures. "It's not his or her real name, but it's definitely a magical signature."

"Which means we may have missed something on the other victim." Jonah smiled tightly. "Time to examine those images of Reeves a little more closely. I'm betting we'll find out there was a signature on him too."

"I'll let you know if we find anything during the autopsy." Paul tucked his folder under his arm. "In the meantime, get out of my hair. I've got work to do."

"Oh, before we go, I'm borrowing your wife this weekend." Carol's cheeks began to heat. "I need to pick up some clothing."

"Oh?" Debbie drawled, linking her arm with Carol's. From the wink she gave, Carol understood she was about to be teased. "Tell me more. What kind of clothing?" She tugged Carol out of the morgue, Jonah following behind them.

Carol shook her head. "Work clothes, ya perv."

"Damn," came softly from behind her.

Carol turned to stare at Jonah. "Did you just say—"

"Nope." Jonah coughed into his hand. "I didn't say a word." He wasn't meeting her eyes, though, and his cheeks were as red as hers probably were.

Carol turned back around. "Maybe I can shop for some non-work clothes," she muttered.

"Yay!" Debbie hugged her. "You have no idea how much I'm looking forward to this." Debbie took off cackling, so happy she even smiled at her husband's secretary.

The secretary to scowled for about two seconds before turning a bland smile their way. "Oh, Detective, Ms. Voss. Are you leaving already?"

Carol almost rolled her eyes. Now that Debbie and Paul were no longer visible, the secretary's tone couldn't be more bored. "Jonah? Be right back." She ducked back into Paul's office. "I'm going to eat your secretary."

"Huh?" Paul looked up from the pile of paperwork on his desk. "Why?"

"Why? She irritates your wife, and she was barely polite to Jonah and me. That isn't who you need greeting people who come to the morgue, especially family members who have to identify the deceased." She was hoping that professionalism would win over Debbie's obvious jealousy. Maybe if someone other than Debbie complained, the woman would get fired.

Paul sighed. "You're right, and thank you. I've needed a real reason to get rid of her, but no one other than Debbie has

190

complained. If you and Jonah do, I can fire her with justification."

"I'll talk to him. I'm sure she's been less than pleasant to him in the past." Carol waved goodbye. "Oh, if you and Jonah want to join us this weekend, you're welcome to."

Paul grinned, looking so happy she thought sparkles might start dancing around his head. "Nah, we'll pass. Maybe I'll take him for burgers while you ladies shop."

"Sounds good. See you later." Carol left the office, certain she'd done her new friend a solid.

Jonah was waiting by the elevators reading something on his tablet. He smiled as she approached, seemingly relaxed. "Everything all right?"

"Perfect." She pushed the button to call the elevator. "Paul is going to ask you out for burgers while Debbie and I shop."

Jonah glanced at her, his expression relieved. "Good, I was thinking of tailing— I mean, going to the mall too."

Carol chuckled. "I think I'd notice you, senpai." She tapped the side of her nose. "I've got your scent."

Senpai? He chuckled softly. His familiar apparently liked anime. A senpai was an older classmate or teacher, one who usually mentored the younger person, or kohai. He tugged at her magic, then took hold of her hand as they stepped into the elevator. "That's okay. I've got yours too."

191

Chapter 19

Jonah took a huge bite out of his burger and moaned. "Jesus, that's good."

"Mm." Paul swallowed his own bite and turned to stare at the crowds in the mall. They'd chosen this restaurant because they could meet up with the women once they were done shopping. The girls had told them they'd grab a bite to eat in the food court, not wanting to waste much time on food when there was money to be spent and clothing to be tried on.

Jonah smiled. Carol had been so excited on the way to the mall she'd been bouncing in her seat. She'd run up to Debbie the moment she caught sight of her, chattering away a mile a minute. If he didn't know better, he'd think her a chipmunk instead of a wolf. "Carol was looking forward to this all day."

"So was Debbie." Paul put his burger down. "By the way, do me a favor and write your complaints about my secretary down so I can fire her ass and not get sued for it, okay?"

"Huh?" Jonah shook his head, amused. "Is that what Carol was talking to you about?"

"Yup." Paul took a bite of his burger. "Om, beh da muay—"

"Hold it right there." Jonah shuddered in disgust. "Eat, then speak, you ass."

Paul swallowed. "Yeah, whatever. Listen, the magical signature we found in those runes. I can't get it out of my head. I get the feeling there's something significant to it, more than what we originally thought."

"Oh?" Jonah pulled out his tablet, scrolling through images until he came to the one with the signature. "What about it caught your attention?"

Paul wiped his hands before handing over his own tablet. "Take a look at the enhanced picture."

Jonah stared at the runes. They'd been magically enhanced and enlarged. "There's runes within the runes, not just the signature Carol thought she saw." He blinked, the image dancing before his eyes. The way it had been done was dizzying, but if he focused, he could ignore the sensation of being off-balance enough to understand what it was he was examining.

"Yeah. Whoever did this is a master, Jonah. I'm going to be checking Reeves's body for the same thing just in case we missed them."

"Meaning Carol could be wrong about the Eat at Joe's thing." Jonah sat back, thinking hard. He munched on a french fry while his mind raced. "Like I said, I'm not a rune expert, but this is significant. It seems that the runes are different from the ones used to hide them."

"Using non-magical language to hide magical language," Paul concluded. "I'm having my expert double-check Ms. Miller's photos as well. It's possible there's more than one hidden message that we've missed."

"Check for Egyptian magic specifically." Jonah sat forward and picked his burger up again. "Since we're dealing with Apep, it's likely we'll find Egyptian hieroglyphs or hieratic script."

"Good point. If we do, I'll send them to your Egyptologist contact and get them interpreted." Paul glanced out the window again. "We might need to sit down with her and ask some questions. This is getting more and more interesting, isn't it?"

Jonah picked up Paul's tablet again, sending himself the images Paul had shared with him. "More and more confusing, you mean."

"Hmm. If you were to take a diamond and cut it in half, you'd have two triangles," Paul muttered, drawing something on the window with his finger. "A triangle in three dimensions is a pyramid."

"That's one way to…" Jonah stared at Paul's finger as it traced a triangle over and over again on the glass. "Shit. Apep, funeral flowers, baseball diamond… He's creating a death pyramid."

"Maybe, maybe not. It's just a theory though." Paul turned back to Jonah. "I could be wrong."

It made sense. Pyramids were the tombs of pharaohs, who were considered immortal gods. The pyramid was said to be designed to help the soul on its journey, and to help it return to its body. Using the baseball diamond to create a pyramid of death with the pitcher's mound as the capstone would work, but for what he still wasn't sure. "I agree. The dead people, not just their souls, but if he's a follower of the Egyptian gods…" He was rambling, his thoughts tumbling over one another, trying to follow the trail that Paul was on.

Paul's gaze turned to his tablet. "Wait. I seem to remember that there's more than one soul for an Egyptian, isn't there? I remember from watching some mummy movies that there's the *bâ* and the *ka*, right?"

Jonah brought up a web browser and began searching for beliefs of the ancient Egyptians when it came to the soul. "It says here that there's the *jb*, or heart, created from a drop of blood from the mother's heart. It was the seat of will and intelligence as well as emotion." He continued to read. "Then there's the *sheut*, or shadow. Every shadow contains something of the person it represents. Statues were often referred to as shadows."

"Which is why, if you wanted to erase someone, you chiseled away at their statues," Paul replied.

Jonah nodded and continued. "*Ren* was the birth name of the person. If you erased the name, you erased the person, so they were careful to protect it."

"More chiseling, to get rid of a person." Paul was writing something down, but Jonah was too busy reading to check it out. Besides, Paul would tell him his theory once he was done forming it.

"The *bâ* was the personality of the person and was one of the aspects that would remain after death. It would join the *ka* in the afterlife."

"That's a lot of souls," Paul muttered.

"There's more." Jonah scrolled down, wondering which aspect of the soul contained the magic. "The *ka* was the vital essence, that which made a person either alive or dead. If the *ka* fled, the body died. The last bit is the *akh*, which…" Jonah whistled. "Okay. The *akh* was thought to be living thought, intellect as a living entity of its own."

"The spirit of the person, right?" Paul leaned over to stare at Jonah's tablet. He began to read out loud. "So, the *akh* replaced the *khat*, or physical body, in the afterlife by joining with the *ka* and the *bâ*."

"Hmm. It says here that in the spells left in Egyptian coffins the *bâ* could eat, drink, and even have sex. The *bâ* could even perform everyday tasks in non-corporeal form, returning to the mummy at night." Jonah shook his head. "I don't think the *bâ* is what this guy was after though."

"Or the *ren*," Paul added. "He did nothing to try and hide their names."

"Probably. Hmm. I'm thinking that it's probably not the *sheut*, either, since capturing someone's shadow is more difficult than it sounds. Shadows are closely linked to Terra Noctem, making them almost impossible to control. Even if you make a statue of the person, you won't get the whole shadow, just a fraction. If the *sheut* acts like a normal shadow, then I doubt it's what this guy is looking for." Jonah tapped his finger on the tablet. "So, we're left with the *ka*, the *jb*, and the *akh*. Which one holds mana?"

"I have no idea, but if I were to hazard a guess, I'd say the *ka* or the *jb*. The *akh* is more of a traditional ghost in my mind."

"The *ka* is the vital essence, and the *jb* is the personality of the person." Jonah stared at his cooling burger, his appetite fleeing. "The *ka*."

"It has to be." Paul picked up his own tablet. "Which part goes to the afterlife to face Ma'at?"

"The *jb* is the part that's placed on the scales," Jonah muttered. "Oh, shit." He glanced up at Paul as his blood ran cold. "The *jb* is the part that's devoured if it isn't lighter, or at least the same weight as, Ma'at's feather."

"So, it's a matter of figuring out which part of the soul our mana comes from, the heart or the soul." Paul picked up one of his fries and swirled it in the ketchup. "I'm thinking that the magical signature will answer that question for us."

"I agree, though I'm leaning toward the *jb*. Apep devours the heart if it isn't judged worthy of the afterlife, and that's whose symbol we're finding on the victims." Jonah picked up his burger and took another bite, his appetite returning with a vengeance. "If we can find the blood sorcerer before he completes his pyramid, we'll stop whatever ritual he's performing."

Paul nodded as he bit into his ketchup coated fry. "Hell, if we can figure out what his ritual is for, we might be able to stop him without needing to find him."

"If we could come up with a counter-spell, that would lead us to him as his spell rebounds back on him." Jonah took the last bite of his burger, swallowing before he continued. "We need to talk to that Egyptologist pronto. Maybe she'll be able to help us figure this out." His sister could help with the runes, but Egyptian souls, religions, that sort of stuff, she'd be lost on. They had to find an expert in the subject to check out his and Paul's theory.

"Yeah, the Internet only goes so far." Paul used a fry to point to his tablet. Luckily, it hadn't been diving into the ketchup pool yet. "We might be able to find some scholarly papers on there, but I doubt either of us will fully understand what we're studying without an expert's help."

"Especially when it comes to funereal rituals." Jonah swiped some of Paul's fries, ignoring his friend's protests. "One thing I noticed, in Egyptian rituals, the mouth was opened to release the *bâ*, but our victims' mouths were closed."

Paul grunted. "Damn it. We just don't have enough information that will lead us to what he's after, the soul or the mana."

"Without that, figuring out the ritual will be nearly impossible."

They finished up their meal in near silence. Jonah's thoughts were going in circles, trying to figure out the motive of the murderer. Normally, with a blood sorcerer case, it was simple. The sorcerer was after the mana.

This case was different in so many ways he couldn't even begin to list them. It might turn out to be one of the toughest cases of his career. He was certain it would be one of the most memorable.

Each of them ordered dessert and coffee. Paul's phone dinged, and he checked the message, smiling at Jonah when he was done. "The girls are having a good time."

"Oh?" Jonah sipped his coffee, smiling at the thought of his familiar roaming the mall, credit card in hand. "What are they up to?"

"According to my wife, you'll be broke in about half an hour if she has anything to say about it."

Jonah laughed. "Let them have fun. I can afford it."

"You say that now, but wait until you get the bill." Paul shuddered. "A woman given an unlimited credit card and free rein? You're going to be bleeding from the anus, my friend."

"Carol's had nothing but secondhand clothes for years. Let her get what she wants." Jonah wanted Carol's time with Debbie and Rose to be both fun and stress-free. "I'm hoping she isn't worried about the amount of money she's spending."

Paul saluted him with his coffee cup. "It's your wallet's funeral."

Jonah rolled his eyes and changed the subject to small talk. The girls would signal when they were done. Until then, he was just going to enjoy spending time with one of his friends.

Chapter 20

"Oh, dear gods and goddesses, put that down." Carol grabbed the couture Badgley Mischka dress—careful, mustn't wrinkle it—out of Debbie's hand and stared at her like she'd lost her mind. "Where the hell would I wear a twenty-five-hundred-dollar dress?"

"The policeman's ball?" Debbie glanced at the woman in the private dressing room who'd begun bringing them clothing. "Am I right?"

"She'd be stunning in that ivory gown, especially with her red hair." The saleswoman had a professional smile on her face, one that hadn't been there when Carol, Rose, and Debbie had first shown up in the store.

The saleswoman had taken one look at Carol's secondhand Gap jeans and "vintage" T-shirt and had immediately begun to direct them to the discount racks found all over the huge, high-end department store. One look at the tattoo on Carol's wrist and the woman had become all smiles, directing them to the private dressing room they now sat in.

Carol was about to have a heart attack. Jonah was going to kill her if she spent that much money on a single dress. Debbie was a crazy woman, and she was only sorry she hadn't noticed it earlier. "I told you I need work clothes, not—"

"Yeah, yeah," Rose dismissed her protest with a wave of her hand. "Honey, my friend needs a complete wardrobe overhaul."

"I agree," the saleswoman said, her gaze traveling up and down Carol's outfit with a quickly dismissed air of disdain.

"She *does* need some clothing appropriate for an officer of the law, but she needs other outfits as well," Debbie added. She must have noticed Carol's discomfort and hopped in to save her.

Then she ruined Carol's warm, fuzzy feelings by continuing, "Cute things she can wear that won't make her appear inferior to a Sound sorcerer."

Carol's protest froze on her tongue.

With an evil look, Debbie continued. "Especially for when she meets the parents."

Game, set, match, damn it.

The woman nodded and left briskly, leaving behind the admittedly gorgeous gown.

"He's gonna kill me," Carol muttered, falling back into the provided chair. "I'm gonna spend so much money I'll be in debt three hundred years after I'm dead."

Rose put her hands on her hips and kicked Carol gently on the shin. "He told me to take you here, silly. Said his parents always do this for his new familiars. It's on them, okay? Now, enjoy the experience, 'cause it will probably never happen again."

Carol closed her eyes, utterly embarrassed. She didn't belong in this part of the store with its designer clothing and six hundred-dollar shoes.

"After this, we'll take you to Sephora," Debbie crooned in her ear.

Carol sat up immediately, her mind racing with all the makeup she'd been dying to try. "Let's get this show on the road. There's a Tarte eyeshadow palette just waiting for a loving home."

Debbie chuckled. "Damn straight."

Outfit after outfit was brought out for Carol to try. Some of them she refused outright after being shown the price tag, but others she tried on with an air of inevitability. She tried her best to keep the amount of money the girls wanted her to spend down, but in the end, she spent far more than she'd wanted to.

Who knew a simple pair of jeans could cost that much?

By the time they were done, Carol was ready to head somewhere that she'd be far more comfortable in. "We're going to Target next."

"Fine," Debbie whined, her shoulders drooping and her feet dragging. "I still say you could have spent more."

"Three hundred dollars for jeans, Debbie? Seriously?" The only part she'd truly enjoyed about the experience was that they were going to deliver the clothes she'd bought to Jonah's house. "That's so stupid, I can't comprehend how stupid it is. Jeans are meant to be lived in, not framed in a museum."

She'd put a stop to *that* set of protests immediately. The trip to Target was for everyday wear, while the department store had been for the parties she'd been told she'd have to attend as Jonah's familiar.

It wasn't that she was truly unhappy with her purchases so far. They'd wear well, and she'd done her best to pick pieces that would never truly go out of style. She just wished she'd spent her own money on the clothing, not Jonah's. Not that she'd ever have the same amount of money he did. She'd have to win the lottery for that to happen.

"I'm picking up some wear and tear clothing there, stuff that if it wrecks, I won't start weeping in my Cheerios." Carol was determined to keep this part of the trip down-to-earth. "And I need some sensible shoes, ones I won't care about scratching up. Ones I can run in."

"I agree, actually." Debbie dropped the pouty act and caught up to Carol. "Seriously though. Jonah's not going to be upset, I swear."

"That doesn't stop me from feeling guilty." Carol strode into Target, glad that it was part of the mall. "Now help me find some real people clothes."

"I swear, the people who shop at that department store are real people." Rose glanced around and grabbed a cart. "Except their boobs, lips, butts, tummies…"

Two hours later, Carol had jeans, underwear, some tank-tops and T-shirts, and a cute pair of shoes she'd been unable to resist. At a shoe store, she found a pair of loafers she could wear that wouldn't look out of place on an officer of the law and went with the several pairs of work slacks she'd picked up. The soles were sturdy rubber, good for running if need be.

"All done?" Debbie grabbed hold of her arm before she could respond. "Good. Let's get some makeup."

Carol didn't resist being dragged to Sephora. She'd been in one more than once, dreaming of what she could pick up if only she had the money.

By the time they were done, she'd spent more on skincare, haircare, and makeup than she had at the department store and Target combined. She clutched a striped shopping bag, cackling like a maniac. "It's all mine, Precious."

Rose laughed.

Debbie just shook her head. "Ready for the food court?"

Her stomach rumbled on cue. "Yes, please." She whimpered and whined, giving Debbie her best puppy-dog eyes. "I want a huge-ass pretzel and some ice cream."

"How about real food?" Debbie once again grabbed her arm and began dragging her along.

"If I drop my makeup, I'll hurt you." Carol clutched the Sephora bag tighter with one arm, the Target bags and shoe store bag held in the other. She ignored the way those bags kept banging against her leg as she practically ran after Debbie. Rose trailed behind them, still cackling.

Real food turned out to be mall pizza, her coveted pretzel, and a hot fudge sundae. By the time she was done, she was leaning back in her chair, rubbing her stomach in contentment. "That hit the spot." And she'd paid for it with her own money, making it that much more satisfying.

"I texted the guys and told them that we're almost done." Debbie picked up their trash and heaped it on one of the trays.

"Almost?" Rose glanced around. "Where else are we headed?" Her eyes lit up. "Oh, scented candles? Or the jewelry store?"

Gods, Carol hoped not. She couldn't imagine the amount of money the crazy duo would try and convince her to spend in a jewelry store. Carol stood, too, grabbing her bags before following after Debbie and Rose. She was starting to get used to following them around.

Hell, she was afraid she was learning how to heel. Soon, Debbie would be tossing her Scooby Snacks for being a good girl.

"Yup." Debbie's expression was wicked. "There's one more thing you need to make me happy."

Uh-oh. "And that would be?"

"A haircut." Debbie dumped the trash and placed the tray on top of the trash can. "I made an appointment for..." She checked her watch and groaned. "Now. Let's go."

"Wait, wait, wait!" Carol ran after Debbie, doing her best to avoid banging into the mall-goers. "Why do I need a haircut?"

"When was the last time you had a trim?" Debbie kept going without looking back.

"Uh…" Did she have to admit she cut her own hair?

"That's why." Debbie pointed. "There. That's where we're going." She swerved and entered a shop that smelled of hair coloring chemicals, perm solutions, and wet hair. "Sheila? I've brought you something interesting!"

Carol groaned. "What have you gotten me into this time?"

A woman popped her head around a partition, smiling and waving at Debbie. "Hey there! Is that her?"

"Yup!" Debbie put her arm around Carol's shoulders. "She's Jonah's newest."

"Oh?" The woman came around the partition, scissors in hand. "Hmm. This one's cute."

"She'll be cuter without the dead ends, am I right?" Debbie winked and took Carol's bags. "Follow Sheila, sweetie. She'll make you look like a goddess."

"I just want to look like Carol," she muttered in reply. She followed Sheila obediently, ignoring the way Debbie was cackling to herself. Rose was conspicuously absent, probably hunting down cinnamon-apple-scented candles. The bitch. How dare she ditch Carol in the chemical hell of a hairdresser's shop?

Half an hour later, Carol had to admit her hair appeared much healthier than it had before she'd entered the salon. For a moment, she even contemplated forgiving Rose for her desertion. "I didn't realize having someone else cut your hair could make such a difference."

The twin looks of horror on Sheila and Debbie's faces made her laugh out loud.

Sheila went to the register and grabbed a card, scribbling something on it before returning it to Carol. "Here's your next appointment." She leaned in close, her eyes narrowing. "You *will* keep it."

Carol shrank back from the crazy lady with the scissors. "Yes, ma'am."

Sheila handed a second card to Debbie. "You too." The glare she sent Debbie wiped the grin right off her face.

Debbie twitched into a salute. "Yes, ma'am."

"Now then." Sheila returned to her previous, happy demeanor as she stared at Carol. She tilted her head, fingering one of Carol's curls. "Have you ever considered highlights?"

"Wolf shifter. The smell of the chemicals makes me sick." Just being in here had her nose twitching with the urge to sneeze. That, and she'd never once thought of dyeing her hair. She loved her red hair as it was.

"Honey, when the grays start showing, you'll suck it up. Believe me, I've seen it plenty of times." Sheila pointed to her own perfectly streaked dark mane. "You think I come by this naturally?"

Fifteen minutes later, Carol slunk out of the shop, her tail between her legs and appointment card clutched in her hand. "That woman scares me."

"Me too, but her skills are out of this world." Debbie linked arms with Carol and began dragging her along. "Now, let's get the boys and get out of here before I start shopping for me."

"Why would that be a problem?" Carol obediently followed Debbie.

Debbie grinned. "Not all of us have the credit limit Jonah has, and one of the dresses in that department store was being *way* too seductive."

Carol chuckled. She was damn glad Debbie had agreed to come shopping with her. The woman was a blast.

"There you are." Debbie glared at Rose, who'd just appeared out of the crowd. "Where were you?"

Rose stared at Carol. "You're alive!" She hugged Carol tight. "I thought you'd die in chemical hell."

Carol smacked Rose on the shoulder. "No thanks to you, Chicken Little."

"When the cluck fits," Rose replied, laughing.

An evil, devious thought came to her. "Debbie? I think Rose needs to meet Sheila."

The two shared a calculating grin. Oh, yes. Rose would get hers.

Debbie turned back to the salon and shouted, "Stella!" in the best Marlon Brando style.

Luckily, earth elementals didn't run very fast, and Carol's revenge was both satisfying and smelly.

Carol grinned as Stella bullied Rose into a second appointment, snickering behind her hand as Rose stood at attention and saluted.

Definitely worth it.

Chapter 21

Jonah seemed confused as Carol held out the receipt with a shaking hand. How was she supposed to explain this? She still couldn't believe she'd let Rose and Debbie talk her into all of this...stuff.

"I'm sorry."

She couldn't look at him as he glanced over the receipt. She should have turned down so much of it, but they'd been insistent that Jonah wouldn't mind. The guilt had nearly overwhelmed her more than once on the way home. How could she have been so greedy?

Jonah's warm hands cupped her cheeks. She glanced up at him through her lashes to see him smiling gently at her. "It's fine, sweetheart. I expected you to spend more, actually."

"Huh?" She blinked, shocked. "What did you do, dip into a trust fund?"

"Something like that," he replied, shocking the fuck out of her. "I earn my own money, and I live on that, but my parents like to spoil my new familiars. They're paying for this." He kissed the tip of her nose. "And they don't take no for an answer either."

"But—"

This time, he kissed her lips, stopping her protest. "I double-checked with my parents. They were thrilled when I told them what was going on." He scowled, looking more wolf-like than ever. "They said you should be spoiled more often, and I agree with them."

She shook her head, unsure if she was charmed or if he was totally off his rocker. She decided to go with both. "The trust fund is for what, exactly?"

He put his arms around her, tossing the receipt onto the floor. "Well, spoiling my lovely familiar is now top of my list." He twirled one of her curls around his finger. "I like the haircut."

Oh God, he noticed! Sawyer *never* noticed when her hair was cut. She squinted up at him, eager to tease him. "Are you sure you're not gay?"

He chuckled. "First off, that's sexist." He kissed the tip of her nose before she could protest. "Second, I think I proved that not too long ago." He dug his fingers into her hips, the pressure just enough to send a throb of desire through her. "Want me to prove it again?"

His voice had deepened, making her swallow the puddle of drool that was threatening to escape. "Sure. That works."

He put his hands under her ass and lifted her into the air. She wrapped her legs around his waist, holding tight as he carried them upstairs. "Get the door for me."

Jonah's voice was calm, but his pupils had dilated. His stare held her captive, making her fumble as she tried to do as he commanded. She finally grasped the doorknob, turning it and pushing the door open.

"Good girl." He transferred her to the bed and began methodically stripping her of her clothing. "Now, I want you to put your hands on the headboard and hold them there."

Carol's eyes widened. What game was he playing? And did she want to play along?

The sexy smirk on his face convinced her. Whatever he was doing wasn't going to hurt her, far from it. He wanted to have fun, so she'd see where this went.

If she didn't like it, she could always flip him over and make *him* put his hands where she told him. She had a couple ideas already.

Placing her hands against the headboard, she grinned. "Now what?"

"Don't. *Move*." His voice had roughened, his Adam's apple bobbing as he swallowed. "Christ, you're sexy."

She shivered as his gaze roamed over her naked body. He sat up, watching her as he undressed, standing only long enough to remove his pants and socks.

Carol held still as he loomed over her once more, his hands braced on either side of her head. He kissed her softly before moving to her breasts, sucking one of her nipples into his hot mouth.

It was hard, keeping her hands on the headboard when all she wanted to do was bury her fingers in his hair and hold him in place. The suction on her nipple was driving her crazy, making her writhe under him. His hand dipped between her legs, rubbing at her clit in strokes too soft to truly satisfy her.

He moved to her other breast, treating it a bit more roughly, his teeth grazing her. She moaned, arching her back for him, thrusting her breast into his mouth as best she could. With her hands firmly planted on the headboard, it was all she could do not to scream when he released her.

"Want something?"

God damn him for teasing her. He licked her nipple, reminding her of how good the suction felt. When he blew across the wet tip, she shivered. She had to respond, or he'd just keep tantalizing her. "Suck me."

"My pleasure," he whispered. But instead of taking one of her nipples in his mouth, he kissed down her body.

"Oh, yes." Carol moaned as his wicked mouth took her in, nibbling and licking her clit in devilish ways. His fingers dug into her ass, lifting her to where he wanted her, leaving her open, vulnerable. She dug her feet into the mattress, lifting to his mouth, her eyes closing when the pleasure became too much to bear.

She bit her lip, almost desperate to come, to ride his mouth to ecstasy. Jonah was relentless, pushing her closer and closer until she exploded, crying out as her vision went white.

Soft licks brought her gently back down, quivering from his mastery over her body. Animus thrummed along her skin as their magic entwined, tickling fingers of amber and gold that touched her all over. He breached her with his fingers, muttering an incantation under his breath as he did so, one that raised the hairs on her arms.

All of a sudden, her body tingled with warmth and desire. The amber light became plucking fingers, teasing her nipples while Jonah once more concentrated on her clit.

"Holy gods." She gasped when one of the tendrils stroked a particularly sensitive spot just behind her ear. "Where the hell did you learn to do that?"

He chuckled. "Do you want to talk practical magic now, or do you want to fuck?"

"Fuck. Definitely fu-huck." Despite the fact that his lips had left her body, it was as if he was still sucking on her, leaving her gasping for breath.

She barely noticed him sliding up her body, but she definitely did when his cock glided into her, filling her completely. It was like being fucked in an amber mist that touched her all over, leaving her breathless as Jonah rocked into her over and over again.

He kissed her, sharing her taste and his own. His warm skin brushing against her added to the sensory overload. Their legs tangled together, Carol needing an anchor in the storm Jonah had started with a few whispered words.

Jonah's mouth left hers to descend on her neck, biting and sucking as their rhythm became faster.

Close. She was so close, eager for the orgasm she was chasing so desperately. She tilted her head, baring herself to him, to his teeth, earning a deep groan from the man above her. A sharp nip rewarded her for her submission.

His fingers tangled with hers, pulling her hands off the headboard and by her ears. All she could hear were their deep pants, the soft sound of flesh on flesh and the whispers of their magic encasing them. All she could taste was him as she licked his shoulder, salt and male mingling on her tongue. Jonah's scent enveloped her, marked her inside and out, leaving no doubt who she was fucking.

Her body began to tremble as the orgasm came closer and closer, threatening to drive her insane. Jonah's teeth closed over her earlobe before he once more took her mouth, kissing her roughly, sloppily, their mutual pleasure far too close for subtle movements.

He let go of her hands and grasped her inner thighs, spreading her wider, allowing him deeper access. She braced herself against the headboard once more as he pounded into her. She watched him, his head thrown back, his eyes closed as he chased their mutual orgasm.

Carol's claws dug into the headboard, her teeth clenching as spasms rocked her body. Her toes curled as pleasure blinded her, racking her body and wrecking her mind. Her voice was strangled, trapped in her throat as breath itself escaped her, leaving her gasping and trembling in the throes of the best fucking orgasm she'd ever experienced.

When she could finally breathe again, she looked up, only to find Jonah's face was clenched. He was thrusting into her body with short, sharp jabs, spilling inside her as his orgasm washed over him. He was beautiful when he came, bathed in the amber light of their shared magic.

He gasped for breath and let her legs go, falling on top of her and almost crushing her. "Holy shit, we need to do that again."

She giggled, wrapping her arms around him. "Hell yes." She kissed his damp cheek as their magic receded, finally letting her body go. "That spell *rocked*."

"No." He lifted his head just far enough to look into her eyes, his own dazed yet content. "You did."

She blushed, his meaning not lost on her. "You've used the spell before."

He nodded wearily. "Mm." He nuzzled her neck, sending shivers down her spine. "Gimme a few minutes, and we'll try it again."

"Just to be sure, right? That it's us, not the spell, I mean." Carol was already trembling with anticipation.

"Exactly. For science."

She sighed happily. "I fucking love science."

Chapter 22

Carol grimaced as yet another conversation died the moment she strode through the break room. She kept her head held high as two men in suits stared at her, eyeing her badge before returning their gazes to her face. She grabbed the mug she'd brought to the precinct with the image of a wolf on it.

The two men left her alone in the room, but it wasn't long until she heard their voices once more. They must have thought they were out of earshot, but her wolf hearing allowed her to pick out their conversation easily once they mentioned Ian's name.

"Did you hear about Matsumoto?" One of the men was talking about Ian, Jonah's new partner. The unknown detective's tone was sympathetic, as if Ian's transfer was either unwanted or disagreeable.

The other detective sighed. "Yeah, that's gotta be rough. Being sent to MCU to work with…" the man's voice drifted off.

"The wolf?" The other man chuckled. "You can say it. I bet she can't hear us with the guys in the background."

Shit. This wasn't about Jonah or Ian, but about her.

She poured her coffee, pretending to ignore them. By law, there wasn't anything that could remove her from her sorcerer's side other than their consent, so whenever she ran into conversations like these, she tended to do her best to overlook them. Besides, she'd been to the academy and had been hired to be a cop. Either way, when her year and a day was up, she'd still be in this job. It wouldn't do to make enemies of the other cops.

"Yeah. You heard what Wheeler and Ridgely have been saying?" The first detective's voice had gone lower. Carol had to strain to hear him.

"She growled at them, didn't she?"

What? She froze, almost pouring too much creamer into her coffee. She quickly set the creamer down on the counter and focused solely on the conversation somewhere in the hallway.

"That's what I heard. And worse, I heard she's not the only one." The first detective cleared his throat. "Rumor has it that the higher-ups are ignoring the problem, and Wheeler's going to do something about it."

Carol kept her growl sub-vocal. The last thing she wanted to do was confirm Wheeler's account.

"One of these days they're gonna go feral, just like that dude Lionel Geyn," the first detective continued. "Then the county will see what we've been saying all along was right."

Shit. Of *course*, they'd bring up Lionel Theodore Geyn. Stories of the feral shifter had been dogging both the shifter and familiar communities since the 1920s. He'd gone full-on Leather Face, killing people, eating their flesh and making household décor out of their tanned skins and weathered bones. He'd been caught when he'd made the mistake of kidnapping a popular shop owner, skinning and dressing her like a deer in his barn.

His community had been horrified, and he'd been diagnosed as feral. He'd been put to death.

There was no known cure for going feral. It was as much a mercy for the shifter as it was a visible reprisal for the grieving families of the victims. Him, and others like him, were often used as examples of why all familiars and shifters needed to be shackled and treated like second-class citizens.

"Worse, I heard that the wolf is fucking Sound already," the second detective snickered. "Someone overheard Kramden warning Sound to watch his back."

The first detective chuckled. "She's going to eat him in his sleep."

Carol ground her teeth together. She wished she'd paid more attention to the detectives, at least enough to get their badge numbers. That kind of talk went against all of the non-discrimination laws, not to mention that there were rules inside the precinct about that sort of thing.

Human supremacism was alive and well, though not as widespread or as universally accepted as it had once been. Despite the laws, she was different, so she was looked at as dangerous. That was the catalyst the specists needed to try and drive all non-humans out of the police force, or indeed any emergency services they deemed too "volatile" for non-humans to handle.

"Any idea what Wheeler has planned?" The second detective's voice had dropped to the level of the firsts.

"I'm not sure, but it's gonna be epic." The first detective now sounded gleeful.

"Why can't a sorcerer come up with a way to bond with their familiar without the damn animal following them all over the place?" The second detective's tone was full of frustration.

"No idea, but they should get on that as soon as possible, before they go feral in the middle of inmate processing."

Carol rolled her eyes. She'd heard that one before. No matter how many times it was proven that sort of device wouldn't work, the specists would bring it up again. It was like the conspiracy theorists and their belief that shifters were used to spy on people in their animal forms and report back to the CIA.

She was willing to bet that, because of those rumors, spies were taught how to recognize the subtle differences between familiars, shifters, and normal animals. They'd be stupid not to.

The men's voices began to drift away, and Carol took a sip of her cooling coffee, wondering what to do about the things she'd overheard. She could go to Jonah or Ian, but this involved all three of them, and she didn't want either of them to overreact.

Okay, she didn't want *Jonah* to overreact. She had no idea how Ian would handle things.

"Hey."

Carol blinked at the sound of her boss's voice behind her. She turned, smiling. "I need to talk to you." She kept the smile on her face as she tried her best to subtly gesture out of the break room.

Captain Anne Ford followed her out of the break room and right into the captain's office. Cpt. Ford sat behind her desk, steepled her fingers, and stared at Carol with a penetrating gaze. "What did you need to speak to me about?"

Carol took a deep breath. "I overheard two men talking while I was making my coffee," she started. "They were saying that Detective Wheeler was going to 'do something'"—she made quotation marks with one hand, the other still occupied by her almost forgotten coffee—"about my presence on the force."

"Shit." Cpt. Ford's expression didn't change, but her tone was vicious.

"They mentioned feeling sorry for Ian for being transferred to our unit." She ignored the way Cpt. Ford's narrowed gaze made her want to squirm. "They also said that they believe I'm sleeping with Jonah."

Cpt. Ford sat back in her seat, her hands falling to the arms of her chair. "Are you?"

Carol nodded once. "It's consensual, I promise."

"But still a problem," Cpt. Ford muttered. "Especially since we can't separate you for the year and a day."

Carol closed her eyes, feeling a chill go down her spine. "Is it because I'm a wolf?"

"No!" Cpt. Ford sounded so fierce Carol opened her eyes in surprise. "It's because you're work partners. It wouldn't bother me if you were, say, a detective in Vice. But you're here, in MCU, working with your sorcerer and lover. Worse, when the year and a day are up, you might become a uniform in order to work your way back up. That would put you below Jonah in status, thus putting an onus on him."

Carol's shoulders slumped. "I want to stay here, but if I can't, I could go to a different precinct."

Cpt. Ford relaxed. "We'll see." She pointed sternly at Carol. "First, prove yourself. Once your year and a day are up, *then* we'll talk about your placement."

"And Wheeler?" Carol wanted to take a bite out of the Homicide detective for making hers and Jonah's lives difficult, but for the same reason she'd gone to Cpt. Ford, she couldn't go after Wheeler. She had to do this officially.

Man, some days being a grown-up sucked.

"Leave him to me." Cpt. Ford smiled. "I'll have a few friends of mine keep watch of him for a while. If what you overheard is true, it's a civil rights' violation and needs to be investigated by the proper authorities."

Carol bit her lip. "Internal affairs?"

"Or, worst-case scenario, the FBI, yes."

"Okay. So, back to work for me?"

Cpt. Ford grinned. "Yup. Get your ass out of here, Voss."

"Yes, ma'am." Carol swiftly turned, opened the door, and strode back into the bullpen. She sat at her desk and set her lukewarm coffee down.

"What did the captain want with you?"

She glanced up to find Jonah staring at her.

"Nothing major." She'd keep her ears open from now on. Nothing was going to hurt Jonah on her watch, not even other cops.

His gaze seemed to penetrate her, seeking out her secrets. "Are you sure?"

She nodded. "I promise." Her fingers were crossed in her lap, but what he didn't know wouldn't hurt him.

She hoped.

Chapter 23

"Hello, Jonah." Lessa's tone was warm, her voice excited. "I think I've got something for you. Get your ass here pronto."

Hallelujah, his sister had come through with the runic research. It was nice, having an expert in the family. Jonah started gathering his things, motioning for Carol to do the same. "We'll be there soon." Jonah hung up, making sure he had everything before texting his boss where they'd be. She poked her head out of her office.

"Jonah! Take Matsumoto with you."

"Yes, ma'am." Curious. She only assigned him temporary partners when he didn't have a familiar. He'd have to talk to Ian to find out if he knew what was going on.

When he glanced at Carol, she shrugged. "Ya got me."

"God, I hope so," he muttered, following her out of MCU and down the stairs to Homicide. He ignored the glares of Wheeler and Ridgely as he approached Ian's desk. "Morning, Ian."

"*Ohayou*, Jonah, Carol." Ian grinned at them, his posture laid-back.

"Oh hai what?" Carol wrinkled her nose. She was so cute, he wanted to snuggle her close, but he didn't have time. Damn it. Maybe later that night he'd pull her into his arms and just...be.

"*Ohayou*. It means good morning in Japanese." Ian wrinkled his nose right back at her. "Don't you watch anime?"

"Good lord," Jonah sighed. "Never mind that. Our runic expert called and has something for us on the campus murders." Jonah waited while Ian logged off his computer and gathered his things. "Not sure what, but my boss wants you with us to find out."

"Sounds good to me." Ian waved toward the exit. "Lead the way."

Jonah pulled out his car keys as they got to the garage. "Any idea *why* my boss wants you with me?"

Ian shrugged. "Because I was on-scene when the second body was found? My captain was on the phone with yours not too long ago, so I figured we might be working this case together."

"Hard to hide something from a detective, huh?" Carol climbed into the passenger seat, leaving the back seat for Ian.

"That's me, Detective Conan, boy genius." Ian settled into his seat with a smirk.

"Who's that?" Carol asked curiously.

Jonah started the car, heading toward his sister's place. "Isn't that an anime character?"

"Yup. He's a teenage detective who winds up somehow being turned into a little boy, but he continues to solve crimes with the help of some friends." Ian leaned forward and patted them both on the head, earning a snarl from Carol. "Friends like you."

Carol rolled her eyes. "I am *not* Scooby-Doo, asshole."

Ian cackled while Jonah just shook his head. "Behave, children." If Ian didn't, Carol might just bite him.

The two bickered amiably about anime while Jonah made his way to his sister's place. He pulled up in front of Lessa's condo, eager to find out what she'd discovered. "C'mon, let's go." He led the way up to his sister's front door and rang the bell.

Lessa opened the door, her hazel eyes lighting up as she saw them. "Come on in." She gazed curiously at Ian. "You are?"

"Detective Ian Matsumoto, Ms. Sound. I'm currently working the campus case with your brother." Ian held out his hand, shaking Lessa's when she presented hers. "Nice to meet you."

"Nice to meet you too." Her tone was friendly, but Jonah saw the way she stared at Ian. She was sizing him up, just as she did everyone she was introduced to. "Are you a sorcerer?"

"No, ma'am, just a homicide detective." Ian's smile was easy, his posture relaxed as he gazed around at Lessa's home.

"Our bosses decided it might be a good idea to make this one inter-departmental," Jonah informed his sister.

She rolled her eyes. "Oh, I get it. Play nice together, boys, and maybe you'll get a lollipop."

Jonah shook his head. "Pretty much."

Ian gazed at Lessa curiously. "Let me guess. You work in academia."

226

Lessa blinked, obviously startled. "How did you know?"

Jonah bit back a smile as Ian explained. "See your coffee table? It's littered with paperwork with red pen marks and grades. Your bookshelves don't hold the usual high school textbooks or paraphernalia you'd expect, but it does hold college-level stuff. Also, you've got a note from your TA stuck to a paper that fell on the floor. Since high school teachers don't get TAs..." Ian shrugged. "Not that difficult to deduce that you work in a college or university environment."

Lessa's gaze was less wary and more impressed. "Not bad, Watson."

He winked at her. "Besides, you were in the news like two days ago, Miss Sound."

She chuckled, and Jonah relaxed. They'd get along just fine.

"So. What do you have for us?" Jonah settled on the couch, ignoring the papers on the coffee table. He whipped out his notebook and prepared for whatever she was about to reveal.

"Remember how you told me that your coroner friend thought that there might be a magical signature buried in the runes?" Lessa parked herself next to him, leaving two chairs for Ian and Carol. "Well, he was partially right."

"Partially?" Great. This case seemed to take one step forward, two steps back, then cha-cha'd all over his nerves.

She searched through the papers until she came up with the symbol that Ian had drawn. It seemed Ian had quite a bit of

227

talent. The symbol was damn near perfect in every detail. "See here?" She pointed to where the signature was supposed to be. "If you examine this under a magnifying glass, you'll find the symbol of Apep repeated several times in the calligraphy, but also two symbols other than his."

"What symbols are they?" Carol leaned forward, her expression fierce. His little wolf was on the hunt.

"That's the problem." Lessa sat back with a scowl. "While I could read that they were names, the names themselves are obvious pseudonyms."

"How can that be?" Carol bit her lip. "In order for a spell like this to work, there have to be clear pathways and sympathetic magics involved. If he uses a pseudonym, wouldn't that cause the spell to either cancel out or be cast on someone other than the intended recipient?"

"That depends on whether or not he incorporated blood or other bodily fluids in the signing of the name." Lessa folded her hands in her lap, her tone the one she frequently used when lecturing her students. "If the caster did so, it would negate the possibility of the spell being mistakenly cast on someone else. The blood would tie the caster to the spell, the blood of the recipient doing the same."

"Shit." Jonah sat back, his shoulders slumping. And here he'd thought they'd found something. Instead, it was a big, fat nothing.

"Don't be so down, brother. It's possible a DNA signature would—"

"Not possible," Carol interrupted. "The rune and the signature were completely obliterated by a wither with a knife."

"Well. Fuck me." Lessa slumped, her hands falling to her sides. "Unless you can figure out who the pseudonyms belong to, they're useless."

"Not entirely." Jonah held up the picture, staring at the two names Lessa had pointed out. "It's evidence that can be used at trial."

"I get to testify again?" Lessa held up her fist, the gesture reluctant, as was her voice. "Yay."

Carol smiled at his sister's antics. "It's better than jury duty."

Lessa snorted in disgust. "Wait until you've been cross-examined by someone determined to destroy your credibility and we'll talk again." Lessa rolled her eyes. "Just because Jonah and I are related, they'll say I made things up. As if I would damage my own career just to bolster up an already rock-solid case. Hmph."

Ian held up his hand. "Professor, I have a question."

Lessa blinked at him. "Go ahead."

"What, exactly, *are* the pseudonyms?"

Jonah almost smacked himself in the forehead. How could he have forgotten to ask something so obvious?

Ian winked at him. "This is why you bring us non-magic folk with you."

Lessa snatched the paper away from Jonah, almost cutting him. "The names aren't really *names*, actually. Not in the sense you mean. Roughly translated, the larger one is *Apep, Lord of Rebirth*, and the second one is *Bennu, Lord of Jubilees.* The first is a reference to Apep, but not one usually made. The second refers to the phoenix as the ancient Egyptians saw him. They're...titles, I suppose."

"The phoenix? That's a creature of rebirth." Carol shuddered, her voice barely above a whisper. "Then we were right. Whoever is doing this is trying to bring someone back from Terra Noctem."

Chapter 24

It had been a few days since they'd met with Lessa. Their Egyptologist had gotten back to them and informed them that Lessa's interpretation of the signatures was correct. Worse, they hadn't found anything new in the pictures of Reeves, disappointing both of them. The autopsy had confirmed the cause of death, so they had that at least. *Death by magic— homicide* was the official listing.

Jonah stretched, checking his watch when he was done. They'd come home from the precinct and immediately headed for their shared home office to sift through their notes once more.

"Shit." He stood, collecting the pictures of the baseball field he'd been studying into a pile. "We need to get ready, or we're going to be late for dinner."

Carol froze. "Dinner?"

"With my parents." He tilted his head and stared at her. "You remember? It's tonight."

She blinked, her face paling. "Oh. Was that today?"

She wasn't fooling him one little bit. She was nervous as hell. "Yup." He sauntered around his side of the desk and stopped beside her, holding out his hand. "M'lady."

She rolled her eyes, took his hand, and stood. The pictures she'd been studying were still sprawled across the top of her side of the desk. "I want to examine these a bit closer. There has to be *something* we missed, right?"

"Not necessarily." Jonah led her out of the office, ignoring the way her feet seemed to drag. "The sorcerer could have simply decided that this victim would receive his signature, or Reeves was an experiment."

"Ugh, I hope not. It's bad enough he had to die in such a shitty way, but to be the warm-up guy?" Carol shivered. "Not cool."

"Go get ready. I'm going to grab a shower and change too." They'd come home from the station early but just couldn't stop staring at the photos of the victims.

Jonah made his way to his bedroom, more than ready for a shower. He'd hoped talking about the case would keep Carol calm, but just mentioning dinner had made her tighten up like an overwound spring. "Don't forget, Rose will be there too."

"Sure. Yeah." She stumbled into her room and shut the door.

An hour later, Jonah was ready to storm her room to get her out of it. "Are you done yet?"

"Typical male," she shouted back. "Getting curly hair to behave takes time."

"Open the door, woman." He kicked the bottom of the door gently, not wanting to damage it. "You're dressed, right?"

"Yeah."

"Damn," he muttered.

"I heard that." She opened the door and glared at him.

Jonah whistled. "Woah." He pulled her out of her room and turned her, ignoring her irritated grumbling. "You're beautiful."

She glared at him over her shoulder, catching him in the act of checking out her ass. "My eyes are up here, stud."

He chuckled, remembering Officer Bob and his wandering gaze. "Those jeans should be illegal."

"Hmph." She turned back around, showing off her amazing cleavage. She'd chosen a dark pair of jeans paired with a V-neck silk peasant top. She'd done her hair up in some complicated, braided updo that had him wanting to free her curls just for the fun of watching them come down. She'd left some wisps free, making his fingers itch even more. She'd kept her makeup simple, just the way he liked it. The slick of rose-colored gloss on her lips made him want to kiss it away so he could view her mouth's natural pink coloring. How long it would take? Would the gloss make her lips taste sweet?

"You do. You're gorgeous." He kissed the tip of her nose, loving her little squeak of surprise. "I'm glad you went shopping with Debbie." He grinned, enjoying the way her cheeks turned red. "Now, let's go before they serve dessert, and Rose eats it all." He started down the stairs, all ready to head out.

"Wait! I have to grab my shoes." Carol turned back into her room. She rummaged around for a moment before she ran

233

out, carrying a pair of sandals. She sprinted down the stairs, her cheeks still pink. "Okay, I'm ready."

"Then let's go." Jonah grabbed his black shoes and slipped them on. He'd found they both preferred to go barefoot inside the house, so for the most part, their shoes were left by the front door. He assumed that the sandals she was strapping on would soon join the others in the shoe rack he'd set up for them. When it was just him, he hadn't even cared where his shoes landed when he got home, but one day an Amazon box had appeared, and a shoe rack had been inside. Apparently, Carol liked their shoes neatly placed by the door.

Carol finished putting on her sandals and stood. "If we can figure out the signature hidden in the runes, we'll have our guy."

"Unless it's a false name, in which case we won't. Always keep an open mind, or you'll run the risk of missing something important." Jonah glanced at his watch again. "You ready?"

"Yeah." Carol took a deep breath and approached the front door. "Seriously. I don't need to meet them tonight, right?" Despite her words, she waited for him to let them out and lock the front door behind them. "I think I'm coming down with a cold anyway." She sniffed, rubbing the tip of her nose.

"You're not going into enemy territory alone, soldier." Jonah took hold of her hand and led her to the car. "You've examined dead people without flinching. I think you can handle one middle-aged sorcerer and his wife. Oh, and my sister.

Maybe my brother. I'm not sure if he's back from his trip yet or not."

"You suck," Carol muttered, getting in the car.

"Only if you ask nicely." Jonah shut her door and strode around the hood. He climbed behind the wheel and grinned. "Off we go!"

Carol leaned back in her seat and closed her eyes. The only sign she gave that she was still unsure was the way her arms wrapped around her waist. She had a death grip on the bottom part of the seat belt.

"We don't have to go. If you're that scared, I'll stay here with you. We'll order pizza and binge Netflix until we're blind." Jonah put his hand over hers, willing her to set aside her fears. She'd get along with his parents if only she had the courage to try.

She stared at him, seemingly studying his face. Whatever she saw there must have reassured her because she let go and gave him a brief smile. "I'm okay. I just have issues with parents, that's all."

He started the car and began the drive, not willing to give her time to change her mind. He wanted to rip the proverbial Band-Aid off for her. "Well, I can understand that. If you want, you can talk to my mom about it. Since she's a predator, too, she'll understand."

Her smile broadened. "I keep forgetting your mom is a raptor."

"She's unique, even for an eagle." Jonah adored his mother, even if she did flit around more like a hummingbird than a majestic bird of prey.

"How so?" Carol's tone was still slightly off, but she was slowly relaxing as he drove through the night. His parents' home was close to his own, so the drive was a short one. He hoped that fact would also ease her fears. The less time she had to fret, the better.

"You'll see." Jonah pulled up to his parents' house. It was a four-bedroom Spanish colonial that his parents had purchased recently. It had been built in the nineteen-thirties and still had curved archways, dark hardwoods, and colorful adobe tile. His mother had done her best to maintain the charm of the home while adding the modern comforts they enjoyed in other homes. "Here we are."

"Oh boy," Carol muttered, clutching the seat belt once more. She was staring at the house like it was filled with spiders and she was a raging arachnophobe.

"You'll be okay, I promise." He took hold of her hand and gently pried her fingers off of the seat belt. "I'll stay by your side. Plus"—he pointed to Rose's electric car parked neatly in front of the garage doors—"Rose is already here. You have someone to fend off the Mongol hordes for you."

She took a deep breath and blew it out slowly. "Okay. I can do this."

"You can." He got out of the car and walked to the passenger side door. He opened it and held out his hand. "You're my familiar. I'll protect you even from my family."

Her head whipped around. Her gaze landed on him, gaze steady as she took his hand. "I bet we could take them."

He chuckled, pleased. She'd said *we*. "I know we could." He kept hold of her hand as he led her to the front door. "They're old."

"Am not!" The front door opened, displaying his mother's cheerful, smiling face. "Jonah!" She wrapped her arms around him, pulling his head down for a kiss, then pulled back and scanned him from head to toe. "You look happy."

"Thank you, Mom. I am." He hugged her back, her tiny frame filled with more strength than any woman he'd ever met save one. "I've got a keeper this time," he whispered. He pulled away from her and gestured to Carol. "This is Carol Voss, my familiar." He wondered if Carol perceived the pride in his voice as he introduced her to his mother. "She's a great partner and has a degree in law enforcement."

Carol, still edgy, held out a shaking hand. "Hi, Mrs. Sound."

His mother grinned. "Finally." She grabbed Carol's hand and shook it with such vigor Carol's wispy curls bounced. "Nice to meet you."

"Nice to meet you too." Carol's eyes were wide as she stared at Jonah's mother.

Jonah's mom was taller than Carol but much thinner, almost model thin. A lot of bird shifters tended to be that way. She had bouncy blonde hair and a wide smile she gave anyone who hadn't pissed her off.

Jonah tried to never piss her off.

"Lessa is here already. She just lost her familiar, so she'll be searching for a new one soon." His mom was dragging Carol behind her and talking a mile a minute. "You have a brother, right?"

"Yeah."

Carol barely got out the answer before his mother was off again. "Great, let's introduce them. Oh, and call me Tanya."

"Um, okay." Carol squeaked as she was hugged from behind.

"Carol!" Rose had grabbed hold of Carol's other hand. She helped his mom drag Carol into the living room. "Lessa, this is Carol, Jonah's new familiar."

"We've met before. Lessa pushed her glasses up her nose. Her golden hair was pulled back in a long ponytail. "Hi."

"Hi. Nice to see you again." Carol's last word was grunted as Rose and his mother practically pushed her into a chair.

"Now you sit tight while I get Benny." And his mother was off, still talking. "You'll love my husband. Benny!"

Jonah tried not to laugh as Carol sat there, obviously stunned. "And you wonder why I'm so quiet."

Carol nodded. So did Lessa, who smirked at Jonah. "Mom can talk the ear off a rabbit."

"And that's a lot of ear," Rose added, settling on the sofa next to Carol. "Hey, Lessa? What happened to this one?"

Lessa snorted. "He tried to seduce me."

Rose tilted her head. "And? Was he uglier than a blobfish?"

"Ugh." Lessa wrinkled her nose. "No, but he couldn't tell the difference between a sigil and a rune."

Carol leaned toward him, muttering, "What *is* the difference?"

Lessa's brows rose as she answered. "Your familiar doesn't know that?"

Jonah wanted to growl. His sister could be a bit of a snob when it came to magical knowledge. He wasn't going to let her insult Carol. "Carol's degree is in law enforcement, not magical studies."

Carol smiled, but it was a little more strained than before. "I took some low-level courses because I figured I'd be working in the MCU once I had a sorcerer, but mostly I use my wolf instincts and my Google-Fu when it comes to that kind of thing."

"Ah." Lessa sat back. That Carol had even tried taking some of the lower-level courses eased some of Lessa's snobbishness.

He'd have to tell Lessa about Carol's background. She'd back off once she found out that Carol was the living embodiment of what their mother fought against.

Carol nodded. "I learned some runes through self-study, and I can recognize some of the more common dimenic languages on sight, even read a little of some of them, but that's it."

"Hmm." Lessa nodded, her disdain disappearing. "What degree does your brother have?"

"He's a nurse," Carol proclaimed proudly. "He's working as a nurse practitioner right now, but if he gets a sorcerer, he'll have to quit to accommodate whoever pairs up with him, at least for the year and a day."

"That's…encouraging." Lessa sounded intrigued—a good sign. "He's not paired at the moment?"

Carol shook her head. "He's a lion. Not many sorcerers are willing to approach us." She frowned thoughtfully. "Although, if you'd rather have a scientist type, you might like my friend Brent. He's gone on arctic expeditions investigating claims of lost magical artifacts."

"Really?" Lessa drawled. Now she seemed thoroughly intrigued. "Tell me more."

As Carol spoke of her friend, Jonah watched curiously. By the time his mother returned with his father they were exchanging phone numbers, something they hadn't done previously. Carol was promising to contact Brent about meeting Lessa.

Interesting. Already Carol was changing his family's lives, and he'd only had her a few weeks. He hoped that, over time, she'd lose her fear and truly become a member of his family.

In fact, he was counting on it.

Chapter 25

Carol was slowly starting to relax. It helped that Rose made sure to sit next to her, with Jonah on her other side. Across the table were Lessa, Benjamin, and Tanya Sound.

Benjamin Sound had the same dark hair Jonah had, with the same dark blue eyes. Jonah's features were more like his mother's side of the family, however, sharper and slightly sinister, just enough to intrigue without turning someone off.

Benjamin held out his hand, taking the mashed potatoes. "What is it you do again?" He spooned some onto his plate and passed it to Tanya.

Carol was waiting for everyone else's plates to be full before she dug into the fantastic smelling pot roast. "I've got a bachelor's in law and, if things work out like I hope, I'll soon go to the police academy."

"You're well-matched with Jonah in career aspects." Tanya's cheerful voice piped up. She wasn't very predator-like. She was more like a sun parakeet, talkative, friendly, and eager to make friends. "You're already working together, right?"

Carol nodded. "Yes. We're working a case right now."

"No cop talk over dinner." Lessa shuddered. "I still haven't recovered from last time."

"Oh, the Crispy Critter case?" Jonah chuckled. "Yeah, that was a doozy."

Carol and Rose laughed as Lessa gagged. She threw a dinner roll at her brother. "Asshole. I still can't eat barbecue."

"How many other sorcerers have you been paired with?" Benjamin began to eat, signaling the beginning of dinner.

"None." Carol moaned at the taste of the roast. "This is so good."

"Thank you, dear." Tanya smiled broadly. "I'll email you the recipe. After dinner, give me your contact information."

"I'll get it to you," Jonah responded before Carol could. He pulled out his cell phone and began typing.

"Uh, Jonah?" Carol was willing to give his mother her info, so why was he doing it?

Tanya's question distracted her from finishing her question. "So, Carol. Tell me about your family." Tanya's grin was still wide, but now it was a lot more predatory.

Guess it was time for the Mommy Inquisition. "I grew up in an orphanage with my brother, Sawyer. We're both predators, and my parents didn't think they could handle us." That was an understatement. "Our lives weren't too bad, but we didn't have a lot of things, and it was pretty much us against everyone else."

"That's horrible." Lessa's expression was one of disgust. "Who throws away their children like that?"

"Some parents do, others don't, when it comes to the larger predators. Most of us were tossed away if their parents weren't also predators." Carol shrugged. "At least I had my brother."

243

"True. Family can make any struggle easier." Tanya's face was also a picture of disgust. "Still, I'd like to get hold of your parents and peck their eyes out."

"That's carrion birds, not eagles, dear." Benjamin patted her hand. "Pick them up, fly really high, then drop them on rocks."

"That's for turtles, Dad." Jonah had finally put his cell phone away and picked up his fork. "Besides, she's got me now. She doesn't need her parents. They can go die in some horrible accident involving hornets and fire ants."

"Ooh." Rose grinned. "Why not include lava while you're at it?"

"I like how you think." Jonah grinned at Rose. They both had reasons to hate the prejudice surrounding non-humans.

Carol covered her ears. "I hear none of this."

"Don't worry, sweetie." Rose patted her knee. "We're talking acts of God, not murder."

"Lalalalalala," Carol sang loudly. "Sorcerers can't kill people with hornets, fire ants, and lava. Nope, nope, nope."

"Yes, we—"

"Lalalalala!" Carol shouted, interrupting Jonah's amused reply.

Everyone laughed, and soon the talk turned to idle chatter. She learned about Benjamin's job as a lawyer and Tanya's work as a financier. Tanya also worked in familiar's rights with Benjamin whenever possible.

244

Before she knew it, she'd relaxed completely, even telling stories of some of the mischief she and Sawyer had gotten into over the years. "There was this one particularly obnoxious sorcerer who kept coming to Familiar House. He'd eye all the female familiars but never managed to bond with one. One day he came in and decided that it was my turn to be leered at." The man had been so skeevy all of the female familiars tried to avoid him. Since he wasn't a blood sorcerer and he hadn't abused a familiar, he couldn't be banned, so they were forced to put up with his presence. However, that didn't mean they had to present themselves to him like plushies on shelves. "My brother had had enough of his shit and, well…" She started to laugh. "Sawyer kind of, um…"

"What did he do?" Rose's eyes had gone wide as Carol tried to contain her laughter.

"H-he pissed all over him." Carol glanced over at Rose to find her mouth hanging open.

"I'm betting that *pissed* the asshole off." Jonah was grinning from ear to ear.

"How did he manage that?" Rose's voice was filled with amused awe.

"Let's just say a certain polar bear distracted him while my brother took care of business." Carol still adored Brent for that. "Man, that sorcerer was *pissed*. He tried to kick my brother, but Brent intervened and prevented him from laying a finger on him. Then he shifted to human and told the sorcerer that if he ever showed up at the House again, Brent would turn him into origami."

"Um." Benjamin was obviously trying to frown but wasn't pulling it off all that well. "I'm not sure I can condone such behavior."

"No matter how well deserved it was," Tanya added. She wasn't frowning at all. In fact, her grin was almost wider than Jonah's.

"But I must say I'm going to have to arrange to meet these boys." Benjamin finally allowed his smile free. "I think we should treat them to something nice."

"As long as it's not piss, I think they'll appreciate it." Lessa wiped her mouth with her napkin, but not before Carol caught sight of the Sound grin on her face. They all had a similar wicked smile, but Benjamin's was eviler while Tanya's was more wickedly delighted.

"Speaking of yellow substances, does anyone want pineapple upside-down cake?"

Everyone stared in horror at Tanya.

"What?"

"I swear, woman." Benjamin shook his head in disgust.

"What?" Tanya shrugged. "If you don't like pineapple, I've got brownies too." She stared at her husband, her head tilted at an inquisitive angle only bird shifters could achieve.

Canines could do it, too, but it looked weird on the birds.

"Can Carol have chocolate?" Lessa stared at her with an amused expression.

"Yes, Carol would love some brownies, and some pineapple cake." Carol stood, muttering in disgust. "I'm not a dog, people."

Lessa, Rose, and Jonah followed her to the living room, where Tanya directed them. "And don't come in the kitchen, I'm making out with my man for a few minutes!"

"Jesus Christ, Mom!" Jonah's horrified was nearly drowned out by Benjamin's laughter. He caught up to her and threaded their hands together. "So?"

"You win. Your parents are nice." Carol did her best to sound begrudging, but she was telling the truth.

"Told you." His smug response made her want to tickle him, so she did, only to find Jonah wasn't ticklish at all. He just stared at her like he was bored out of his mind. "If you want to paw me, you should wait until we get home. I'm not an exhibitionist like my parents."

"Oh my God," Lessa moaned, dropping onto the sofa. "Do you remember Dad walking up behind Mom and grabbing her—"

"Nope." Jonah settled into a chair and pulled Carol into his lap. "I have no idea what you're talking about."

Rose, who'd sat next to Lessa, winked at Carol. "Ben has a fascination with Tanya's ass."

Jonah's whole body slumped. "Ugh. Gross."

Lessa shuddered. "Please don't talk about my mom's ass."

"Why? She has a great one." Benjamin came into the room, carrying a tray filled with steaming mugs of coffee, some half and half, and sugar. He set it on the coffee table, ignoring his children's groans. "Best one I ever felt up."

"Mom!" both Sound children shouted at the same time, nearly deafening Carol.

Carol giggled and snuggled closer to Jonah. She couldn't wait for Sawyer and her friends to meet the Sounds. She'd bet it would be one hell of a party.

Chapter 26

"Sound! Matsumoto! Voss! Get your asses in my office *now*!"

Jonah jumped at the harried bellow from his captain. What the hell was she so upset about that she'd call all three of them into her office?

Jonah strode in, doing his best to maintain his calm. He was the senior in their trio, so if they'd screwed anything up, he'd take the heat no matter who'd made the error.

"What's up?" He settled in front of Cpt. Ford's desk, his gaze traveling over her desk for any signs of what might have made her call them in.

"Take a look at this." She turned her monitor around, displaying a live video feed from one of L.A.'s news organizations. "I'll turn up the volume."

The newscaster's voice became audible as Cpt. Ford clicked her mouse. "…and sources say that the presence of these dangerous predators on the force could have potential impacts on ongoing homicide investigations. Already, allegations are being made that Detective Jonah Sound may be involved with one of these creatures in a romantic sense. One he works closely with."

Jonah scowled as the newscaster prattled on. He leaned closer, his anger rising as the newscaster mentioned incidents of shifters who'd gone feral and committed heinous crimes, obviously trying to connect his familiar with the likes of Robert Berm and Lionel Theodore Geyn, both feral serial killers. "The fuck?"

Ian waved toward the monitor. "This is bullshit. You know this channel's guys are always harping on shifters and magical dimens being a danger to society."

The channel the captain had tuned into was a conservative yet mainstream news channel. "If they've gotten my name, that means someone in the force put this out there." That betrayal stung, but he'd been forewarned that something like this could happen. Thanks to that he knew just who to blame. "Wheeler and Ridgely."

Carol and Anne exchanged a wincing glance.

"You two were aware this could happen, then?" Ian sat back, whistling softly. "Why wasn't this story gagged?"

"Because I couldn't gag it," Anne replied. "I did my best, but it still slipped out." She shook her head and muted the sound. "Jonah, Carol, this is going to hit you two the hardest. Be prepared to be mobbed." She leaned forward, elbows on her desk, that direct stare of hers making Jonah want to squirm even though he was innocent of any wrongdoing. "How do you want to handle this? Some of this has to do with your personal life."

Before he could respond, Carol answered. "I don't want any of this to impact either Jonah or Ian." Her expression started out completely miserable, but slowly morphed into determination. She matched Anne stare for stare. "If needed, I can be sidelined."

"What are you saying?" Jonah was aware that his tone had become deadly quiet. "You know we can't be far from each other, not for a while yet."

"I don't need to be a cop right now," Carol responded, never once glancing his way while she spouted her bullshit. "I just need to follow you around. I can do that by just showing my mark."

Jonah tried really hard not to grit his teeth. God damn Wheeler and Ridgely for doing this. "You're not quitting."

"Damn straight." Ian was leaning back in his chair, his expression still easygoing, but there was a hardness around his eyes that showed he was not unaffected by the news story. "Who else will talk anime with me? That guy?" Ian hitched his thumb toward Jonah. "Pfft. He doesn't even know the difference between *Akira* and *Sailor Moon*."

Jonah shook his head. He had no fucking clue what Ian was talking about.

Ian continued, his smile bright and easy, his eyes still hard. "Besides, I hate the idea of letting those assholes win. If you back out, that's exactly what you're doing."

"I'm not backing out," Carol retorted, shooting Ian a black look. "I'm following my dream, just…in the correct order. Get sorcerer? Check." She held up one finger. "Become a cop? Eh, I can wait the year and a day and start over as a beat cop. I can learn from you guys the whole time too. Win-win for the department and me."

"But not me." Anne stood, coming around her desk to stand directly in front of Carol. "I'm the one who agreed to you having not just a familiar badge, but the detective's badge you're wearing. Be honored. I haven't done that for any other familiar, but you're from the academy. This is your dream, just like you said. You throw this chance I've given you away, and you'll never work in MCU again. No one will trust you as a partner if you abandon your sorcerer when the going gets tough."

"I'm not!" Carol's skin had paled so much her freckles looked far too dark.

"Then pull up your big girl panties, because you're gonna need them." Anne set her butt on the edge of her desk. Beside her, the screen still showed the newscaster talking, but now the image was of some accident on one of L.A.'s freeways. "You're going to face this again and again, especially if you and Jonah become life partners as well as work partners. If you can't handle it now, what will you do in five years? Ten? Back down again?" Anne shook her head. "No. We're a team, and you're not leaving without a fight."

Jonah began clapping. "Thank you. I couldn't have said it better."

Carol bit her lip. "Then how *do* we handle it?"

"You get statements ready. You sometimes answer questions. Then, you let it die down until someone else brings it up again." Anne gestured toward Jonah. "Jonah's been around that block a few times. Listen to him, get advice from his parents, sister, and brother, but you stay the course."

"Yes, ma'am." Carol's spine straightened. She even saluted, and Jonah was positive she meant it respectfully.

"Good." Anne stood and walked back around to sit behind her desk. "Now. Tell me how the campus murder investigation is going. Any updates?"

Jonah filled her in on everything they'd learned so far, ending with, "We're waiting on the Egpytologist's reply, as well as the final cause of death from the medical examiner. We're also setting up interviews with professors and staff at the university."

"Update me on some of the other cases you've been working on." Anne turned to her computer and began typing. "What about the Jones case?"

Between the three of them, they were able to catch the captain up on all of their cases, keeping things brief. At the end of their summations, the captain pointed toward the door. "Get outta here. Grab some lunch and discuss how to handle the press."

"Yes, ma'am." Jonah saluted just as Carol had.

"I want Mexican," Ian muttered as they left the captain's office.

Jonah ignored the whispers and looks of the other MCU officers, both sympathetic and otherwise. He was too intensely focused on Carol, who kept wincing.

"She can hear you guys," Ian called out. "If you got questions, just ask."

The room fell silent.

"Thought so." Ian thumped Jonah's shoulder, almost knocking him over. "Tacos or enchiladas?"

"Neither," Jonah replied. "Fajitas are all I need."

"Pfft." Carol shoved between them, trotting down the stairs. "Combo plate, bitches!"

"Ew." Ian shuddered. "I don't want enchilada sauce soaking into the bottom of my taco shell."

"It adds spice," Carol shot back.

Jonah chuckled as he followed the bickering pair out of the precinct. Unfortunately, there were already reporters waiting for them, rushing toward Jonah, Ian, and Carol the moment they were spotted. Shouts of "Detective Sound! We have questions for you," "Miss Voss, a moment of your time!" and "Detective Matsumoto, how do you feel working with a dangerous predator?"

That last one got Jonah to stop. "Carol Voss is a graduate of the police academy. Before I met her, she had already been hired by the LAPD. If you have any questions about her suitability, I suggest you contact the chief of police." With that, he grabbed hold of Carol's wrist and began walking through the throng of reporters.

Ian was behind them, fending off reporters with "No comment" and "The number for the LAPD's chief of police is 213..."

Jonah opened the passenger side door, shielding Carol until she was in the car. It was almost classic police work, keeping the press from a suspect until they had a chance to interrogate them. Except, this time, Jonah was protecting someone precious to him rather than some scumbag piece of work who deserved to rot in a jail cell.

Once they were all in the car, Jonah carefully backed out of the lot. The reporters were kind enough to get out of the way, but they remained close to the sides of the vehicle until Jonah pulled out of the parking lot and onto the street.

"Well. That was fun." Ian leaned forward, placing himself above the car's middle compartment. "Now what?"

"We do what Anne recommended," Jonah replied. "We go over statements or decide whether or not to reply to them at all."

"Sounds like you've already decided." Carol was staring at him, her gaze concerned. "No comment, right?"

"Letting the higher-ups deal with the press is sometimes a viable option, especially right now," Jonah replied. "We need to make decisions, and it won't be easy."

"I say we don't bother trying to hide your relationship," Ian said, his fingers drumming the top of Carol's seat. "They're bound to find out about it anyway, and it makes it look like you're trying to hide something illicit if you're not up-front about it."

"But we're coworkers," Carol muttered, looking down at her hands. "That's what worries me. Will my relationship with Jonah impact Jonah's career? Yours? What do we do then?"

"We deal with it," Jonah replied. "Ian has an out. He could request another partner."

"And miss all this?" Ian waved his hands like a magician. "Hell no. I'm in, good or bad."

Carol smiled. "Okay. Then let's go balls to the wall."

"You have balls?" Ian gasped dramatically.

Jonah bit back a laugh. Ian was gonna love this.

Carol leaned forward and pulled out a chewed-up tennis ball from under her seat. It had been a gag gift from Debbie. She held it up for Ian to see.

"Canine. Gotta have our chew toys."

Jonah shuddered, clamping his thighs together. "Yeowch."

"Dude, I didn't know you were into the rough stuff." Ian cackled like an idiot.

Jonah barely resisted the urge to cup himself. "So, we're agreed? Open and honest?"

Carol winked before putting the tennis ball away. "Yup. Balls and all."

Chapter 27

The weekend had been fairly quiet. Carol had called Stacey and talked for about an hour in her room and had gone shopping with her friends while he stayed home reading. They'd worked on their magic, the give and take coming easily to them.

She was his perfect match, physically, mentally, and magically. They hadn't been together for very long, but he was already willing to put a ring on her finger. Hell, if he thought he'd get away with it, he'd put his name in magical ink on her forehead.

Or maybe across her shoulder blades. Yeah, that was definitely the way to go. *No Touchy! Sincerely, Jonah Sound* was the perfect tattoo, especially if he got it inked on her in his own handwriting. The thought made him grin.

He'd make her wear halter tops all the time just to expose her ink and his claim.

"Jonah?"

He blinked, his thoughts of nakie time with his familiar interrupted. He shouldn't have been thinking about that in the first place, not here, anyway. Jonah and Carol's getting-to-know-you grace period was over, and now both of them were required to be in the office Monday through Friday as well as being on-call, just like every other detective pair.

"Yeah?"

"Dr. Ramsey is can to talk to us today. Her office called and said we can come over." Carol was standing over him in her work clothes, appearing both serious and hot as hell.

Damn. When he found black slacks and a striped shirt hot on a woman, he had it bad.

"Then let's roll." Jonah picked up his badge and gun and headed stairs. Around them, the rest of the office chatted on phones or typed on keyboards.

On the stairway, they met up with Ian Matsumoto. "Hey, guys, I was just coming up to talk to you. You off to talk to the dimen expert?"

"Yup." Jonah nodded to the detective. "You coming?"

"Yup," Ian echoed. "I've been assigned as your permanent partner."

Carol growled.

Ian just laughed in response. "Until you're through your on-the-job training, your boy here still needs a full-fledged detective as a partner, remember?" Ian slung his arm around her shoulder. "After that, I'll probably be paired with someone else, so love me while ya got me."

"Hmph."

Carol's displeasure vibrated through their bond. Jonah decided to address it by showing how proud he was of her. "Carol's been a big help already. She's the one who recognized the symbol of Apep."

Ian whistled. "How'd you identify it?"

"Internet." Carol stomped down the stairs, her expression fierce. "And Jonah only has one partner. Me."

Jonah couldn't help but grin at her possessive tone. The fact that she responded to him so strongly was a good sign for their future. Not to mention, the sex was spectacular. "You're special, Carol. Remember that. You're the first familiar I've ever had who went through the police academy. If you'd had more training under your belt, Ian wouldn't be here." Jonah got out his keys and unlocked the doors. They climbed in, Ian taking the back seat as if he always sat there. "So, if Ian is now my permanent partner, all three of us will work together. That means he's your partner, too, and you can pick his brains as well."

"Huh." Carol relaxed a bit at that news.

"You completely up to speed on the case?" Jonah asked Ian as he headed for the campus where Dr. Ramsey worked.

"I think so. Two vics, each stabbed repeatedly to remove the Apep symbol, each with a different flower in their hands, and it's possible that this is part of some sort of ritual using pyramids and diamonds." There was the sound of rustling papers as Ian continued. "We're going to be talking to..." Ian muttered something under his breath. "Right. Dr. Rosemary Ramsey, professor of dimenology and dimenic languages at UCLA. Dr. Hill set it up for us."

"She's emailed us some useful information." Jonah headed for the college, keeping an eye on traffic while he listened to Carol and Ian double-check their facts of the case. Before they were done, they were pulling up in front of the main administrative building. He got out of the car and waited for his partners to do the same. "Let's go chat up a professor."

Carol and Ian followed him up the steps. He had forgotten which office Dr. Ramsey might be in, so he planned on asking at the front desk in the central campus office. No one stopped them this time, unlike when they'd met Dean Hill.

The young man at the front desk smiled at them, the typical professional smile of receptionists everywhere. "Can I help you?"

"Hello, I'm Detective Jonah Sound, and these are my partners, Detective Ian Matsumoto and FD Carol Voss. We've got an appointment with Dr. Ramsey."

The young man typed at a computer before nodding. "She's in the department of languages, office 305." He pulled out a map and circled a building. "Go to the parking garage near Rosenfeld Library, then cross Royce Drive, past the North Campus Student Center and take a right toward Campbell Hall A." He gave them a stern look. "That's *A*, not B."

"Thank you." Jonah took the map with the marks the receptionist had made and walked back out of the building. He followed the provided directions, marveling at the sheer size of the campus. He'd gone to a much smaller college than UCLA, and he didn't regret the experience. Gas alone had to cost a fortune for the students.

"Man, this brings back memories." Carol was glancing around with a wistful expression.

"Miss school?" Ian was doing his best to be friendly with Carol.

Luckily, she was responding in kind. "Hell no. I miss some of the friends I made who moved back home. It was the first place I felt accepted, even normal."

Ian, who didn't know about the bullying Carol had gone through, gave her a concerned glance. "What do you mean?"

Carol shrugged. "Let's just say my life hasn't been a bowl of cherries, but it wasn't all bad."

"Cherries?" Jonah glanced back curiously.

Her expression turned horrified. "Do you know how much a bed of roses costs?"

Ian snorted out a laugh. "Oh yeah, I'm going to like working with you guys."

Carol shook her head. "Idiot." But her tone was fond, making Jonah bristle a bit. Before he could say something he'd regret, Carol pointed. "There's the building."

On the surface of the brick building were silver letters, denoting it as Campbell Hall A. Across from it was an identical building, but this one was marked B.

Ian held up a finger. "Remember, *A*, not B, children."

Carol snorted, clearly amused. "They must have magical and non-magical languages separated."

"Wouldn't want to accidentally blow up the kids learning Spanish." Ian took the lead this time. Jonah happily fell back to walk next to Carol.

They entered the building and took the stairs to the third floor. Finding the professor's office wasn't difficult. Voices from inside meant she wasn't alone, however.

"Dillon, you'll be fine. Remember what I told you, and don't screw up the order of the words, or you'll summon Belial. No one wants Belial at a graduation party."

Carol's brows rose. "That *would* be one hell of a party," she muttered.

Ian knocked on the door. "Dr. Ramsey? It's Detective Matsumoto. We're here for our appointment."

A tall, somewhat gangly man opened it, his cheeks bright red. "Um. Sorry. I needed to double-check something with the professor."

"Yeah, you wouldn't want hell-spawn drinking all your beer." Ian shook his head. "I hate it when they do that, especially when they leave the cheap stuff and drink all my IPAs."

The boy's cheeks heated further. "Um. Yeah. I'll just…go." He glanced behind him, his tone changing from embarrassed to respectful. "Thank you, Dr. Ramsey."

"You're welcome, Dillon." The professor's voice was deep for a woman. It reminded him a bit of Emma Stone. "Come in, Detectives."

Dillon left, rapidly walking down the hall without a glance back. Ian, Jonah, and Carol walked into the professor's office.

The room was small, the desk, two chairs, and bookcases taking up most of the space. Each bookcase was filled to overflowing. Magazines were stacked on the floor by one of the chairs.

Jonah sat, pulling out his tablet. Ian hesitated for a moment, but Carol stood behind Jonah, obviously guarding him from whatever might come up behind him. Instead of suggesting she take a seat, Jonah nodded for Ian to take the other one. "Thank you for agreeing to speak with us. I'm Detective Sound, and this is my familiar, Carol Voss, and my partner, Ian Matsumoto."

Dr. Ramsey held out her hand. "Nice to meet you."

After everyone had shaken, Jonah got down to business. "What can you tell us about the writing found on our victim?"

The professor grimaced. "Yeah, about that. There's some weird shit going on here."

"No, really?" Carol murmured. "Can you tell if the person left us, oh, I don't know, their real name?"

The professor chuckled at Carol's question. "No, they didn't. However, I can tell you that it's definitely an aspect of Apep you're dealing with. While your sister did a nice job with the magical runes, the hieroglyphics give us some of the ritual your murderer is performing." Dr. Ramsey pulled a sheet of paper toward her. "This is what I've been able to translate." She cleared her throat and began to read. "Apep, serpent of rebirth, you who devour the barque of Ra, who battles Set yet is never vanquished. He who was spat out, roar to the heavens thy defiance. Children of Apophis, come forth! Drink of this offering, that thy power may fill this vessel."

"Holy shit," Carol breathed. "That's bad."

"It's not the complete spell." Dr. Ramsey put the paper down. "Are you sure there wasn't writing on the first body?"

Jonah shook his head. "We didn't find any, but…"

"Invisible writing?" Carol stared at him, but she wasn't observing him. Her gaze was distant as she continued speaking. "Like lemon juice ink? When you put the paper to a heat source, it turns brown. Otherwise, it's invisible."

"That could be it, but the body has already been released to the family," Ian replied. "If that was done, it's been washed away by the mortician."

"Not necessarily." Jonah was well aware that there were other ways to write something invisibly. "Dr. Ramsey, what do you think this could mean?"

She shook her head. "I couldn't tell you without the beginning of the spell, but I could hazard a guess. Either this person is after power, or he's trying to raise the dead."

"The price being parts of a soul." Ian swore softly. "Dr. Ramsey, if we find anything more, can we bring it to you?"

"Of course. I'd be delighted to help, Detective." Dr. Ramsey stood. "Once you have more of the spell, please bring it to me. Even without the start, I might be able to figure it out before it's too late."

"Too late for what?" Carol asked.

Dr. Ramsey clenched her hands. "The apocalypse."

Chapter 28

Carol watched closely as Jonah sat cross-legged on the floor, his back against the wall. Before him were the autopsy photos of Louis Reeves, as well as hair clippings from the body that they'd gotten from Paul. They'd promised to call him once Jonah's spell was complete. He'd been just as horrified as they were to discover that the words written on the second victim's body weren't a signature but part of a spell.

They were back in the precinct, in the spell chamber the detective-sorcerers used when they needed to cast. The magic wouldn't leak beyond the room, making it similar to the shielded room where they'd viewed the tape of the wither.

Ian sat next to her, watching Jonah with a curious gaze. "How often have you watched him use his magic?"

"Most of the time, we've concentrated on blending our anima and animus to strengthen our bond. Other than that, he's used it to send a wither away."

Ian stared at her in disbelief. "A wither? I thought magic didn't work on them very well."

"It doesn't, but Jonah didn't use it on the wither. He used it on the lights. He made them so bright the wither ran." Carol smiled fondly as Jonah tugged on her anima, aligning it with his magic. "He's almost ready."

"What do you think he'll find from a photograph that wasn't found on the body?" Ian truly sounded curious. People who had no magic often challenged it, but Ian seemed utterly charmed by it.

"He might be able to use sympathetic magic to bring up any spells or symbols that were done invisibly." Carol held up her hand before Ian could ask. "Sympathetic magic is magic that uses effigies, like straw dolls or photographs, to represent the person being targeted. Something belonging to the victim, like hair or toenail clippings is added. The sorcerer then casts the spell to affect the target."

"In this case, poor Mr. Reeves," Jonah added. He'd begun to sparkle with the amber glow their combined magic created. "Now shush. I'm going to cast."

Carol nodded and closed her eyes, concentrating on the link between them. The language of the sorcerers echoed through the room, Jonah's deep voice vibrating along their bond. Their magic flowed much more freely between them than it had the first time they'd practiced together. Jonah's determination to find anything hidden in the autopsy photos that hadn't been discovered yet firmed her own resolve to help him any way she could.

This spell would cause those hidden things to flare to life, visible to anyone in the room. Ian would write down anything that glowed because Jonah and Carol would be too busy maintaining the spell to take notes.

Jonah's voice rose in volume, the tone demanding. Soon, she sensed Ian scribbling away, meaning they'd found something. Jonah's voice continued to drone on, keeping the spell active.

"Got it. You can stop." Ian's voice was quiet. Either that, or the magic was drowning him out.

The tug on her anima slowly dissipated, leaving her weak. It was a good thing they'd done this sitting down because she didn't think her legs could hold her. She opened her eyes to find Jonah leaning back against the wall, his face pale and sweaty.

"That was rough," Jonah muttered. "Something fought me."

Carol scowled. "I didn't sense anything like that, just the normal flow."

Jonah grinned weakly. "Because I didn't let you get caught up in it." He slumped over, lying down, his legs still tangled together. "Sorry."

"Ass." She crawled over to him, placing his head on her lap. Her movements scattered the spell components, but she didn't care. They didn't need them anymore, and they could clean up once Jonah was back on his feet. "You should have let me help." She stroked his hair, and he sighed, closing his eyes.

"How?" Ian's voice interrupted her thoughts of how cute Jonah was as he curled into her like a kitten seeking warmth. "I mean, you're not a sorcerer, so how would that have worked?"

"I could have taken some of the burden from him, or even all of it. It's part of what a familiar does for his or her sorcerer. Shifting pain and fatigue to a familiar is common among those who duel often."

"You haven't done it before." Jonah's voice was soft and sleepy. He must have really put himself into the spell. He'd never appeared this tired after blending their magic before.

"So? I have to do it sometime." She continued to stroke his hair. "One of these days you'll bite off more than you can chew. What will you do then?"

Jonah cocked an eyebrow. "Spit it out?"

She bopped him on top of his head. "Idiot."

"You two get along really well," Ian observed.

"That's because I have the best girl in the world." Jonah snuggled closer, the back of his head now on her stomach, his cheek against her upper thighs.

Ian sighed. "I am so jealous right now."

"Remind me to introduce you to Rose. I think you two would hit it off fabulously." Carol closed her eyes, enjoying the softness of Jonah's hair under her fingers. It was silkier than she'd thought it would be. "She's a hoot."

"Is she a familiar too?" Ian also crawled over to them, but he didn't touch Jonah.

That was good. Right now, Jonah smelled wounded. Even Ian wouldn't be safe if he touched Jonah. "Nope. She's an earth dimen."

"Speaking of dimens, what did you get?" Jonah opened his eyes and tried to sit up, but Carol stopped him by placing her hand on his head and holding him down.

268

"Most of it seems like gibberish to me, but we got the snake symbol and some writing that looks like the stuff we sent Dr. Ramsey." Ian placed the paper he'd scribbled on where Jonah could view it. The bottom of the paper was resting on Carol's knees. "I'll fax it to her once you two can stand upright again."

"I can—"

"*No*," Ian and Carol yelled at the same time.

"Okay, okay." Jonah settled back down. "Sheesh."

"You smell hurt, Jonah. Don't test me right now." Her wolf was riding her hard. It wanted to shift, to protect its wounded mate from anything that might...

Wait.

Mate?

Mate?

Holy shit. Her wolf had laid claim to Jonah in the most primal way possible. If anyone tried to take him away from her, she'd kill them without mercy.

"You two rest." Ian stood, holding the sketch pad. "I'll get this out to the professor. Once you two are on your feet, I think it's time to start questioning people on campus."

"Agreed. We've got a list of those who've been in the botanical class, which our victims shared. We need to talk to that professor as well." Jonah tapped Carol's foot. "What was his name?"

"Elroy Ballenger." Carol continued to stroke his hair, smiling as she stared down at him. He sounded sleepy. The magic must have taken quite a toll on him. "If you don't share the burden with me next time, I'll bite you. And not in a good place."

Ian laughed. "On that note, be back in a few." He left, shutting the door behind him.

"Hmph." Jonah closed his eyes and relaxed once more. "Read me a story."

"What kind?" She'd even read that horrible pseudo-romance novel that was all the rage a few years ago, the one that had half the romance community in an uproar and the other half in defense mode. She'd gag—she was firmly in the yuck group—but she'd do it if he asked.

"The kind where I learn everything we have so far on Professor Ballenger."

Ah. She should have realized what he was going to ask for, but she'd been so distracted by his scent and his hair and his weight—really, his everything—that she hadn't been thinking straight.

"Mm. I have to get up to get my bag. Think you can lie on the floor for a second?"

"Sure. I'm not a delicate, withering flower." Jonah snorted in derision. "Just don't drop my head."

"Did you know that the human head weighs roughly eight pounds?" Carol got up, careful to do as he asked.

"You know the weirdest shit," he muttered.

"I'm just explaining why my leg is going to fall asleep by the time we're done." She got her tablet computer and settled back on the floor, once again placing Jonah's head on her lap. "All right. Professor Ballenger, age forty-six, has tenure. He's been a professor here for twelve years now. His field of specialty is green magic." Those who preferred to cast spells involving plants and their growth, illnesses, and pests, called themselves green sorcerers. They were much in demand in the agricultural field as well as in pharmaceutical industries and forestry. "I'll need to check the familiar registry to check if he currently has one."

"Good idea. Let's check all the professors on campus." Jonah hummed quietly. "I've got a feeling that it's someone onsite doing this, not someone off-campus. Someone familiar with the magic here and how to work it."

"Someone familiar with the placement of the cameras?" Carol followed the thought trying to elude her. "Otherwise why have the wither dump the body?"

"Huh. Interesting thought. We'll run it by Ian, find out what he thinks. If he can't poke holes in it, I think we're on to something."

"I hate to say this, but we need to add anyone on the security team to the list as well." That was what had been bugging her. "They'd be able to access information on where all the cameras are, and some are bound to be sorcerers."

Jonah opened his eyes. "You think Chief Rivers is a suspect?"

Carol shrugged. "He's as good as any of them. He was there when the wither came, he runs security on campus, and he mostly slept while we were going over the security videos. He's just too relaxed about all of this."

"Okay, then. Add him to the list. I trust your instincts."

Carol smiled and began to type. She hoped her partnership with Jonah would never end.

Chapter 29

Ian had agreed with them that the odds of the perpetrator being a professor were remarkably high. He hadn't been as enamored of Carol's theory that Chief Rivers was somehow involved, but he agreed to check it out anyway.

They'd split up to question the professors. It would be a long, grueling task, but Jonah trusted that both Ian and Carol would do an excellent job.

Jonah had decided to question Professor Elroy Ballenger rather than leave it to his partners. He wanted to gather what the professor had to say for himself, despite his lack of knowledge in herbs and plants. Carol was going to speak to a Professor Rodney Ackerman, a specialist in crystals, while Ian talked to one of the magical language professors.

Jonah hadn't taken herbology in college. He'd chosen to study planar entities instead, believing he'd find that subject more useful as a cop in the MCU. Therefore, he'd have to make sure to really question the professor about what herbs could have been used in the murders, then research for himself to find out if he was lying. So far, Professor Ballenger was their best suspect, as he had both victims in his class.

Jonah knocked on the classroom door to get the professor's attention. He'd been told that the class would be over by the time he'd get to the room, and the front desk had been right. Students swarmed around him as they left, glancing at him curiously on their way out.

A tall, thin man with brown hair, dressed conservatively, was cleaning up some papers on a desk as Jonah stepped into the classroom. "Professor Ballenger?"

The man glanced up. His appearance was average, with brown eyes and a radiant smile. "Hello, Detective. I've been expecting you."

That smile was out of place. "Really? Did someone tell you I was coming?"

"I thought…" Professor Ballenger shook his head, the smile fading to a frown. "I'm afraid not." Then his eyes went wide. "Oh, dear. Does it have to do with…" He glanced toward the doorway. "Damn." He pointed toward the seats. "Let's sit and talk."

Jonah took Ballenger up on his offer. Something weird was going on here.

When the professor joined him, he began questioning him. Jonah opened his notebook. "I'm here to question you about the murders of Mr. Reeves and Ms. Miller."

Ballenger sighed. "I'd hoped you were here for a different reason."

Jonah's brows rose. What was the professor talking about? "And that reason would be?"

Ballenger's frown deepened to a scowl. "I filed a report with Chief Rivers about a theft from my on-campus greenhouse." Ballenger pulled out some papers from his bag. "Here, look at this."

Jonah read through the paperwork. "Why would someone want stinking nightshade?"

"It's used in a variety of ways," Dr. Ballenger replied. "It's a hallucinogenic, leaving one feeling dizzy and drunk as well."

"So, it's a real hit with the frats?"

Ballenger didn't smile. "It can be used as a date-rape drug, yes."

Shit. Not the answer he wanted. He made a note of the professor's answer. "What else can it be used for?"

"It's been used as a form of painkiller and a sedative for centuries." The professor leaned forward, his expression going from upset to calm as he taught Jonah about the plant. "It contains three tropane alkaloids: atropine, scopolamine, and hyoscyamine. They block the neurotransmitters that handle the involuntary nervous system."

"Which makes one dizzy."

"It's also a muscle relaxant. Insane asylums used it often to calm so-called maniacs. It would cause their muscles to relax and their behavior to calm. The effects could last up to two days. However, if given the wrong dose, it can cause accelerated heart rate, convulsions, vomiting, extremely high fevers, delusions, coma, and even death."

In the case of the first victim, it appeared as if the perpetrator had wanted to lessen Reeves's pain. He would have to find out if there was nightshade in the man's tox report. "How is it used as a painkiller or sedative?"

"Let me think." Dr. Ballenger began drumming his fingers on his thigh. "The leaves of henbane, along with mandrake, opium poppy, and hemlock, could be boiled in water. A sponge soaked in the resulting liquid is then left out to dry. Once it's needed, you'd soak the sponge in warm water and place it under the patient's nose, causing it to act as a soporific. However, the amounts used would have to be carefully calculated based on the patient's weight and the location and time of year. The efficacy of the plants would be determined by these factors."

"If you mess up?"

"Death." Dr. Ballenger's fingers stopped moving, and his expression was grim. "You're talking about four very toxic plants. While this method was used in both the early Arab world and medieval times, it was hit or miss at best."

Jonah made another note to ask Paul to research all four plants. "Can you detect its use post-mortem?"

Dr. Ballenger shook his head. "I doubt it."

There went that idea.

Dr. Ballenger continued. "However, there's some ways to find the effects of poisoning if you understand what you're searching for. The intestines will be a bit irritated, there will be less saliva, and both pupils will be dilated. But that's if it's used long-term, and the effects are minor. It's *very* difficult to detect if it's only used once or twice."

"What about magically?" If he could find it that way, it would make things much easier on him.

"It depends on whether or not it was used in a magic potion. Of course, potions with nightshade are often used to induce prophecies from oracles. Considering the hallucinogenic properties of henbane, if one were trying for a prophecy, they might combine it with other ingredients to induce a meditative state." Dr. Ballenger's fingers were tapping again. "That state could well produce prophecies if combined with nightshade."

Interesting. "Could it be used any other way magically?"

"Hmm. I suppose henbane could also be used to induce a state of meditation similar to sedation. Mixed with certain herbs, it can induce a hypnotic state." Dr. Ballenger frowned thoughtfully. "That would make the subject susceptible to commands, even taking actions they might not normally perform. The potion would overcome inhibitions on morally objectionable actions."

Damn. It was entirely possible henbane was used on at least Reeves. "I have a few more questions for you, if you don't mind."

"Not at all." Dr. Ballenger smiled, but it was strained. "I do have a class in about twenty minutes, so we'll have to keep it brief."

Jonah nodded. "Very well. I need some information on the victims. What can you tell me about Louis Reeves?"

Dr. Ballenger sighed. "He was a good student, very eager to learn. He was particularly proficient in potions and tinctures."

"Tinctures?" He'd been in planar entities classes, not alchemy or herbology.

Dr. Ballenger gave him a small, somewhat sad smile. "A tincture is an extract of a plant or animal substance mixed with a solvent, usually alcoholic like ethanol, but not always. Tinctures are applied directly to the tongue using droppers, so it enters the bloodstream more quickly."

"Ah. Would that show up in a toxicology report?"

"Only with repeated use, as I said before." Professor Ballenger sat back and ran his fingers through his hair. His gaze was distant, focused on something only he could see. "I enjoyed having him in class. His poor familiar's grades have been dropping, but I'm doing everything I can to give him breaks because of his loss."

"Thank you for that. I can't imagine what it would be like to lose someone so closely tied to you." As far as he was concerned, he never would. Jonah would jump into the fire rather than watch Carol singe even a tuft of her fur.

Professor Ballenger nodded. "I lost one due to cancer. It was…" He glanced away, his expression grave. "It was the worst time of my life."

Jonah made a note. "I'm sorry for your loss, professor."

"Thank you." Ballenger cleared his throat and turned back to Jonah, his expression once more vaguely cheerful. "I have to tell you something about Mr. Reeves, some gossip I overheard by accident."

"Oh?" Gossip could lead to a dead-end, or it could become something very important to the case. Either way, he'd have to check it out.

"Yes. It seems Mr. Reeves was something of a ladies' man. He'd have two or three women he rotated between at any given time." Ballenger held up his hands. "Now, this was just campus gossip, so I have no idea if it's true or not. His familiar would be able to give you more information on that."

"Thank you." Jonah would have a chat with the familiar after he was done talking with the professors. "Now, we need to discuss Ms. Miller."

"Ah, yes. Ms. Miller." Ballenger smiled. "Very strong-willed, that one, quite stubborn when she thought she was right. She had no trouble arguing with me about salves, but when proven wrong, she had no trouble apologizing. She was quite the refreshing character."

Hmm. Hadn't Carol mentioned that the flowers represented certain things? He flipped through his notes. Lilies, Rose had said, represented returned innocence, while gladiolus were strength of character and integrity. Shit. The flowers were more important than they'd thought. "Have you ever taught the language of flowers?"

The professor's eyebrows rose. "No, I'm afraid it's not something I believe in. Flowers are flowers." He chuckled softly. "Besides, I'm quite allergic to them. Just being in the

279

same room is a misery for me. I tend to avoid large events like weddings because they always have fresh flowers everywhere."

"I see." He could be lying, but Jonah doubted it. His gaze had been forthright, his answers quick and sure. He didn't fidget or play with his fingers, and not once had he clutched his stomach or reacted defensively. None of the signs of a liar were there. Still, he'd check with Dean Hill about the flower allergy. "Anything else you can add about either student?"

Ballenger's expression turned thoughtful. "If I recall correctly, Ms. Miller had just ended a contract with a familiar. She appeared somewhat down about it."

"Are you sure?" Sorcerers didn't have tattoos like familiars. There was no tell that gave them away when they had ended a contract.

"Very. She mentioned it when I asked why her familiar was no longer in class with her." Professor Ballenger shrugged. "I told her that this sort of thing happens and that she'd find the familiar meant to be hers soon enough."

"Sometimes it takes longer than you'd think." Jonah stood and held out his hand. "May I call you if I think of any other questions?"

Ballenger took his hand and shook it. "Of course. Anything I can do to help. I don't want to lose any more of our students to this monster."

"Thank you." Jonah put his notebook away. He had Ballenger's number from Dean Hill's list, so there was no need to ask for it.

"You're welcome." Ballenger peeked at the wall clock. "My class will soon be starting."

"I'll get out of your way, then." Jonah strode toward the door, thinking about everything Ballenger had said. Once out in the hallway and a bit of a distance from Ballenger's classroom, he pulled out his cell phone and dialed Dean Hill. After getting through her secretary, he asked his question the moment she picked up. "Can you tell me if Ballenger is allergic to flowers?"

Dean Hill was silent for a moment. "Detective Sound?"

Jonah glanced around as the sound of Carol's voice came from one of the classrooms. "Yes, sorry. I'm a bit distracted right now. Can you tell me if Ballenger's allergic to flowers?"

"Yes, he is. He's infamous for it, actually. He wears a face mask every spring when the flowers bloom on campus, and one time during a fundraising event, he sneezed all over one of our largest donors because he was wearing a boutonniere. His briefcase is full of antihistamines."

"Huh. Thanks." Jonah smiled as Carol came out of one of the classrooms, an irritated frown on her face. "I need to go."

"Call me if you have any other questions. I'm happy to help."

Jonah said his goodbyes and hung up. "Well?"

Carol was scowling. "That man's an asshole." She wrinkled her nose. "He smells like one too."

Jonah shook his head. "What did he say about the students?"

"Not much, other than Miller had a great ass but a bad personality, and that Reeves was a man-whore." She shook her head. "We need to talk to Hill about him."

Jonah checked the room she'd been in. "Professor Ackerman?"

"That's the one. I'll let you listen in when I transcribe the notes. Then you'll understand why I thought about biting him."

"I can hardly wait." Jonah glared at the doorway before putting his arm around Carol's waist. "You're seeing Dean Anthony next, right? If you need me to, I can go with you." He could reschedule his next meeting with...Professor Smythe? Smith? He'd have to check his notes, but right now he was focused on Carol and what she needed.

"Nah, I got this." Carol leaned against him for a moment, her head on his shoulder. She murmured something so quiet he couldn't quite catch it, but her shoulders relaxed, and her eyes closed. The tension seemed to seep out of her as they stood quietly together. "Mm. I needed that."

The moment she moved away, he wanted to pull her back, but they were on the job and Ian would be joining them soon. "Let's get these interviews over with and go home, maybe order a pizza, and watch a movie."

"Yeah." Carol shivered. "I have a bad feeling about this."

That stopped him cold. "What are you sensing? A wither?"

"No, not that. It's just…" She glanced around. "Something is seriously off on this campus, and it's getting worse every time I come here."

"You think the campus is the focus of the spell?" Jonah hadn't thought of that, but mass murder on such a scale would be monumentally bad. That was the only thing he could think of as to why the campus, and not the baseball field, would be part of the spell.

"I'm not sure. What do you sense?" She gazed up at him as if he held the answers to life, the universe, and everything.

Jonah closed his eyes and focused. Their magic began to swirl together as he adjusted their bond to suit his needs. He opened his inner eye and stared around him, searching for something out of place.

Everything was tinged with gray, the gray of death. The gray of Terra Noctem.

"Shit." This was overwhelmingly bad.

Chapter 30

"I wonder how much of this Dean Anthony is in charge of." Carol gazed around, noticing that they were in the same area as Chief Rivers. Now that she had a moment to look around, she read the various plaques as she walked through the corridors. The doors were labeled with such things as Greek Affairs, Community Services, Off-Campus Services, and Veteran's Affairs.

"Dean Anthony deals with campus life experiences," a familiar voice responded behind her. Carol turned to find Dean Anthony's secretary standing there, her expression haughty. "For instance, campus security reports to him." Her tone was pointed, as if she were mere moments from calling Chief Rivers and having Carol thrown from the building.

Carol held out her hand. "FD Carol Voss, LAPD." She flashed her shiny badge and watched the woman sniff somewhat disdainfully. "I have an appointment. I'm here to talk to Dean Anthony."

The secretary "This way, Ms. Voss."

Carol ignored the way the woman pointedly did not call Carol "Detective," instead opting to quietly follow after her. They passed Chief Rivers's office, which seemed closed, continuing down the hall. "And you are?"

The woman ignored her question, keeping her pace brisk, as if Carol couldn't keep up with the taller female. "Dean

Anthony is an extremely busy man. He's also in charge of returning veterans, assisting our students who live off-campus or on, and student activities such as the student government and our various clubs. He has men and women under him who deal with the day-to-day governing of these offices, but they all report to him."

Carol stopped, remembering suddenly something the secretary had said when they'd first met, that the murders happened *off*-campus. "You knew about the murders beforehand because of your connection to the dean?"

"That is correct, Ms. Voss." Her brisk pace slowed as they neared the end of the corridor.

"But how did you know that the murders were committed off-campus? We hadn't released that information yet."

The woman stopped, pointing toward a door marked *Dean Frank Anthony, Ed.L.D.* Just outside the double doors was a desk where the name plaque *Laura Butler* sat. The secretary sat there, picking up the phone. "One moment, please, while I make sure the dean is ready to see you."

Carol took one of the two seats next to the secretary's desk, going over what had been bugging her about the secretary. The fact that the murders were done off-campus had been kept from the press, but it was possible that Chief Rivers had figured it out and informed Dean Anthony. But why would the dean tell his secretary? Was it just an official line, or was there more to it? She'd have to ask both Dean Anthony and Chief Rivers about it.

It was possible that the homicide detectives who'd first been there had let slip the fact that the body had been ditched on home plate.

"Ms. Voss? The dean will see you now." Firmly in her place of power, Ms. Butler was serene as she set the phone back in its cradle.

"Thanks." Carol stood and went to the door, pulling it open.

"Ah, Ms. Voss." The dean looked behind her, obviously expecting Jonah to be right behind her. "So, my secretary was correct. I was surprised to hear you were the one to come and interview me."

Carol sniffed discreetly, surprised to find that the room smelled...odd. Sooty.

The dean smiled. "Caught that, did you? I'm afraid I had a bit of a run-in with a djinn, and, well, you know how their tempers are."

Huh. Having never pissed off a djinn she wasn't sure of that. Then again, she'd never smelled a djinn before either. Carol nodded her greeting rather than shake hands with the man. Something about him made the hairs on the back of her neck stand on end, an instinct she'd thought set off by the wither the last time they'd met.

He seemed to be your average, badly dressed professor. So why did she instinctively want to snarl at him?

Carol took a seat. She pulled out her recorder and showed it to the dean, turning it on. "Dean Anthony, we wanted to speak to you because Chief Rivers reports to you, and you are in charge of campus life."

She discreetly sniffed the air again, ignoring the scent of papers, wood, and dust. It wasn't just the room that held the scent of soot. Dean Hill smelled like ashes. "Did the djinn try to take a bite out of you?"

He seemed startled for a moment before he replied. "Yes, actually. Your nose is quite acute, Ms. Voss."

"Thank you." She glanced around, taking mental inventory of the room around her. "Can you tell me when Chief Rivers spoke to you about the murders?"

"I was aware that a body had been found almost as soon as Chief Rivers found out," Dean Anthony replied. His demeanor was calm, as was his tone. His gaze remained steady on her.

"But Mr. Reeves's familiar informed your office that his sorcerer was in trouble, yet he says that you dismissed his concerns without investigating. Shouldn't that have been looked into before it led to his death?"

Dean Anthony frowned, appearing concerned, but something about his demeanor didn't sit right with her. He shifted in his seat, his gaze darting away from Carol and back again so quickly she almost missed the movement. His cheeks were turning red. Perhaps he was embarrassed by his lack of action?

"Yes, well, sometimes we have new familiar-sorcerer pairs where the familiar senses distress and tries to report it, only to find out that the sorcerer in question was simply late for class that day. It happens more often than you think."

That answer didn't satisfy Carol. Ronnie Stewart hadn't struck her as the type to run off half-cocked, no pun intended. "So, because you felt he was overreacting, you refused to send anyone to investigate his report?"

"That wasn't my call, it's policy." The dean sighed. "If we inspected every report of a distressed sorcerer we've gotten from a familiar, Chief Rivers would never get anything else done." His gaze returned to Carol, his expression sorrowful. "I'm sure you understand what I mean."

Carol's brows rose. This was exactly why she'd chosen law enforcement, to better the plight of familiars, and here was a prime example of the system not working. "Do I?"

The dean studied her expression for a moment before clearing his throat. "Pardon me, but our familiars are quite young, and usually in the throes of their first bond. Most familiars I've met are emotional during that time. I've noticed that, after more than one partner, their emotions tend to settle down. Bird shifters, especially someone like Mr. Stewart, are a little more…flighty than their counterparts. You must remember how it was with your first bond, am I correct, Ms. Voss?"

Carol didn't, as Jonah was her first bond. She decided to change tacks to discover whether or not she could surprise the man. So far, he'd been pretty unflappable. "Sir, what can you tell me about your secretary?"

"Laura?" Dean Anthony stiffened, his brows lowering. "Why would you need information on her?"

There was a not-so-subtle warning in his tone that had Carol's hackles rising. "Well, she was the first person on campus we spoke to the day we found Mr. Reeves's body, and she said some things that made us curious."

The dean sat back slowly, his movements cautious. It was more than obvious he didn't like Carol's change of inquiry. How close was he to his secretary? "She's been with me for several years now. She knows the ins and outs of campus life almost as well as I do."

"Can you tell me whether or not she's a sorcerer?" If she was, they'd definitely have to research her background more thoroughly.

"I… Yes, she is." The dean's hesitation didn't go unnoticed. Something fishy was definitely going on between the dean and his secretary. "She has an Associate of Applied Science in Administrative Assisting. I believe she uses her magic to help keep the office running smoothly. She's not a strong sorcerer, but she's discovered a way to make it useful in her everyday life."

"Does she have a familiar?" Carol would like to speak to that person.

"She does, though I've never met her." The dean was slowly relaxing as Carol continued asking innocuous questions.

"What does her familiar do for a living?"

He seemed to think about that for a moment before giving a reply. "You know, I have no idea. As I've said, I've never met her, and Laura doesn't speak much about her. I'm not certain how long they've been together, but I've been given the impression that it's been years."

Carol nodded. She'd need to confirm whether or not Ms. Butler was a fairly weak sorcerer or not. She glanced behind the dean and saw a picture of him, his arms around two women, one around his age and one much younger. She smiled at the big grin on the younger female's face. "Is that your family?"

The dean tensed again, barely glancing behind him. "Ah. Yes."

Carol tried her best to get him to relax once more. "They're lovely."

"Thank you." He must have still been upset about something because he fisted his hands before hiding them below his desk.

"I'm sorry, I seem to have brought up a sore subject." Perhaps he was divorced and didn't get to see his daughter—obvious from the shape of their eyes—as often as he would like.

He sighed, his shoulders relaxing as he slumped in his chair. "My daughter, she's…not alive anymore."

Carol's ears perked up. As much as she didn't want to poke at an open wound, they were looking for someone who might want to bring someone back from the dead. A beloved daughter would certainly qualify. "I'm sorry to hear that. You have my sympathies."

"Thank you, I appreciate that." He took a deep breath and straightened, a tight, fake smile on his face. "Was there anything else you wanted to ask?"

"How closely do you work with Chief Rivers?" She was certain that Jonah would be interested in the answer.

"We meet once a week to go over campus security, along with the heads of the other departments." He returned his hands to the desktop, clasping them loosely. "Normally, it's a boring meeting dealing with campus drinking and the occasional young man or woman who complains about noise in the dorms. I have a great deal of respect for the man. He's gone through the same sort of loss I have."

Carol blinked at that bit of news. "Chief Rivers has lost a child?"

"Indeed, though his son was a suicide while my daughter was lost in an accident." He shook his head, his face sagging in misery. "We go drinking together on the anniversary of each of their deaths. He's been a comfort to me in times where I think I can't endure the pain anymore."

"I see. While the circumstances are horrible, you must be happy to have such a good friend working with you."

The first genuine smile she'd seen crossed his face. "Indeed." He glanced at the clock on his wall and grimaced. "I'm afraid I've given a little too much of my time. I have an appointment in a few moments." He stood and held out his hand. "If you have any more questions, I'd be more than happy to answer them."

She stood as well, shaking his hand. Again, it was just a tad too firm. "I appreciate the offer. I'll let Jonah and Ian know, just in case I missed something."

He chuckled and let go of her hand. "As a teacher, I'm glad I was able to aid you in your endeavors to become a detective, Ms. Voss. I'm certain you'll do just fine."

"I'll see myself out, Dean Anthony." She turned for the door, only to be stopped by his voice.

"Ms. Voss? Please be careful if you talk to Chief Rivers about his son. It has been years, but the topic is quite painful for him."

"I'll handle it as delicately as I can, I promise." Carol would do what needed to be done, but the dean didn't need to know that. "Thank you for your time, Dean Anthony."

"You're more than welcome, Ms. Voss."

Carol headed into the hallway, waving farewell to Ms. Butler, who was on the phone. Ms. Butler ignored her, but Carol didn't care.

She had two dead kids, both of whom had parents working in campus security. Could one of them be the killer?

Chapter 31

It had been a couple of days since they'd questioned the professors. While Jonah wanted to talk to Chief Rivers and was planning on doing just that, Carol had bigger questions since hearing the results of his own interviews. "This has been bugging me."

"What has?" Jonah was trying to catch up on emails, something she was supposed to be doing herself.

"The entire campus is being, what, dragged into Terra Noctem? How?" Carol had tried her best to digest what Jonah was telling her, but she just couldn't imagine it. The kind of power needed for something that humongous would be staggering. The people without the power to walk the realms would be destroyed by the denizens of Terra Noctem. Of those that could, the weaker ones would fall within an hour as they were swarmed by withers and other denizens of the dead realm for their magic. "That doesn't make sense. Apep doesn't dwell in Terra Noctem; he lives in Terra Caelestes, the realm of the gods, doesn't he?"

"I'm not sure that's what's happening. I think it's more that the ritual the perpetrator is conducting is somehow…bringing Terra Noctem closer to the campus, not sucking the campus in. It's thinning the veil between the realms, making it easier to cross over. But the problem is, we don't know *what* is crossing over, or which way it's going." Jonah shook his head. "Everything about this case is giving me hives."

Her tablet pinged, signaling that she'd gotten an email. She returned to her desk and opened the email, gasping as she read the contents. "Jonah? We got something from the Egyptologist."

"Oh?" Jonah scooted his chair around their adjoined desks so he could view her monitor. "Oh."

Carol shivered as she read the text. "Apep, spirit of darkness, he who devours the twelve souls, who coils around the barque of Ra. Child of Neith, cast your eye upon this vessel that darkness has created."

"That darkness has created?" Jonah scowled. "What the fuck does that mean? And cast your eye upon this vessel? The spell calls for Apep to watch, then to devour the sacrifices."

"Devours the twelve souls. Does that mean there will be twelve victims?" Carol bit her lip. "We need to forward this to Dr. Ramsey."

"Agreed." Jonah gestured toward Ian, who was just coming into the room, munching on an apple he'd probably gotten from the break room. "C'mere, Matsumoto."

"Whatcha got?" Ian leaned between them. "Holy crap. Is that the first part of the spell?"

"More than likely, since it was the writing you copied from Reeves's body." Carol started to forward the email. "Any specific questions for Dr. Ramsey? Other than whether or not this gives her a better idea of what's going on."

"Not that I can think of." Ian rubbed his nose. "This is more your gig than mine."

"Nope, not really. This is priest bullshit, which is a hell of a lot worse." Jonah started backing up, forcing Ian to move. "Have you gone over all the case notes?"

"Yeah, I'm all caught up. Also, I got something from that campus cop you might be interested in." Ian pulled out a notebook from his jacket pocket. "It seems that the cameras around the baseball field have been destroyed."

"What?" Jonah stood. "Has CSI been out there?"

"No. Rivers says that it was cleaned up before he even found out about it." Ian flipped through his notes. "The campus custodians cleared the debris before they reported the vandalism. They must have thought it was kids and not our perp."

"Shit. Someone doesn't want us wither-watching again." Carol sighed. "Maybe if we go over there, I can get a scent."

"Or we can go establish whether or not they got anything on tape." Jonah grabbed his jacket. "Let's go."

The three of them headed for Jonah's car. "Can I drive?" Ian pleaded, his hands clasped over his breast in a dramatic pose that made Carol giggle. "My old partner would never let me."

"Why?" Jonah drawled as he opened the driver's side door.

"I have no idea."

Ian was so bad at faking an innocent guise that Carol couldn't help but laugh again. She really liked Ian. The man had a great sense of humor and seemed to fit in with them seamlessly.

"What?" Ian climbed into the back seat, winking at Carol with a conspiratorial expression.

"Nothing." Carol got into the passenger seat, and they were off on the now-familiar route. "Lunch after this?" She was beginning to get hungry.

"God, yes," Ian moaned. "I call Mexican."

"That's two votes." Jonah beamed. "Not far away, there's this fabulous little Mexican food place that has the best burritos. Instead of ground beef, they use roast beef. It's incredible."

"Mm." Carol's mouth began to water. "Three votes for burritos."

She stared out the window as they drove, thinking about the case. "I keep thinking that there's something wrong with this case."

"Me too. Something's off." Jonah pulled into the parking lot closest to the baseball field. "It's too close to home."

"Huh?" Ian followed as they climbed out of the car.

Carol sniffed, trying to catch any scents as they walked toward the field. "Why here? Why would a professor kill students here, on his home ground?"

"Because he's a cocky fucker who thinks he'll get away with it?" Ian pointed to first base. "Think about how quickly he's doing this. We've had two victims in less than two weeks. That's pretty quick for a blood mage, isn't it?"

"Not if he's working with a wither or a god," Jonah replied, his tone absent as he glanced around. "There. The remnants of the broken camera haven't been removed from the pole yet."

"Right above home plate. That must be the one the wither showed up on." Carol shivered at the memory of the cold presence of the wither.

"Don't think about it too much, or you might catch its attention."

"Wait, what?" Ian glanced between the two of them. "You mean that extradimensional asshole can find us just because we think about him?" He appeared absolutely horrified.

"It's more likely to be attracted to Carol or me, not you, but still I'd avoid it if I could. All human beings have either anima or animus in them to differing degrees." Jonah stared at the broken remains of the camera. "Carol, can you smell anything?"

She shifted, scenting the air. Something strange tickled her senses, sending her toward the tall pole the camera had been attached to. Around the base was a familiar scent, but other scents were also there, all of them recent. She shifted back, scowling. "Chief Rivers and some others I don't recognize, but he told Ian that he'd been here, so I doubt that counts."

"You have the scents of the unknowns, so that means we can eventually find them." Jonah stroked her cheek. "Good job."

Her cheeks heated at the praise. "You pat me on the head and call me a good girl, and I'll pee on your shoes."

"Pfft." Ian turned his back to them.

"Aw, you're so cute." Jonah tugged on one of her curls. "I want you to check around. Follow those scents to wherever they lead, then get back to me."

"They probably belong to the cleanup crew." Carol sighed. This was going to be so damn boring.

"Probably, but it's better to check and find nothing than not go and miss something important that could break the case open. Ian, go with her. I'm going to Rivers's office to ask if I can get a copy of the video." Jonah strode off, not waiting for a response.

"Think he was upset about your threat?" Ian was watching Jonah stride away.

"Nah. That's a pretty light threat as they go. Pooping in his shoes? *That's* serious." Carol turned back to the pole and took a deep whiff. "Okay. I've got the scents. Let's go for a stroll, Detective."

"Gotcha."

Ian followed behind as Carol as she followed the first of the three scents. It led to the administration building. Carol went into the building, ready to follow the scent down a corridor they hadn't been down before. Others moved past them, either ignoring them or nodding brief greetings as they went about their way. The badges around their necks were worth cursory glances at best and were probably the reason some secretary hadn't come out to shoo them away.

"Wait. Let me go first." Ian stepped in front of her, leading the way.

"I'm a wolf, Ian. I can protect myself pretty well." She let him lead though. Something about the scents in this corridor were making her hackles rise. "Listen, whatever we find down there, I want you to listen to me, okay? Something's really off."

Ian gulped. "Should we call Jonah?"

She frowned, sniffing the air once more. "I don't think so. Not yet, anyway."

He took a deep breath and began walking forward. "First whiff of a you-know-what and I'm dialing."

"Agreed." Carol followed closely behind Ian, her eyes practically closed as she tracked the disturbing scent signature with her other senses. "We're getting close."

"We're just outside custodial." Ian opened the door.

Carol shivered. "It's much stronger here." Going on instinct, she pushed Ian behind her. "I lead now."

"Any idea what it is you're sensing?"

"Nope, other than it's giving me the heebies."

"Right." Ian whipped out his phone. "Calling Jonah now."

A hum began to build within her head, drowning out almost everything else. High pitched, the sound vibrated down her spine, causing her to shudder. "Where are you?" She followed the sound, barely aware that Ian was close behind her.

The hum became a whistle as she walked down the hallway. Doors on either side of her held no interest as the sound remained ahead of her. The scents from the crime scene were stronger as well, assaulting her nose with the stench of death and decay.

By the time she reached the end of the hallway, the whistle had become so loud that she had to cover her ears. Higher pitched than that of a tea kettle, the whistle had become a shriek she couldn't escape from. She crouched down, panting, trying to overcome the pain in her head so she could go on. She couldn't let Jonah down. She couldn't leave Ian unprotected.

She had to find the source and end it before it affected them too.

A cool hand landed on her forehead. Whispered words entered her mind, the language familiar yet mysterious. Golden light infused her, forcing the shriek back down to a tolerable whistle.

Carol opened her eyes, surprised that she'd closed them in the first place. "Jonah?"

He smiled at her gently. "I'm here." He glanced behind him, toward the door she'd stopped in front of. "Is it here?"

She nodded. "It hurts, Jonah."

"Shh." He caressed her cheek, brushing her hair back. "Wait here with Ian. I'll deal with this."

Fuck. That. She stood, almost knocking him on his ass. "I don't think so."

"Yeah, me neither." Ian pushed past her to give Jonah a hand up. "I'm your partner. I've gotta face this shit sooner or later. Besides, I'd rather be at your back than out here alone."

Jonah grunted, clearly annoyed. "Fine. But stay behind me."

She could live with that, for now. But if anything came out of that room to bite him, she was going to rip it to shreds.

She was the only one allowed to lay a paw on Jonah Sound.

Chapter 32

He hadn't even had a chance to get to Rivers's office when Ian's call had come in. "Get here now. Carol's hackles are rising."

He'd practically run, following the pull of her anima until he'd found them. His animus was vibrating in a disturbing way, making him shudder. This definitely wasn't right. Worse, the closer he got, the louder a strange humming sound became. Only it wasn't his ears picking it up. His human range couldn't detect it, but where was it coming from? And why was his animus vibrating along with it? "What's up?"

Carol was shivering, her face pale. "Whatever's behind that door is bad. I *really* don't want to go in there, but I'm sure it's the source of the…" She bit her lip. "Sound? The horrible sensations?"

Jonah stared at the door in front of him. Nothing marked what was behind it. No plaque, no number, no exit sign. Nothing. It was a blank door at the end of the custodial hallway.

So where did it go?

Jonah opened it cautiously, his senses humming along with Carol's. The sound was in her mind, unheard by those without the spark of active magic. He winced at the increasing decibel level. He'd managed to tone it down before, but he couldn't force it away from her. Instead, he'd taken half of it himself, allowing him to perceive what she did. As her sorcerer, it was something only he could do.

"Any idea what's in there?" Ian had a flashlight in one hand and his service pistol in the other.

"None. Just stay close, and don't shoot any professors." Jonah stepped into the room, fully expecting to be attacked the moment he did so.

The room was dark, filled with metal shelves, dusty boxes, and cleaning supplies. Larger than he'd first thought, it appeared to be some sort of storage room. He felt along the wall to his right for a light switch, flipping it when he did.

The light was dim, barely illuminating the room. He squinted at the light fixtures, checking if they were lit or not.

They were, but something else in the room was keeping it from reaching the floor. Jonah moved farther into the room, his animus thrumming along his skin in response to whatever was in this room with them.

"It's getting louder again." Carol's voice was strained. He peered back at her, noting how her freckles were even more prominent against her pale skin.

"Can you tell which direction it's coming from?" Because he couldn't. It was too pervasive.

"No, but the scents…" She lifted her face and closed her eyes, sniffing at the air. "I think it's that way."

Ian shone his light in the direction she pointed. "There are just more shelves."

"Let's check it out." Jonah began navigating through the shelves, following Carol's directions. The farther they went, the deeper the twilight became. The whistling sound became closer to a shriek once more. If Carol had come in here without the spell that had allowed him to share her pain, the decibel level might have killed her.

Following the source of the sound, he navigated around the metal shelves, trying to use both his magical and human senses to detect the source. Ian was beginning to wince, showing that the sound was even beginning to affect non-magical beings.

Jonah had no idea how anyone could be in this room without being affected by the sound, even non-sorcerers. It was spine-chilling the closer he got to it. Goose bumps erupted all over his arms, his animus rising in protest to the vibrations emanating throughout the room. There was a shadow creeping into the spaces around him, tendrils of dark and gray that frightened him more than anything he'd ever encountered.

"Jonah?" Carol clutched at his sleeve, her fingers digging into his arm. Her anima was entwining closer to his, almost hiding beneath his own. If she'd been in wolf form, she would have been crouched, her tail tucked between her legs and her teeth bared. She'd also have tried to push him behind her. Not that he'd have allowed that. "We're close."

He glanced at her. Carol's nose was wrinkled as if she smelled something foul. "What are you sensing?"

"Death. Decay." She lifted her face, her expression one of utter disgust. "It smells like rot."

Shit. Shit, shit, shit. He'd understood that this was possible, but he'd never before met anyone who had to deal with it. "Breach."

Carol blanched just as Ian gasped. "You mean…"

"Terra Noctem is coming through somehow." He glanced around. "A pinhole in the Veil between our world and theirs would make this sound."

"Like if we were in space and someone put a pin-sized hole in our ship." Ian moved ahead of them. "Even I can feel the pressure difference, and it's freaking me out."

"Carol."

She sat immediately, closing her eyes. Her essence began to wrap around him in a less frightened way, shoring up his power. He'd need every ounce she could give him before they were done.

"Ian, guard the door. Don't let anyone in."

"What about out?" Ian put his hand on his service weapon.

Jonah grimaced. "If anything gets out of that hole, we'll have a lot more to worry about than you guarding the door."

"Shit." Ian loped off, presumably to take up position in front of the door.

Jonah opened his senses, following the trail to where the pinhole was. Dear Lady, it was horrifying. The shadows moved in sinuous ways, tentacles of gray slithering through the air, reaching for Jonah. He batted them away, his hands glowing as he contemplated the hole in reality he'd found.

This was going to be tricky. "Carol!"

Soon enough, she was standing beside him. She took his hand instinctively. He had to wonder if she understood how much closer this would make their bond. He'd need to be as tightly tied to her as possible, and vice versa, for this to work, or one of them could get sucked through the hole. He could barely keep the tendrils off of him as it was.

A terrible thought occurred to him. Had anyone gone missing? The hole was so small that anyone going through would die a horrible death.

No, not possible. Terra Noctem was coming through, not sucking in Terra Mundus. If anything, the room would repel the living, much like it had Ian. The man couldn't get away fast enough, and he *knew* what was happening. If they didn't, or couldn't sense the magic flowing through that hole, they'd get the sensation that for some reason they shouldn't be there. The hair on the nape of their neck would stand up, goose bumps would run up and down their arms, and an inexplicable chill would cause them to leave so quickly that they'd run for the exit before they even realized their feet had moved.

He took a deep breath, studying the hole. Some things required caution. This…this would require brute force. If that hole stretched even a millimeter wider, it would take several sorcerers to close it.

He raised the hand held tightly in Carol's. Their magic hummed through him, singing the song of life itself. He spoke, a language even he didn't fully comprehend as the magic flowed, guiding him in healing the wound in the Veil.

That was part of learning to control his magic. He had to learn when to let go, to let it guide him in the task at hand and when it needed to be guided. This time, he had to allow it to be what it needed, guiding and shaping it in the right direction. Instinctually, he raised his free hand, pulling from Carol's magic as well as his own to create a healing patch that would slowly dissipate over time.

It took everything he had to remain upright as the hole attempted to pull his magic through rather than allowing the patch. Damn, it was worse than he'd originally thought. If he fell now, Ian would have to come back with a fucking posse of sorcerers.

He couldn't allow himself to fall. Not while he was linked so closely to Carol that he could make out her wolf whimpering in fear. He'd drag her into the void with him no matter how strongly he struggled against it.

Their anima and animus blended even more closely together as he forced the anima to flow. Amber light swirled around his outstretched hand. The battle cry of a wolf echoed in his ears, almost drowning out the high-pitched whistle. He could scent the dust in the room, the decay and death coming from the hole, and almost gagged. For just a second, he understood what it was to run on four legs instead of two.

What the fuck was going on?

Jonah did his best to ignore the sensations bombarding him and concentrated on the patch. An ankh appeared in the swirling amber as he imposed his will on their combined magic, forcing it toward the pinhole.

The flow slowed as the patch settled, closing the hole. Amber magic smoothed over the tiny, jagged edges, blending into the world of Mundus. He would have to ask the dean to keep an eye on the patch. The fact that it was an ankh that appeared confirmed who'd created the breach.

Their murderer's ritual was ripping through the Veil. Whether intentional or not, the stakes had gone way higher than Jonah had anticipated when he'd first come on the case.

Letting the magic go, Jonah hit the ground, passing out before he could even take a breath.

Chapter 33

Carol groaned, her head hurting so badly she was afraid to open her eyes. Nausea roiled through her, making her reluctant to move. She couldn't remember what she'd done to cause herself to suffer like this, but whatever it was she was never, ever doing it again.

Ever.

"Carol? You awake?" The quiet, concerned voice sounded familiar, but Carol couldn't quite place it. "I swear, if you killed her, Jonah, I'm going to hurt you."

"I didn't, Mom, I swear." A warm, masculine hand gripped hers. Magic flowed over her, driving some of the pain into the background. His scent wrapped around her, calming both her and her wolf.

Her mate was there, taking away her agony. She opened her eyes, smiling softly, even that much movement making her wince. "Hi." Beyond Jonah, she caught a glimpse of an unfamiliar dresser, a doorway, and Jonah's mother, Tanya.

"Hey, pretty lady." With his free hand, he pushed her curls off her forehead. "How are you feeling?"

"Like a giant decided I'd make an excellent hacky sack." Even her hair hurt. "What the hell happened?"

Jonah winced. "I, uh, closed the hole in the Veil."

"And almost killed you both in the process." Jonah's mother stepped into view, scowling fiercely at her son. "You should have called for help."

"I thought I could handle it before it got to the point of needing multiple sorcerers." Jonah's voice was as quiet as his mother's, but the contrition was clear as day. "I'm sorry, my little wolf. I pulled too much mana from you."

"And yourself. If not for Ian you'd both still be in that room, unconscious." Tanya's scowl wobbled. "We had to call Lessa and Rose and pool our magic to save you."

Carol bit her lip. "It was that bad?" Sorcerers who became doctors often had to deal with mana drain. They would pool their mana together, forcing it into the patient to relieve the symptoms. Too much mana loss would result in death. And to involve Rose, who didn't even use mana but the ley lines, adding foreign energy into the mix?

No wonder Tanya was upset. Jonah really had almost killed them.

Tanya nodded firmly. "Yes. Ian got someone to help him carry you both to the car and then drove you both here."

"Why not a hospital?" Carol attempted to sit up, but Jonah stopped her with a hand on her shoulder.

"You are in a hospital, sweetie." Tanya smiled, but the expression was strained. "The doctors couldn't get you to accept their animus, so it was thought that family would be better. They believe your wolf was behind the rejection because of your strong link to Jonah."

That made some sense. Her wolf considered Jonah their mate, so none other than family would do. If Sawyer, her brother, had been there, he might have been able to help, but he would have needed assistance as well, since he was also a familiar.

Now that her senses were beginning to work, she could smell antiseptic and sickness all around her. "This room is really nice for a hospital."

"Only the best for my son's familiar." She glared at Jonah, making the man hunch his shoulders against her displeasure. "You take better care of your familiar, you hear? You know better than to pull too much magic from her. You could have damaged her wolf."

"Yes, Mom."

"Don't *yes, Mom* me. Do you want the House to forcibly break your contract?" Those caught abusing their familiars often got sanctioned. One of those sanctions would be breaking the familiar contract, either with or without the familiar's consent.

"No!" Despite the pain, Carol sat straight up. She growled, her wolf coming out as she hopped out of bed and pushed Jonah to the ground. She crouched over him, growling fiercely.

No one would take him from her. They could die while trying.

Tanya backed up, her eyes wide. "Oh." She held up her hands. "I'm not the one who will do it, but the doctors will report this."

Carol snarled. Fuck that shit. If she claimed Jonah, no one would be able to separate them, not even the House. She leaned down, sniffing at his neck and licking a line from his Adam's apple to his chin.

"Hey, little wolf. Can you let me up now?"

Growling again, she stared right into his pretty hazel eyes.

"I guess that would be no?" Warm, golden light surrounded her, attempting to soothe her.

The threat of separation was too great. Her wolf refused to back down, not on this, not ever.

"Jonah, don't move. I'm getting your father." Tanya slipped out of the room.

Carol huffed and sat on Jonah's midriff.

"Oof." Jonah dug his hands into her fur, scratching her behind her ears. "Who's a pretty girl."

Carol chuffed. She wanted to be miffed at the term, but the skritches behind her ears were just too good.

"Think you can get off me? I'm having trouble breathing."

Nope. She liked being on top of him too much to move, but she could compromise. Carol moved down his body until she sat on his thighs.

"Or you could do that." Jonah sat up, smiling widely. "Goof."

Carol lay down, her head at his crotch.

"Watch the teeth, Cujo." Jonah sat up, leaning over her as he petted her back. "Don't worry. No one will take me from you. I swear." His power pulsed, growing stronger as it swirled around her, mingling with her own. "When we closed that hole, our magic became one. We're bonded now." He tapped her paw, right where her tattoo was. "Change back, and you'll see."

Carol did as told and lifted her head. Being that close to Jonah's package while in wolf form was one thing. Being that close in human form was just asking for trouble, especially since she could already sense Tanya and Benjamin coming down the hallway. She glanced down at her wrist, wriggling in delight.

The House symbol was gone, replaced by two crossed wands with a howling wolf beneath. Under the wolf was Jonah's name.

It was something familiars only dreamed of, a fairy-tale come to life. It was like winning Willy Wonka's golden ticket.

She clenched her hands to keep from wrapping them around him. She was afraid if she did, she'd never let him go. "We're one."

Jonah grinned. "Yup." He put his arms around her waist. "So, no more talk of us being separated, right, Mom?"

Carol jumped, peeking over Jonah's shoulder to find Tanya and Benjamin staring at them in shock. "Hi."

"You're soul-bonded?" Benjamin whistled. "I've heard of that, but it's so rare that I've never met a soul-bound couple before." He entered the room and knelt at their side. "Welcome to the family, Carol."

"Thanks." She caressed the mark on her wrist. "He's my mate."

"I kinda figured." Benjamin winked at her. "Especially when Tanya told me how you reacted."

"I had no idea," Tanya huffed. It was obvious that if she'd been in her eagle form, her feathers would have been ruffled. As eagles were apex predators, not much could throw them off their game. Finding out her son was soul-bonded seemed to be one of the few things that could. "I thought soul-bonding was a myth."

Benjamin waved his hand at Carol and Jonah. Carol startled back. If not for Jonah's arms around her waist she would have fallen off his lap. "Meet the myth." He frowned thoughtfully. "I wonder... Could your proximity to Terra Noctem while closing the rift have caused this?"

"Who knows? It's not my field of expertise." Jonah chuckled, then tapped Carol on the nose. "Think you can stand?"

"Maybe?" Her headache was fading, so that was a good thing. "I did as a wolf, anyway."

"Let's check out if you can do it as a woman." Benjamin stood and held out his hand. "C'mon, kiddo. Once the doc clears you, we can take you home."

Carol took his hand and allowed him to pull her to her feet. She wobbled a bit, but Benjamin helped steady her.

Jonah pulled her tightly to him the moment he was on his feet. Carol didn't want to protest the change. Cuddling with Jonah was on her top ten list of favorite things to do.

It even beat out makeup shopping.

Speaking of which, she needed to call her bestie and tell her what had happened. Stacey was going to flip her lid once she found out. She should also double-check with Jonah if that was all right. She didn't want to jeopardize either his career or the investigation. "Can I tell people about this?"

Again, Benjamin appeared shocked, but Jonah merely smiled. "Shout it to the world if you want. Hell, tattoo it on your forehead."

"Will that affect the investigation at all?"

Jonah frowned as if that thought hadn't occurred to him. "No, but we might become very attractive targets to blood mages."

"Or less attractive," Benjamin interrupted, his tone far more thoughtful than Jonah's near growl. "It will be damn near impossible to drain Jonah without also draining Carol and vice versa." He held up his hand before Jonah could give him the reply Carol could practically envision vibrating through him. Jonah didn't like that thought one bit. "However, together you're stronger than apart. I think any sorcerer attempting to drain you would be in for the shock of their lives." The evil grin that crossed Benjamin's face made Carol take a step back. "And I'd dearly like to witness what happens to them if they try."

It seemed Jonah's alpha tendencies came from his quiet father, not his predator mother.

Chapter 34

"Mm. Mine."

Carol was nuzzling him, nipping at him playfully. She was squirming against him, definitely making him think of things other than dead bodies and soul bonds. If she kept this up, he'd be fucking his new mate in his parents' home in two seconds flat. "You might wanna stop that."

"Stop what?" Her tone might be innocent, but the hand she snaked toward his dick wasn't.

"I don't want to fuck in my parents' house." He might have said that, but for some reason, he found he couldn't stop her from kneeling at his feet. It might have been her innocent yet wicked gaze or the way she gazed up at him so lovingly.

Or it might have been the fingers nimbly pulling down his zipper and fishing his cock out.

Yeah. That might have had something to do with it.

Jonah muttered something under his breath, releasing the magic to lock the bedroom door and put up a "No Trespassing" feel around it. He didn't need his mother knocking...

His...

Holy *shit*, she could suck cock.

Carol had wrapped her lips around the crown of his cock, driving all thought from his head other than *more* and *mine*. He grasped her head, holding her right where she was, showing her without words just how much he was enjoying her ministrations.

"Mm." The vibration of her moan shivered through him, making him tighten his grasp on her. She didn't complain, didn't pull back, just sucked harder. Her tongue caressed the underside of his cock, stroked the head, keeping his attention firmly fixed on her.

A bomb could go off, and he was pretty sure he wouldn't care. If he even noticed it.

When the teasing licks and sucks became too much, he began to thrust, keeping it shallow so as not to choke her. He kept his hands buried in her curls despite the need to see her naked.

And why couldn't he? He was a fucking sorcerer after all. What was magic for if not to make his mate naked whenever he wanted?

Jonah grinned and chanted, almost laughing as her eyes went wide in surprise. The suction on his dick stopped for a brief second before resuming, allowing him to enjoy the sight below him.

Pale and pink, perfect for him in every way, Carol embodied everything he'd dreamed of and more.

Part of him wanted to spill into her mouth, let her love on him until they were both satisfied, but that wasn't what he needed. He had to be buried inside her, had to feel her clasping him as she came. Watching her as her orgasm overcame her was becoming one of the greatest delights of his life. He mustered

318

the will to stop himself from overindulging in her soft, warm mouth. "On your feet."

Carol pouted but let him go, standing in front of him without an ounce of embarrassment in her expression. She tilted her head, waiting for him, for his command.

He quivered, anticipating what he would do once he got her on the bed. "Lay down on the bed, but keep your legs over the edge."

She seemed confused but obeyed, draping herself almost exactly as he wanted her. He tugged on her legs, pulling her until she was just the way he wanted her. "Perfect." Kneeling, he kissed her pussy, eager to taste her once more.

Having her come apart under his mouth was his first goal of the day.

He started gently, just licking her in smooth strokes. After a few moments, her hips began to gently rock, her hands drifting over her breasts to play with her nipples. Her eyes were closed, but he could sense that all of her attention was on him, on what he was doing to her body.

It was odd, but the pleasure slowly building inside her echoed in his own body. It wasn't as intense as receiving head, but it was good, so good, that he found himself eagerly pushing his pants off. If he began stroking himself, he'd come when she did, and it would be all over.

He lifted his mouth from her body long enough to remove his shirt, then dove back in. Her soft sighs and moans drove him on, her chants of "yes, please" and "more" telling him when and where to lick and suck to drive her mad.

When she came, he felt it, his dick throbbing with the need to fuck her and find his own release. He held back, wanting more than a quickie. He wanted her to moan under him again the way she had when he'd cast that spell.

Oh, the spell. He should use it again, see how it felt now that their souls were joined. He whispered the words to form the mist, allowing it to flow over both of them instead of just her. He wanted just as much as she did, and he'd indulge himself this time.

Her anima flowed over him, golden and pure, mingling with the darker gold of his until it glowed amber. For a moment, he almost lost control as tendrils of magic wrapped around his dick. Tiny fires licked along his skin, driven by both of them to fulfill their desires. He blew out a breath, bringing himself slowly back under control.

Carol was crying out, her body bowed as the magic crawled along her skin. Her fingers pinched at her nipples, her hips moving erotically, enchanting him. He needed inside her, had to fuck her this instant.

He positioned himself over her and sank into her body, groaning as she came around his cock. Her spasms were so strong he had to hold back, only the tip of his cock in her body. He gritted his teeth. The spell was so much stronger now, so much more intense than he'd anticipated.

"Should I stop it?" He would, if it was too much for her.

"No." Her claws dug into the bedspread. "Don't you fucking dare." She bared her teeth—no, fangs—at him and snarled. "I will end you if you do."

He was in no mood to disobey. "Yes, ma'am." For once he'd let her run the show, allow her to be the one in control.

Her teeth receded, becoming human once more. "Good boy." She shifted, drawing him deeper into her warmth. "You can fuck me now."

The evil leer she shot him was belied by the laughter she was barely holding back. "Definitely my treat," he replied, finally sinking all the way in.

She was so tight, so hot, he had to close his eyes. Tendrils of magic drifted over him, making him gasp. When he opened his eyes, hers were wolf-gold, enticing him closer.

He kissed her, not caring whether or not her teeth were human or wolf. He was so deep inside her his balls were pressed up against her, not a millimeter between them. "It's gonna be quick and hard."

She nodded, panting, her breasts already covered in a fine sheen of sweat. She gave him a shaky thumbs-up. "Go for it."

He couldn't help but chuckle. Even now, when they were both so turned on that he could barely see straight, she managed to make him laugh.

Jonah grabbed hold of her thighs, lifting her legs up so he could anchor himself in her. He stood, pulling her to him as he fucked her hard and fast, driving them both closer and closer to the edge. He sunk into her over and over again, the slap of flesh and their moans filling the room. Amber magic stroked his skin, directed not by thought but by instinct. He bent forward, putting his hands on the mattress, her legs moving until they rested on his arms. He couldn't think beyond the overwhelming necessity of fucking this particular woman. He had to come inside her, fill her, listen to her scream his name until the whole world understood just who she belonged to.

Carol grabbed hold of his forearms, her nails digging into his flesh, stings that were wiped away by the climax that hovered just out of reach. His legs nearly gave way when she cried out, her whole body tightening around him, squeezing him tight. He grunted, his orgasm ripped from him by hers, thrust after thrust, spilling inside her until there was nothing left of him but his peak.

"I fucking love that spell," Carol panted. At least he thought it was Carol. He couldn't quite see yet, and hearing was optional.

"Science rocks," he replied, smiling at his own breathless voice. He nuzzled something covered in soft curls, pretty sure it was her head.

"We need to experiment more often." Warm arms encircled him, holding him tight.

Jonah opened his eyes. "There you are."

She shook her head. "Silly man."

He cocked a brow at her, some of his senses returning now that the incredible climax was over. "Silly, huh?" He tickled her side, earning not only a giggle but a firm clasp from her pussy.

Jonah groaned. "Jesus, woman. Are you trying to kill me?"

"Nope." She kissed him softly. "Just love on you."

"Mm." He tugged on one of her curls. "Mine."

Unexpectedly she sighed, her gaze dreamy. "Yours."

Chapter 35

Once downstairs the following morning, Jonah stretched. Last night had been unbelievably good. They might not have made any more progress on the campus killer case, but making love to Carol was nirvana. He'd been able to experience everything she did through their bond, making the whole thing that much more intimate. He'd taken her twice last night, talking softly in between bouts of mind-blowing sex about anything that popped into their heads.

Turned out they both loved playing fantasy-based video games. Jonah was a chocolate chip ice cream lover, while Carol loved cherry vanilla drizzled in hot fudge.

And she had a beauty mark on the back of her thigh that made him crazy.

He needed to call her House and register their bonding. Carol was officially off the fucking market for the rest of their lives. If he had his way, she'd be his even in the afterlife.

He'd never been so possessive of someone before, but he couldn't help it. She'd rocked his world, and now he wanted to hand it to her on a golden platter.

"Jonah?"

He turned to find a sleep-rumpled goddess gliding down his staircase. "Good morning, sweetheart."

She smiled, so shy and cute his teeth ached. He wanted to leave his mark on her in some way like she had him. The spot

324

where she'd bitten him had already begun to scar. His shirt kept brushing against it, making him more than aware of its presence. Every time it happened the sensation that his mate was touching him distracted him. He'd need to learn to work with it, as it would be impossible to ignore it.

Carol glanced toward the kitchen. "Please tell me you made coffee?"

He whimpered. "Oh, god. Coffee." Right. *That's* what he'd been planning to do before he got distracted by thoughts of his new mate.

"I'll take that as a no." She moved past him into the kitchen. She was wearing a pair of sleep shorts so small the bottom of her delectable ass was practically hanging out. Her tank top moved as her breasts bounced underneath it. Even her bare feet demanded his attention. She'd painted her toenails a bright metallic purple.

How had he missed that last night?

She started the coffee, yawning into her fist as the first cup began to brew. "What's on the agenda for today?"

He grimaced. "Work, work, work." He wrapped his arms around her from behind, grinning when she leaned back against him. "Is that all that's on your mind?"

"As much as I'd like to spend the day in bed, we have to earn our keep."

"Damn it. Stupid mortgage." He kissed her shoulder when she giggled and stood back, releasing her. "We need to go over to the campus and begin interviewing students, as well as follow up on that lead that Dean Anthony gave you about Chief Rivers. After that, we need to head to the precinct and check up on some of our other cases." No matter how much he wanted to concentrate solely on the campus murders, he couldn't let his other cases slide. Carol needed to catch up on where he was with them. So far, she'd been a trooper, combing through records and notes without too much complaint.

"Gotcha." She pulled the cup toward her and started the next one, putting the pod in before starting the machine. "The students have to be freaked out."

"I would be, if I were them." Jonah waved her away when she went to hand him the cup. "You have that one, I'll take the next."

"Thank you." She added sugar and an ungodly amount of creamer. "Coffee makes my world go around."

"Hmm." When the maker was done, he pulled his own mug free. Watching her savor her morning coffee was a religious experience. She leaned back against the counter, her eyes closed as she sipped at her brew. Her dainty feet were crossed at the ankles, the tiny shorts showing that, despite how short she was, her legs were long and smooth. Her skin had a healthy glow to it, and without makeup, her face appeared younger, more vulnerable. Her curls were clipped up, exposing the back of her neck, the tiny red hairs at the base of her head inviting his fingers.

Jonah rubbed the back of her neck, almost moaning when she leaned into his touch. He could sense her contentment through their bond, the peaceful moment only broken by the ticking of the clock he'd hung on the kitchen wall.

With a sigh, he pulled his hand away. "We need to get ready for the day."

She opened her eyes and smiled at him. "Maybe today's the day we get the clue we need to catch this rat bastard."

"Maybe." He tapped his fingers on the side of his mug. "Something's been bugging me since the other day."

"What?" She stood, rinsing her mug out and preparing another pod. She was a two-cup-a-morning girl, while Jonah preferred to follow up his first cup with juice.

"Why did the pinhole appear in the custodial rooms so far from the ritual space?"

She froze for a moment before pressing the button to start the coffee maker. "Huh. Good point. It should have happened a lot closer to the baseball field, but it was all the way on the other side of the campus."

"Exactly. The power surge that caused the pinhole should have manifested closer to the baseball field. So why there? Why not in, say, the parking lot we use when another body is dumped?"

"Or the stands. Could the ritual space be somewhere else?" She pulled out the fixings for cereal. Apparently, they were going without eggs and toast in favor of a quicker meal. "We need to check out that closet."

327

"Agreed. I'll call Dean Hill and get permission to bring in a few CSI guys. You call our chief and Ian."

"Think we'll need a warrant?" She'd fixed two bowls and handed him one, then went to the fridge and got the juice he preferred.

Jonah took a seat at the table. "Maybe? So far we haven't had issues thanks to Dean Hill being on our side." He quietly thanked her when she handed him his juice. "What's near that custodial hall?"

"We need a map of the building. Or a blueprint." Carol sat across from him, a thoughtful frown on her face. "That, we might need a warrant for, just to make everything kosher."

"We could pick up a student map, but I doubt it will do more than show the buildings."

"There might be interior maps posted inside the building. There were in my alma mater, mostly to show where the fire exits were. We could check for those and photograph them for reference."

"Good idea." Jonah ate some of his cereal, his mind racing. He hadn't been in enough of the building to make a mental map of the place. "Searching the whole building won't make us any friends."

Jonah quickly finished the rest of his breakfast and headed for the stairway. "We need to get dressed and go check this out. Call Ian, tell him to meet us there."

"Got it." She picked up her mug and headed for her bedroom, where her phone was currently charging.

Jonah dressed quickly, barely taking time to brush his teeth and wash his face, let alone shave. That could wait. For now, he had a suspect to question. He made a note of where they were going and why, then headed for his bedroom and called his boss.

As the phone rang, he glanced around. Carol would be moving in as soon as possible. He didn't like that she was in a different bedroom. He needed her in there, with him.

"Hello?" Captain Ford's voice was clipped, professional.

He set aside his plan to hijack her clothing when they got home and put his mind back on work. "It's Jonah. Carol and I are headed to the campus. We need blueprints of the building where the pinhole was."

"Oh?" That had piqued his boss's curiosity.

"Yup. We want to find out what's close to where the pinhole popped up. If we can see the blueprints, we might be able to figure out where the murders took place. We also need to talk to Chief Rivers about the boy that Dean Anthony says he lost."

"Carol already called. Ian's on his way out now to meet you at the campus. He's been here since dawn, going over case notes."

Jonah grinned. He was really beginning to like Ian. "He's a good partner. Carol likes him too."

"Glad to hear it. Keep me posted, and I'll get started on getting your blueprints."

"Yes, ma'am."

"Oh, and Jonah? If you run into another pinhole, *call me*, or I swear to the goddess of magic I'll bust you down to meter maid. Not Carol, not Ian. Just you. Understood?"

Jonah winced. "Yes, ma'am. Loud and clear."

"Good. You risk your familiar again like that, and I'll personally kick your ass." Captain Ford's voice to her normal, no-nonsense demeanor. "Now get said ass in gear, Detective. I expect your call in two hours."

She hung up before he could say goodbye, but she was like that with all of her detectives. If she liked you, she was a mother hen. A very busy, very brusque hen who pecked at anyone who hurt the men and women under her.

Carol strolled through the bedroom door, her shoes in her hand. She'd dressed professionally, her curls bound up at the nape of her neck, her makeup understated but there. She had a pair of sunglasses perched on top of her head, and her badge and ID were hanging between her breasts. "Ready?"

"I am." He opened the cabinet he kept his gun and shoulder holster in, strapping the holster in place before holstering his gun.

Carol grimaced. "You think you'll need that?"

"In a magical college, against a magical opponent? Sometimes using a physical weapon gives me an advantage." He'd surprised more than one blood sorcerer by using his service weapon. For some reason, they seemed to think magic solved all problems.

Carol blew out a breath. "Okay, then. Prep for battle mode."

"Maybe, but be aware all we've got to go on is a hunch that the murders took place near the pinhole." He slid his jacket on and strode past her toward the stairway. "For now, we take notes, check things out. We only arrest him or her once we have enough evidence."

She followed him, her footfalls silent on the wooden steps. "Ian agrees with our hunch. He said, and I quote, 'Well that's suspicious as fuck.'" When they were by the front door, Carol slipped her shoes on.

Jonah reached for his own. "Let's go. Our boss wants a status update in less than two hours."

"Shit."

Jonah opened the front door. "Yeah, she sounded pissed. She's still upset about the pinhole thing."

Her eyes went wide with fear. "Double shit. We should bring donuts as sacrificial offerings."

"And coffee. Lots of coffee." Jonah shut the front door.

"Driving!" Carol took off toward his car, waving his keys and cackling like a loon.

Jonah followed. He was pretty sure he'd follow her even into Terra Noctem.

Chapter 36

Jonah smiled as Carol snapped pictures of the posted maps by the elevators in the administration building. He still wanted blueprints, but they could use this as well to make sure everything matched up.

"She's doing a great job, isn't she? It was like she was born for this." Ian was studying Carol with obvious admiration. "We couldn't have picked a better partner, am I right?"

"What's this 'we' shit?" Jonah glared at Ian. "That's *my* girl over there."

Ian shot him the worst innocent look Jonah had ever seen. If the man had been in the interrogation room, Jonah would have arrested him on the spot. "But we both work with her, so that makes her ours."

Gods, Carol was right. Ian probably didn't look innocent even as an infant. "Keep that up, and you'll find out how good I am at transmutation magic. You never know. You might enjoy life as a frog."

Ian cleared his throat. "Right. Cute redhead is yours."

Jonah patted Ian's arm. "Good boy."

Carol waved them over. "You guys coming or not?"

"Don't say a word," Jonah growled at Ian.

"Mnut fayin anamfin." Ian's lips remained sealed even as he mumbled something unintelligible.

"What's going on?" Carol's glance between the two of them was filled with suspicion.

"Absolutely nothing, sweetheart." Jonah put his arm around her waist and shuffled her into the elevator. "You have any idea what questions you want to ask Chief Rivers?"

"Hmm." Carol tapped her finger on her lips. "I promised Dean Anthony I'd go easy on him. Apparently, the loss of his son is still a painful topic, so we either bulldog it or be delicate."

Ian's brows rose. "Bulldog it?"

"Go in guns blazing. Be pushy assholes. That sort of thing." She frowned. "Although every bulldog I've ever met has been sweet as pie, so I don't get why people use that phrase."

The elevator doors opened, and Ian led the way. "Sometimes I really wish I was a sorcerer just so I could have a familiar." He sighed sadly, putting his hand over his heart. "Maybe I'd find my soulmate too."

Jonah coughed. "It's a good thing you never tried becoming an actor, Ian. You'd suck at it."

Ian blew a raspberry at him, making Carol giggle.

They were nearing Chief Rivers's office. "Game faces, people."

Both Carol and Ian's shoulders straightened as Jonah knocked on the door.

"Enter."

Jonah opened the door. "Chief Rivers? We have some questions for you."

"Come in, come in!" Chief Rivers waved, then pointed to the chairs in front of his desk. The thing was huge, just like the man. "And call me Larry, please."

"Thank you." Jonah, Ian, and Carol sat, Carol starting up her recording device while Jonah took out a paper notepad. "I don't think you've met Ian. Detective Ian Matsumoto, meet Chief Laurence Rivers, head of security here on campus."

"Nice to meet you." Ian shook hands with the chief.

"Nice to meet you too." Chief Rivers sat back, studying them curiously. "What can I do for you?"

"First, I need any security tapes of the destroyed camera over home plate." Jonah was hoping he'd find something useful on the videos.

"Done." Chief Rivers turned to his computer and tapped. "I'll email you the file. It's not that large, so I don't think you'll need to put it on that special thumb drive you've got."

"No withers on the tape?" Ian asked, scribbling already.

"Nope. Just looks like some kids with baseball bats." Chief Rivers shrugged. "I hate to say it, but that happens all the time. Either the high school kids come and vandalize the campus, or Greeks have their pledges do it while wearing stupid-ass masks so we can't identify them."

"Which do you think this was?" Carol leaned forward and placed the recorder on the edge of Chief Rivers's desk.

"Honestly? Greeks." Chief Rivers turned back to them, his hands clasped on the desk. His posture was relaxed, his expression one of easy camaraderie. "You'll see what I mean when you get a glimpse of the masks." He shuddered dramatically. "I never wanted to see a plastic First Lady that close before."

Ian chuckled. "Ah, the good old days."

"You were in a fraternity?" Chief Rivers stared at Ian curiously.

"Chi Pi Sigma. It's small, but it was just for criminal justice students, so it was a lot of fun as well as a great learning opportunity." Ian sighed wistfully. "I kind of miss those days, to be honest."

"I think we all miss college in one way or another," Jonah replied, glancing at Carol to note her reaction. She was smiling, so her college experience must have been a good one. She hadn't talked much about it other than to say she missed it too. Jonah shook off the need to ask her about her campus life. He could do that at home. Right now, he had other things to ask about. "Chief Rivers, I hate to bring this up, but—"

"My son?" The smile left his face. He stared down at his hands, his shoulders slumping. "Frank warned me that you'd be asking about Sean."

"I'm sorry to ask this, but what happened?" Carol's tone was quiet, her brows furrowed in concern.

"Sean was bullied, physically, mentally, and magically." Chief Rivers looked up at Carol, then glanced back down. "You might have noticed, but my family isn't completely human. Our dimen side is giant."

"That's nothing to be ashamed of, Chief." Jonah had met some fine giants in his day. They were larger than humans, stronger, but slower and not as agile. Unlike the myths, they weren't stupid at all. Intellectually, they were a match for humans.

"You know how kids can be, Detective. Anything they view as different is cause for bullying. Sean didn't have any magic, unlike his mother. The kids bullied him for that too."

"Who is his mother?" Ian asked, scribbling furiously.

"Anna. Anna Templeton."

Jonah whistled. Anna Templeton was the Neil deGrasse Tyson of dimensional magics, famous for giving lectures that even non-magical folk could not only understand but enjoy. He'd seen her on television more than once, learning things he hadn't realized he'd needed to. She was a champion of dimen rights, as well, earning Jonah's respect. Rose worshiped the ground Anna Templeton walked on.

"Don't get me wrong. Anna loved Sean as much as I did, but nothing we said or tried got through to him. He got more and more depressed. We took him to a psychologist who suggested we remove him from the school, but the bullying continued online, which we didn't even find out about until after he took his life." Chief Rivers's jaw clenched, his eyes reddening. "He hung himself in the garage. I found him when I came home from work."

"Jeez." Ian stopped scribbling and stared at Chief Rivers, horrified. "Tell me the school did something about it."

Chief Rivers laughed, but it didn't sound at all amused. "Two-week suspension for two of them. Expulsion for the worst offender. Nothing happened to the others. The cops said there was nothing they could do since the laws don't consider bullying someone to death murder."

"Shit." Jonah rubbed his hands over his face. "I'll talk to my mother. Maybe there's something she can do through her work to get the laws changed."

Chief Rivers looked surprised at first, then intensely grateful. "Thank you. My wife and I would appreciate that." He sat up straighter, but his eyes were still red with unshed tears. "Anna has been through hell these last few years. Our daughter has done her best to try and fill in the gap, but that's not something a child should have to attempt. I tell her that over and over. So does Anna, but I'm worried about her. We're going to therapy as a family. Harley, our daughter, wants to work in law. She's determined to get things changed for the better, and I couldn't be prouder of her."

"That's good to hear," Carol replied softly. "If she needs any help, please contact me. I might be able to do something with my familiar contacts. She could listen to their stories as well. She'll find a lot of sympathy among them."

Chief Rivers smiled. "You have no idea how much I appreciate hearing that. My son, he was a good kid. He didn't deserve what happened to him."

"No one does," Ian grunted. He looked pissed off. "Now, for the really hard part, and you have no idea how sorry I am to ask these questions, but I have to."

"I understand, Detective. I truly do. Ask your questions."

"Do you think Anna could be involved in the murders on campus?" Ian was going for the throat on that question.

Chief Rivers looked furious for a moment before his expression blanked. "No. As much as my wife and I miss Sean, we would never deprive another parent of their child."

"Yet her work as an interdimensional sorcerer would be a boon to the ritual currently taking place on campus." Jonah decided to back up Ian's play. "How well does she know the campus?"

"Not that well. She's familiar with this building, but she works for UCLA, so she's not here often." He looked thoughtful now, his brows furrowed, his gaze distant. "She's familiar with how to get to my office, Dean Hill's office, and Dean Anthony's. Other than that, I'd say there's not much more of the campus she's visited."

"Has she ever given a lecture here?" Carol's tone was back to normal, curious yet non-judgmental.

"No." Chief Rivers chuckled his expression bashful yet proud. "We can't afford her."

"Would you mind if we spoke to her?" Jonah wanted to talk to Anna Templeton. If rumors were true, she was more than powerful enough to perform the Apep ritual.

"She's in Wisconsin right now. Has been…" Chief Rivers leaned back in his chair with a relieved expression. "She's been there for over a month, working on a dimensional portal project that would allow us to see into Terra Noctem without actually entering it."

"So, she couldn't have killed our latest victim." Carol, still smiling sweetly at the chief, also seemed relieved. "I have to admit, I've admired her for a long time. However, we'll have to confirm her alibi."

"I have no problem with that." Chief Rivers glanced at his computer and grimaced. "Damn it. I have a meeting with Frank in ten minutes. Is there anything else you need to talk to me about?"

Jonah shook his head. "I think we're done. Thank you, Chief."

"Like I said, call me Larry." The chief stood and held out his hand. "I'll admit, I'm going to miss you guys running around campus stirring up shit. Some of the professors here are real assholes. Watching them squirm has been a pleasure." He winked as Jonah shook his hand. "Once everything's cleared up, I'd love to have a meal with you guys."

"I think we can arrange that." Jonah stood back as his partners took their turns shaking the chief's hand. He even heard Carol quietly apologizing for bringing up Sean's death.

The chief patted her on the shoulder. "You know, familiars sometimes come in here and tell me that their sorcerers are in distress or danger. I've been told to ignore those reports, that they're unreliable." His expression turned stern. "I think from now on I'm going to fucking ignore that order instead."

"Who gave it?" Carol's eyes were wide, but through their link, Jonah understood exactly what she was truly feeling. Excitement.

"Dean Anthony." Chief Rivers's expression turned grim. "He doesn't have a lot of respect for familiars, to be honest. He sees them as extensions of their sorcerers rather than people in their own right, with magic we don't completely understand." He frowned, looking confused. "Why didn't I think of that before?"

Something about the way the chief spoke had Jonah's hackles rising. Jonah took hold of the chief's hand. "Let me check something." He began to tug on Carol's anima, blending it seamlessly with his own. The joy that always jolted through him at their connection filled him, made his magic stronger. He spoke the words of a delicate spell to check for mental tinkering.

There. Two dark spots on the chief's head. The first was in the front left-hand side, the second much deeper. "You need to go to a hospital. Now."

"What?" Chief Rivers looked horrified. "What did you see?"

"Two dark spots on your brain. There are signs of magical tampering, but this spell is far more delicate and long-term than something I feel comfortable dealing with." Jonah shook his head. "Someone's been inside your mind, forcing you to forget certain things."

"Shit." Chief Rivers sat back down so hard his chair squealed. "Will it kill me?"

Jonah shrugged, but he couldn't help but feel concern for the chief. His instincts were screaming that the man, and his family, were innocent. "I don't know, but I'd go now to have it looked at."

"See if they can get a magical signature too. That might tell us who cast the spell." Carol glanced at Jonah, her expression showing all the concern Jonah was experiencing.

"I will." Chief Rivers stood. "I owe you, Jonah."

Jonah waved his hand nonchalantly. "Eh, when you get out of the hospital, buy me a burger, and we're even."

The chief laughed as he picked up the phone. "It's a date."

Jonah led Ian and Carol out of the chief's office. "You thinking what I'm thinking?"

"We need more proof that Dean Anthony is responsible before we can arrest him." Ian was scowling furiously as he stomped toward the elevator. "If we took him in now, he'd wiggle his way free before we could say 'lawyer up.'"

"Let's investigate his family situation. What do we know about his wife? What sort of accident took his daughter?" Jonah waited with his partners for the elevator to arrive. "Let's make sure we take this fucker down hard."

"Agreed." Carol, her lip curled up, was showing fang.

Jonah was a sick, sick bastard, but damn. That was hot as hell. He put his arm around her shoulders and whispered in

341

her ear. "Put that away, sweetheart. We don't want someone else seeing it."

She appeared confused. "Huh?"

He chuckled. "Don't you realize? Your fangs turn me on."

Her cheeks turned bright red. "You're so strange."

"Yup." He settled her comfortably against him. "And you love every minute of it."

All he could do was laugh when she snarled playfully at him.

Ian, like the good boy he'd promised to be, said absolutely nothing.

Chapter 37

Once back in the precinct, Carol called the best person she could think of to help her track down Dean Anthony's dead child. Ian was working on the blueprint warrants, and Jonah was… Actually, she wasn't sure what Jonah was up to, but she doubted he was sitting there playing Tiddlywinks.

"Hey, Carol, what's up?"

"Hi, Debbie. Listen, I need your help tracking down a death certificate."

"Really? Whose?" Debbie seemed curious.

Carol stared at the memorial page she'd managed to dig up on a social media site. "It's the child of a suspect."

"What's her name?" Debbie was pure professional now, the sound of a keyboard tinny through the phone.

"Megan Anthony. She was twelve when she passed, and I was told it was in an accident."

"Date of death?"

Carol read off the date of death from the social media site. "Can you expedite this?" She scrolled through message after message of condolences, looking for anything from the parents. "It has something to do with the campus murder case."

"The death was recent enough that it's already been added to our database…ah. Here we go. Megan Anthony. What do you need to know?"

"First, I need you to email me that death certificate, and if possible, Paul's notes. Second, what's the cause of death?"

"It's listed as accidental, just as you said."

"Is the type of accident listed as well?" Carol waved Jonah off when he tapped her on the shoulder.

"Let me check." She heard more typing as Debbie did as asked. "Ah. It seems she died from magical overload."

"Huh." Carol had been thinking car accident or maybe drowning, not magical overload. "What's her species sub-type listed as? Sorcerer, familiar, vamp, or dimen?"

"That's interesting. Familiar."

"Familiar?" Carol sat up straight, her mind racing.

"Don't see a lot of those dying of magical overload. Usually, our animal halves protect us by forcing the excess magic into the earth."

She glanced up at Jonah, who was frowning at her curiously. "She was *twelve*, Debbie. How does a twelve-year-old familiar, who's never had their first bond, die of magical overload?"

Jonah's eyes went wide in shock.

"Shit. Someone was using her, someone she wasn't bound to. She couldn't have been." Carol was beginning to shake with rage. "She was too young to form a bond. Her animal would have refused it no matter who it was."

"Which means the magic was forced on her from an outside force." Debbie's tone had turned frosty, indicating she too was angry as hell. "The father or the mother?"

Carol couldn't say anything, not until they had proof that Dean Anthony had been grossly abusing his child. "I can't tell you."

"Hmph. Fine. But I want the full story once you've caught the bad guy, got it? Let me know if you need any further information. I can talk to Paul, see if he remembers anything about the girl's case."

"Thanks, I'd appreciate that." It was good to have an in with the wife of the chief medical examiner.

"You're welcome." Debbie sounded sulky, but the next moment, she seemed full of delight. "Oh, before you go, guess what?" Carol could envision her friend bouncing in her seat.

"You pierced your nipple?" She winked at Jonah, who was once again staring at her in surprise.

"I…what? No! Ding, dong, the bitch is gone, baby!" Debbie began to crow in triumph.

"Oh. Is that all?"

"Is that all, she says. Hmph. Paul finally fired the bitch. She went too far when she insulted one of the board of supervisors. Apparently, she didn't recognize him and treated him like dirt, all because he was wearing a T-shirt and jeans. The man complained, and poof! The office now runs efficiently thanks to a competent person holding the post."

"Congratulations." Carol shook her head, amused at Debbie's unholy joy.

Debbie cackled again. "We can have a celebratory lunch later this week, okay?"

"Sounds most excellent." Carol said her goodbyes and turned to Jonah. "So, Megan Anthony died of magical overload."

"I heard some of that." Her computer dinged, indicating she'd received an email. She opened it and, with Jonah reading over her shoulder, began to go over the death certificate and notes she'd asked for. "Burns across the left side of her face, down her arms to her hands. Part of her brain was turned to mush."

"The part where our magic resides. She was completely burned out." Jonah cursed softly. "What the fuck was he doing with her?"

"What if it wasn't him but his wife? We don't have any information on her, do we?" Carol glanced up at him to find his face mere inches from hers. She had the urge to lick him, so she did.

He reared back in disbelief. "What the hell?"

She giggled. "I licked it, so it's mine."

He rolled his eyes. "I've been yours, you silly pup." He leaned over her again. "Look at this." He pointed to something in the notes she hadn't seen before.

"A signature." She leaned forward, squinting slightly as even through an email the signature squirmed in front of her eyes almost as if it were alive and not happy to be viewed. "Is it me, or does it look exactly like the one Lessa translated for us?"

"Apep, Lord of Rebirth." Jonah stood up. "It's definitely our killer's signature."

"What the fuck, Jonah? I thought the ritual was to bring someone back to life, but if he was using it before this whole thing even began…"

"Yeah. We're going to have to rethink everything. If it wasn't his daughter he wants to bring back, then who the fuck is it?"

"We need to go farther back, look into his past. Maybe an old lover, another child, even a parent." Jonah grabbed a sticky note and began jotting down notes. "Anyone else you can think of?"

"A bonded familiar?" Carol leaned back in her chair, thinking. "If he'd created a strong bond and then lost that familiar, wouldn't he want that one back?"

"He has no real love for familiars, remember? Which might be why he was so willing to use his daughter the way he did." Jonah ditched the sticky notes and grabbed his notepad. "Did he have a child who was a sorcerer and lost him?"

Carol began to click on the social media pages. "If so, there might be something here. Check birth records for the county. I'll find out where he was born. Maybe something's there."

"Good idea." Jonah ruffled her hair as he returned to his desk. "Good work running this down, Carol."

Her cheeks began to heat at the praise. "Thanks." She hunched over, concentrating on looking for evidence in his social media pages that Frank Anthony had lost a sorcerer child.

An hour later, she was beginning to think that he hadn't. She decided to find out where the man had been born. She started by searching records of his alma mater, discovering that he'd gotten his degree in UC San Diego. From there, she was able to track his home town to Fremont, California. She then searched the public records and confirmed that, yes, Frank Anthony had been born in Fremont to Harvey Anthony, a high school teacher, and Kelly Ann Anthony (née Wallace), a housewife. She leaned back, stretching her arms over her head. She groaned as her stiff shoulders burned with the movements.

She moaned even more as strong hands began massaging her shoulders. "Thanks."

"You're welcome," Jonah murmured. He dug his thumbs into a particularly nasty spot, making her twitch.

"Ow." She leaned her head against his stomach and looked up at him. "What did you find out?"

"No other children, but Ian got us the blueprints. Found something interesting on them while you were working your Google-Fu."

"Oh?" She sighed as her muscles finally began to relax under his skilled fingers.

"The spot where the pinhole formed was under Dean Anthony's office."

She stiffened again, causing Jonah's massage to turn painful. "Owie."

"Relax, sweetheart. This is just one piece of the puzzle, remember?"

"Could he have been killing them in his office?" Carol tried to picture the man's workplace in her mind but couldn't figure out where such a ritual would take place. "Or could he be using a space just below his office but just above the pinhole?"

Jonah's hands froze before he lifted them away. "Good question. What *is* below his office?" He returned to his desk, clicking furiously.

Carol stood, stretching her whole body upward. Gods, it felt good to stand.

"Jeez, woman, don't do that unless we're alone." Jonah was staring at her, his gaze roaming over her until she was once more blushing. Through their bond, she could sense his desire beginning to rise.

"Down, boy." She crossed her arms over her breasts. "We still have work to do."

"Slave driver." Jonah turned back to his computer. "Huh."

"What?" She crossed to his side of the desk and glanced over his shoulder. "Well. What do you know? Looks like it's a storage closet."

"Think we should send in CSI?" Jonah's expression was sinful.

"Most definitely."

Jonah picked up the phone. "Boss? We need a warrant…"

Chapter 38

Carol watched avidly as the CSI guys got to work, sifting through everything in the room. Plastic gloves and little plastic baggies were very much in evidence as they did their best not to contaminate the scene. They even sprayed luminol and used black-lights in the room.

Unfortunately, they found very little blood evidence, but they did find hairs and fibers that they were carefully gathering in little baggies. Jonah was talking to one of the guys who was taking pictures of everything, being very careful not to touch a thing. Ian was taking notes while speaking with another investigator.

Carol had chosen to remain just outside the room to help field the curious. Dean Hill had accepted the warrant with grace and was also in the corridor, making sure none of the staff gave the crime scene investigators trouble.

"Heard from Chief Rivers?" Ian stood beside her, watching the staff watch them.

"Nope. It's been a couple of days. I hope he's okay." She glanced over at Ian. "I did confirm he's at the hospital, however, and his wife and daughter are with him. He's getting those magical growths taken care of."

"I thought his wife was working on a pretty sensitive project."

"Seems she thinks her husband is more important than her contract." Carol turned back to the staff to see Dean Hill and Dean Anthony arguing. "Hmm. I spy with my little eye, something that begins with B.S."

"Oh, I know! Bullshit." Ian clapped his hands. "What do I get for winning?"

"You get to help Dean Hill keep Dean Anthony out of here."

Ian groaned, but instead of arguing he headed toward the duo.

"Excuse me, Ms. Voss?" One of the technicians had taken Ian's place.

"Yes?" She tilted her head, wondering why the technician looked so nervous. Was it because she was a wolf, or because she was Jonah's partner?

The man was frowning, but not in distaste of her. It looked more…academic? Curious? "I hate to disturb you, but I think we could use your nose."

Her brows rose. "My nose?" She glanced back into the storeroom, realizing what it was he wanted from her. "Not a problem. You want me to sniff out something specific, or am I scenting things in general?"

The man immediately relaxed. "A little bit of both, actually. I think there's something in a specific spot, but I don't want to prejudice you. By all means, sniff all over the place."

"And if I happen to find something else in the meanwhile, that would just be peachy keen, right?" Carol winked at the investigator, hoping he'd relax.

It must have worked because his smile was wide and conspiratorial. "Exactly."

She stepped into the storeroom, wrinkling her nose at the smell of all the different people. It would be much stronger once she shifted.

"Need me to clear the room?" The investigator was once more watching her warily.

"Nah." She glanced back at the cameraman. "In fact, make sure the guy with the camera follows me, taping everything I do. I don't want anyone to say we planted any evidence."

The guy nodded. "I'll set that up." His gaze roamed over her body, utterly methodical. There was not a hint of desire in his eyes. "Do you need to strip, or can you change with your clothes on?"

In response Carol shifted, apparently startling him enough that he took a step back. She sat, wagging her tail and allowing her tongue to hang out. Look at the pretty, goofy dog. No predators here, just someone looking for a belly rub and a treat.

The guy laughed, albeit shakily, and gestured toward the room. "After you, ma'am."

Carol woofed, stood, and strode into the storeroom. Behind her, she heard two sets of footsteps following, one of which must be the photographer with the video camera. She glanced behind her, ensuring that yes, it was the technician and the camera guy.

"Carol?" Jonah knelt before her, stroking her ears. He glanced up at the investigator, his tone going from fond to frigid. "Why is my familiar shifted?"

She caught the sound of the investigator swallowing before he replied, "Um, we, I mean I, thought her sense of smell might be useful, Detective Sound."

Jonah turned his attention back to her, his expression once more tender. "Do you agree?"

She woofed and licked his chin.

"Goofy pup." Jonah rubbed her ears again before standing. "Fine. I'm going to go speak to the staff and find out who had access to this room."

She nodded, padding past him as he left. She had her own job to do, and Jonah could take care of himself out there. Besides, Ian was there, keeping the peace between Dean Hill and Dean Anthony.

And if anything *were* to happen to Jonah, she'd sense it through their bond.

Carol put her nose to good use, sniffing everything and anything that crossed her path. She scented a minute amount of blood, ash, soot, and the faint stench of feces and urine, both animal and human. The building had a mouse problem, but human excrement shouldn't be here. She rubbed her nose with her paw to keep from sneezing—and thus contaminating the scene—and kept going.

The scent of death and decay became stronger in the back portion of the room. It was familiar. She could almost taste the desiccated flesh of the wither as its scent danced across her senses. Mingled in with it was the scent of ash, soot, and Dean Anthony. She shifted. "The wither's been here, several times. I also scent Frank Anthony."

The investigator nodded. "We'll check this area more thoroughly, thanks."

"Was this where you expected me to head?"

The investigator shook his head. "Nope. We had a luminol hit over there. What lit up was shaped like what looked like hieroglyphs."

She immediately shifted and headed where he'd pointed, sniffing at the ground for any clue as to what would have drawn hieroglyphs.

The investigator was right. Whatever they looked like they were definitely drawn in blood, but so thinly that she'd ignored it as background noise among the stronger scents. She shifted again. "I need a picture of the hieroglyphs and anything else you find that's out of place."

The investigator nodded. "We can do that." He glanced around. "Anything else catch your interest?"

Carol shook her head. "Sorry, no. It's all so jumbled up in here that only that spot called to me."

"Then I think that's it. If you want to join your partners, we've got things from here. I'll call you back in if we find an area where we need your olfactory senses again." He held out his hand. "Thank you, Ms. Voss. I appreciate the help."

"No problem. If you need me, you know where I'll be." Carol headed out into the hallway, surprised to find more staff outside the room rather than less. Ian appeared harried as he worked with a uniformed officer to keep the crowd away from the doorway.

Worse, it appeared there were fucking journalists beyond the staff. Dean Hill was currently speaking to them, but Carol couldn't quite make out what she was saying. She'd need to shift to do so, and she didn't want to do that in front of this crowd. Outing herself as a familiar could lead to being interrogated herself. The last thing she wanted was to be stuck talking to journalists. Instead, she joined Ian, who was holding people back. "Where's Jonah?"

Ian nodded toward the left of Dean Hill. "Being the face of our little trio." There was Jonah, speaking to the journalists with an ease she envied. Every once in a while, he would gesture toward where she was standing. He was either talking about the CSI guys, or about their relationship, but over the other sounds around them she was having some trouble hearing his words. Ian turned back to her with a wicked grin. "All done with your Scooby-Doo duties?"

She scowled at him, tuning out the reports. "Ass."

"That's beside the point. Are you?"

355

"Yes," she grumbled.

"Good. Then help me with the crowd."

"Gotcha."

Carol and Ian worked with the uniformed cops to keep the crowd in line. As the CSI guys began to wrap things up, Carol's stomach grumbled. She batted her lashes at Ian. "I'm hungry."

Ian nodded. "Me too. Let's—"

Carol held up her hand as an overwhelming sensation of *wrongness* filled her. Glancing around, she couldn't see anything out of the ordinary. She closed her eyes and used her other senses, but again, there wasn't anything she could pinpoint as the cause of her unease.

"What's wrong?" Ian touched her shoulder.

She shook his hand off and concentrated, turning in a circle as anxiety filled her. Missing, something was gone that should have been there, the burning in her wrist—

Her wrist! The symbol linking her to Jonah was burning, warning her of something dire. But what?

"Shit!" She opened her eyes to find herself facing the room she'd emerged from, the room where the murders had occurred. "Ian, where's Jonah?"

Out of the corner of her eye, she saw him glance around, a scowl forming on his face. "I have no idea."

"Fuck." She held up her wrist, and it was red, raw, the symbols etched in gray. "Something's happening to him."

"We need to find him." Ian strode toward Dean Hill, Carol on his heels. The moment they reached her, Ian barked, "Have you seen Jonah?"

Appearing startled, Dean Hill took a step back from the scowling detective. "I... No. He walked away a few moments ago."

Carol exchanged concerned glances with Ian, then showed Dean Hill her wrist. "Something's happening to him."

The dean's eyes widened, then narrowed in determination. "Frank left a while ago." She pulled out her phone and was soon dialing, shaking her head as the rings went on and on before switching to voice mail. Carol could hear the cheerful message and wanted to break the man's neck. "He's not answering."

Carol growled. Her canines descended, claws erupting from her nailbeds.

The enemy had her soul-bound sorcerer, and he was about to learn why predators were feared.

Chapter 39

Jonah groaned and tried to clutch his aching head, but his hands didn't move. He opened his eyes, unsurprised to find the world around him bleary. Something bad had happened recently. Had he found another pinhole and tried to close it? If so, where was Carol? Was she still unconscious?

God, it hurt. Hell, even his fingernails hurt. He closed his eyes again, hoping to fall asleep once more. Worse, there was an odd taste in his mouth, like...herbs?

"Wakey wakey, Detective." An annoying, sing-song voice tried to take his peaceful slumber from him. "You're a little older than I usually take, but that's fine. Once you're dead, the ritual will be nearly complete."

Ritual.

Jonah opened his eyes. "Dean Anthony, I presume?" His vision was still pretty blurry, but it was slowly clearing. Too bad the same couldn't be said for the ache. Anthony must have hit him over the head, same as he'd done to Reeves. He had to applaud the man. The dean had to have hit him exactly right, or Jonah would have fried his ass.

"Yes." A blurry form came closer, resolving into the face of the dean. "Can you see again? I used a bit of magic on you to make you more compliant, but the effects should be wearing off by now."

"What the hell do you think you're doing?" The inability to move was irritating, but more so was the fact that he couldn't sense Carol anywhere nearby. Had the dean taken her as well, or was she safe with Ian?

"Isn't it obvious?" The man raised his arms, his expression reverent. "Immortality."

What? This didn't seem to match what they'd been thinking, but he'd been on the wrong track before. "And you plan to achieve this by feeding the souls of others to a god of destruction?"

The reverence left his expression, replaced by serenity. "You don't understand. I doubted you would. Most people wouldn't be able to comprehend what it is I'm ascending to." The dean settled next to him with a cheery smile, one that looked completely at odds with the position Jonah was currently in.

For the first time, Jonah realized where he was. "This is the storeroom where the pinhole appeared."

"So, your sight is definitely getting better. Good. I'd hate for you to miss the finale."

"The storeroom was a red herring?" He hoped the asshole kept talking. The more he monologued, the closer Jonah's familiar got to chewing Dean Anthony's ass off.

"Your dogs are currently going over the bait I laid out for you." The dean caressed his cheek, the gesture almost loving. "I was certain you'd fall for it."

"They'll soon figure out I'm gone." In fact, Jonah was counting on it. His body might be frozen in place, but Carol's wasn't. She was going to rip this guy a new asshole when she found them.

"In that crowd?" The dean chuckled, apparently amused at Jonah's bravado. "They'll be too busy trying to keep the curious away to notice anything until it's far too late."

Dean Anthony stood, and for the first time, Jonah realized he was not on a bed but the floor. Glancing around, he saw his arms and legs were spread, like Da Vinci's Vitruvian Man. A sacrificial pose that made him tense. To make things even direr, appeared he'd been in Anthony's hands long enough for the man to take his clothing off.

The dean continued, his tone indulgent. "Why do you think I told the staff what was going on?"

"Did you call the media too?" It would make sense, if what Anthony was saying was true. He'd want as many distractions as possible while he completed his mad plan.

"Of course." The man knelt down by him again and began rubbing some sort of oil on his wrists. "This case is bigger than you realize, or it is now, especially since a member of the Sound family is about to disappear forever."

"My partners already know who you are." The smell of the oil was strange, pungent. Myrrh, perhaps? Frankincense? He couldn't tell. Either way, he wished he could move. He'd kill the insane dean before the man even realized what was happening.

"I highly doubt they'll get here before my wither friend has a chance to eat you."

Fuck. He'd completely forgotten about the wither. "How'd you manage to get one under your control?" Jonah had his suspicions, but he needed them confirmed.

"Offer one power, and it will eat out of your hand." The dean stood and moved to his legs, anointing each ankle with the oil. "By the way, just so you are aware, even if your friends attempt to kill me, the spell should be strong enough to prevent it."

He seemed so nonchalant, so sure of himself, that Jonah almost began to doubt that Ian and Carol would find him in time, let alone save him. Almost. Because already he could sense Carol's fury through their bond.

She was coming. All he had to do was keep the dean talking long enough to prevent the wither from arriving and killing him.

"We thought you were trying to resurrect someone." It wouldn't hurt him a bit to tell Anthony what they'd theorized.

"You might, from the bits and pieces you've gathered of the spell." The dean shrugged and crawled to Jonah's side, anointing his forehead. A five-pointed star, then: wrists, ankles, and then the seat of consciousness. No wonder he was spread out the way he was. "Of course, you don't have the full spell, so its ramifications would be lost on you."

"You even fooled our experts." Jonah had interrogated more than one suspect in his day. He was aware when one wanted to brag, and Anthony had been practically begging to do just that.

"I'm sure I did." Anthony shook his head, seemingly disappointed. "Ramsey? Really?" He snorted in disgust. "Might as well look the spell up on Wikipedia."

Jonah barely managed not to roll his eyes. "How did you fool everyone into thinking you were a sorcerer instead of a priest?" It was the only thing that made sense now. There was no partner, no other participant in this crazy little game Anthony was playing. There was only him. Him, and the wither.

"Egyptian magic is exclusive to its priests, Detective." He stood, walking toward something Jonah still couldn't see. The spell was more potent than even Anthony had anticipated if it was still affecting Jonah. "Really, Ramirez, what did you tell them? Ra good. Set bad. Blah blah blah."

His contempt for the professor didn't seem to stop him from continuing on with his plan. Jonah heard him muttering in a language that Jonah didn't understand, meaning it must have been a mundane language rather than a magical one. Was he saying the words of his spell in Egyptian before reciting it in the language of sorcerers? It would make a twisted sort of sense if Anthony did so.

Damn it, he wished he could see what the hell Anthony was doing. He could barely make out that the man was moving his arms, but that was all. Anything else was lost in the haze of the blinding spell. "Immortality? How do you hope to achieve that?"

The chanting stopped. "How many souls is a pharaoh worth, Mr. Sound? Ten? A hundred?" The man stepped close once more, giving Jonah a glimpse of his hands. "A thousand?"

He was holding a poker, the end of which twisted and morphed in a nauseating way. Jonah couldn't focus on it no matter how hard he tried.

"Once my pyramid is complete, I'll be a king." He knelt by Jonah's side once more and set the poker on the floor. "See?" He opened his shirt, revealing dark, desiccated flesh. "It's already begun."

Shit. Dean Anthony was becoming a wither.

"I'll rule over Terra Noctem as its immortal pharaoh." He stroked Jonah's hair, the gesture almost fatherly. "The withers will fall under my command, and the mortal realm will tremble before me."

"Psycho." Jonah couldn't stop himself, the word coming before he could censor it. "It will never work."

Dean Anthony smiled. "They all say that." He picked up the poker and held it over Jonah's chest. "Right before they die."

Chapter 40

Carol held tight to her temper as she listened to the bullshit Dean Anthony was spewing. Ian's expression was horrified. Leader of the withers? A pharaoh?

He'd had lost his friggin' mind.

"How do you want to do this?" Ian whispered just as Dean Anthony raised the strange, icky-feeling poker.

"Fast." Carol shifted and ran, knocking Dean Anthony to the floor.

Unfortunately, that didn't last for long. The side of the poker hit her, pulling a scalding howl of pain from her. Whatever that poker was made of hurt like a son of a bitch. She staggered, her hold on the dean broken.

She growled despite the pain, showing her fangs to the man who threatened her mate, her soul-bound. She'd kill him before he left this room, and anyone who tried to stop her would die with him.

She leaped at the dean once more, but he sidestepped faster than she'd expected, avoiding her entirely. Her teeth snapped shut on empty air.

"Foolish dog. You can die with your sorcerer." Anthony waved his hand.

A sickening wave of wrongness filled the room. Energy crackled along her skin, raising the hairs on the back of her neck even higher. An alien hunger crawled along her spine, making her gag in horror.

Wither.

Carol intercepted the creature's lunge for Jonah, leaving Anthony to Ian. She had to deal with the otherworldly threat before she could help her partner take care of the sorcerer, priest, whatever the hell he wanted to call himself.

The wither bayed, thwarted from its prey. Its hunger slithered through her, forcing her to deal not only with the damage Anthony had dealt but also a staggering nausea that threatened to drive her to her knees. She snarled, pushing at the wither, but it shifted its position and tried to dodge to her left.

Carol intercepted, snapping at the wither's arm as it tried to reach for her fallen mate. Jonah groaned, but she couldn't turn to find out what was happening. She had to keep her attention on the monster in front of her. Shots rang out, and Carol shook her head, the sound far louder than it should have been.

The flickering lights were driving her nuts. It was hard to watch the wither's movements when she was tracking it through staggered strobe lights. Worse, out of the corner of her eye, she could see Ian and Anthony struggling hand-to-hand, and she couldn't determine who was winning.

The wither hissed, its long limbs bent, its hands gnarled as it reached for her. She snapped again, missing flesh as the wither got ahold of her scruff.

Howling agony raced through her, blinding her as her anima was slowly sucked away. While she didn't have the draw of a sorcerer with their vast pools of power, a wither would take a familiar if it could. She was a snack, an hors d'oeuvre before Jonah was consumed. Its pale eyes bored into her as it clasped her skull, its talons perilously close to her eyes.

Another shot rang out, but she couldn't be bothered to look, not while her whole body shook. This was worse than thunderstorms could ever be.

"Carol!"

Somewhere behind her a voice called her name, but…who?

"Latch onto me!"

Latch on?

Strength poured into her, forced into her by someone…Jonah! It was Jonah, giving her the power to pull free of the wither's grasp by sacrificing some of his own animus.

Carol was now well past angry and into cold fury. She was going to rip the fucking wither limb from limb, then shit on it, then bury it. If it was lucky, she wouldn't do it while it was alive.

She leaped onto its chest, forcing it down to the ground. She got her teeth around its neck, ready to rip and tear, but the wither's claws were in her back, her sides, doing the same to her. Her only chance was to kill it before she bled out.

She shredded its throat, her head shaking rapidly to pull chunks of desiccated flesh from its bones. She sank her claws into its chest, digging through until she hit bone. She wrenched her head up, pulling out a huge chunk of larynx and esophagus.

The wither wheezed but continued to fight, sliding its claws vertically to slash along her midsection. Holding back her cries, she dug in once more. Perhaps if she completely removed the head, the wither would fucking die, and this would end.

Blood poured from her onto the wither, making her dizzy. The wither practically writhed in ecstasy as her anima bled from her with her bodily fluids, feeding it in more ways than one. Damn it! If the fucking thing healed, she'd be dead, and so would Ian and Jonah.

Jonah. His power still was in her, but she couldn't use it the way he could.

But she could use it the way *she* could.

Carol used Jonah's gift to sharpen her teeth and claws and enhance her strength. With her newfound muscle, she snapped the wither's rib cage, giving her access to a strangely beating heart.

"Rip out the heart!"

Without hesitation, Carol obeyed Jonah's order. She released its neck and ignored the renewed struggle the wither gave her, snapping her jaws shut on the wither's heart. She pulled it out, its arteries and veins snapping like old rubber bands.

The wither collapsed, a marionette with its strings broken. It's body slowly dissipated, disappearing into a noxious mist.

It had been banished, hopefully for a good long while. Withers might not die on Terra Mundus, but they could be grievously injured. It would take some time for it to heal.

Carol jogged over to Jonah, her tail wagging a mile a minute. She was still in pain, still bleeding, but so proud of herself she wanted to show off before she passed out.

Jonah smiled weakly. "Good girl. Now see if you can help Ian."

She turned to find Ian being strangled by an enraged Dean Anthony. The man was roaring words that made no sense to her but must have for Jonah, because he widened his eyes in fear.

That was enough for her. She crouched low before springing, biting Dean Anthony right through the meaty part of his ass. With her sharpened teeth, she almost took the whole cheek off.

Dean Anthony screamed, releasing Ian to bat fruitlessly at her. Ian, coughing furiously, bent over, picking up his gun. He leveled it shakily at the dean. "You're under arrest, asshole."

Carol growled around the piece of meat in her mouth. If either Jonah or Ian made cracks about rump roast, she was gonna skin them.

Cops flooded the room, their guns drawn, all of them pointing directly at Dean Anthony. Fucking cavalry had finally arrived.

"Jesus, what took you guys so long?" Ian huffed, lowering his hand and leaning back against the wall.

"Um, could you get your dog to let the bad guy go?" One of the uniforms gestured toward Carol.

Carol snarled. She wasn't so sure she wanted to let go. The man needed to die.

"Carol." Jonah's voice, weak but steady, tore her thoughts away from biting the other cheek. "Let him go, sweetheart."

The uniforms looked at her strangely when she huffed but released Dean Anthony. He collapsed, sobbing, onto the floor. He was handcuffed and dragged from the room, the uniforms in lock-step to make sure that he couldn't move. A gag was put around his mouth to prevent him from spellcasting. SOP, but still funny for Carol to see for the first time.

She turned to Jonah and doggy grinned.

He shook his head, obviously amused at her antics. "Ian, I need you to call the chief. Anthony put some sort of spell on me. I can barely see, and I can't move more than my pinky."

"That's not your pinky, bruh." Ian gagged. "And I do *not* like you that way, so stop staring at my amazing beauty."

Jonah sighed. "Ass."

Carol crawled over to Jonah and put her head on his groin, shielding his nether regions from further inspection by a grinning Ian. Those were her goodies. Ian wasn't allowed to make fun of them.

"If you lick him there, I'm leaving." Ian shook his head, his phone to his ear. "That's just sick."

Carol rolled her eyes and ignored him. Releasing the extra energy Jonah had given her was harder than she thought it would be. The pain of her wounds brightened, the pulse a torture she didn't want but was forced to take.

"You shouldn't have done that." A warm hand descended on her head. Jonah's. His scent was all around her, calming her despite the pain. "I could have dealt for a little longer." She snorted, making him laugh. "That tickles."

"And I'm gone," Ian muttered, leaving the room. Carol could hear him talking on the phone, calling for a mage to come and help Jonah.

"We did it." Jonah stroked her head, calming her even further. Much more, and she'd fall asleep. Now that the danger was past, that was all she wanted to do. Sleep, heal, and go home with her mate. Not necessarily in that order.

A sharp tug on her ear snapped her awake. "Don't you dare. Shift. I want to see your wounds without the fur covering them." His voice was stronger, and she could feel him moving restlessly under her.

Carol obeyed, crying out as skin and bone moved with her transformation. "Owie." At least the wounds weren't quite as bad as they'd been thanks to the shift, but they were still not good. She sat up, pushing her hair out of her eyes.

At least she had her clothes on, unlike her mate.

Jonah smiled wearily. "You saved me."

Carol returned his smile, folding his hands over his privates. "It's your turn next time."

He winked. "I'll remember that."

Epilogue

"Anything I can help with, Tanya?" Carol poked her head into the kitchen of her future mother-in-law. Jonah had proposed a week after Dean Anthony had been arrested, and Carol had said yes. It was fast, but their bond was so strong she couldn't imagine living her life with anyone else.

Not to mention, the sex was out of this world.

"Nope, I've got this. Go rescue Ian from Rose." Tanya winked. "I think she wants to eat him."

"Hopefully in a good way," Carol muttered.

"I heard that, young lady." Tanya paused. "Wait! What happened to those two detectives who gave you and Jonah grief?"

Carol grimaced. "Suspended. With pay. They're undergoing an IA investigation." She doubted they'd lose their jobs, but they could be sanctioned for their actions. Hopefully, they'd receive more than slaps on the wrist, but she wasn't counting on it. Speciesism was alive and well, no matter how hard they fought against it.

"Good. I'll tell Ben to keep an eye out for any cases involving them." Tanya grinned lasciviously. "Now, hurry up before Ian winds up as Rose's appetizer."

Carol laughed and left the kitchen, heading for the family room. Sure enough, Rose had pinned Ian down, questioning him about his work with Jonah and Carol. She was leaning forward, practically sitting in the man's lap. Her hungry gaze rested on him like a wolf sighting a particularly tasty deer. Lessa was watching with an amused gaze, sipping quietly at her wine. Benjamin was nowhere to be found, but his scent was strong. He must be sneaking up on Tanya.

A second later, Tanya squeaked, then laughed. The pair of them gave her hope for her own life with Jonah.

"Penny for your thoughts." Jonah's breath tickled her ear as his arms wrapped around her. Through their bond, his contentment hummed.

"Your dad is feeling up your mom."

Jonah shuddered. "Ugh. Never mind, you can keep them."

Carol leaned back in his embrace and yawned. "That new case the boss lady threw at us is killing me."

"Another day, another murder." Jonah rested his chin on her head. "At least we've been finding more of Anthony's kills. We should be able to wrap that case up soon."

Carol resisted the urge to rub the burn scar that case had left on her right arm. Luckily, she hadn't been hit with any of the runes, or she might have needed magical assistance with it. "Hallelujah. Chief Rivers and Dean Hall have been more than helpful. They'll make good witnesses." Carol closed her eyes, enjoying the scent of her mate. "Enough work though. We're here to have fun and relax with family."

"True." Jonah nuzzled her neck. She had to bite back a moan at the scrape of his scruff against her skin. "I know of some fun that leads to being really relaxed."

She lightly slapped his wrist. "Bad sorcerer."

When Jonah's phone rang, she tensed. Please don't let it be work. Please?

"Hello?" Jonah picked up. "Yes? This is Jonah Sound." He pulled away, leaving her mourning his lost warmth. "Familiar paperwork? What…" He groaned. "Shit. We never finished the familiar paperwork."

Carol's brows rose. It had been weeks since she paired with Jonah. "And they waited this long to call?"

He nodded. "We'll turn it in tomorrow. Thanks. Bye." He hung up. "We'll have to register our bond too."

"Great. More paperwork." Carol shook her head. Bureaucracy at its finest.

"At least that will be the last of it, Ms. Voss." Jonah held out his hand. "Care to join me for some wine?"

"Jonah, get your ass over here!" Ian called out, sounding desperate.

Biting back more laughter, Carol answered, "I'd be delighted." She took Jonah's hand, ready to follow her sorcerer wherever he led.

About the Author

Dana Marie Bell wrote her first short story when she was thirteen years old. She's now a *USA TODAY* bestselling author, both self-published and with Carina Press. She lives with her husband, Dusty, their two maniacal children, an evil ice-cream stealing cat, and a dog that doesn't understand the meaning of "personal space." Dana has been heard to describe herself as "vertically challenged" and loves video games and anime. She is also an "invisible illness sufferer," as she has both fibromyalgia and ankylosing spondylitis. Due to this, she walks with a cane or rides in a mobility scooter. She refuses to answer whether or not she's ever attempted to run her children over with the scooter. She will say, however, that they are now very fast runners.

You can learn more about Dana at: www.danamariebell.com

DM
B

Dana Marie Bell Books
www.danamariebell.com

Manufactured by Amazon.ca
Bolton, ON

12316618R00219